Viking Dragon

Book 12 in the Dragon Heart Series

By

Griff Hosker

Viking Dragon

Published by Sword Books Ltd 2016
Copyright © Griff Hosker

The author has asserted their moral right under the Copyright, Designs and Patents Act, 1988, to be identified as the author of this work.
All Rights reserved. No part of this publication may be reproduced, copied, stored in a retrieval system, or transmitted, in any form or by any means, without the prior written consent of the copyright holder, nor be otherwise circulated in any form of binding or cover other than that in which it is published and without a similar condition being imposed on the subsequent purchaser.
A CIP catalogue record for this title is available from the British Library.
Cover by Design for Writers

Contents

Viking Dragon i
Prologue 2
Chapter 1 3
Chapter 2 13
Chapter 3 30
Chapter 4 43
Chapter 5 54
Chapter 6 66
Chapter 7 76
Chapter 8 90
Chapter 9 104
Chapter 10 118
Chapter 11 128
Chapter 12 141
Chapter 13 152
Chapter 14 163
Chapter 15 172
Epilogue 189
Glossary 190
Maps 194
Historical note 195
Other books by Griff Hosker 197

Prologue

We had battled against many foes and enemies and we had prevailed against overwhelming odds. We had slain my nephew, Jarl Erik Eriksson on Man and scoured the island of all those who opposed us. Thorfinn Blue Scar and Gunnstein Berserk Killer now safely ruled Dyflin and Ljoðhús. The north and the west were safe and yet since we had discovered that we had a traitor in our home, I could not sleep. We had discovered, from one of our enemies, that there were those in my land who wished us harm. I would almost have lost the battle than that. I had believed that all those who lived in the land others called 'Land of the Wolf' were loyal; now I knew that this was not so.

Brigid my wife was with child and I hated disturbing her as I tossed and turned, sleeplessly. I had taken to sleeping or spending the nights, at least, before the fire of my hall. All that I knew was that someone had taken messages to Jarl Erik Eriksson on Man and they had raided my knarr. I could not divine who it might be. I trusted all of my men. Aiden, my galdramenn, and Kara, the volva who was my daughter, would normally have used their powers to help me but my granddaughter Ylva occupied both their time and their powers. It was as if their thoughts and their eyes looked within. When my granddaughter grew she would be more powerful than either of them. *Wyrd*.

It would soon be the time of the new grass. Already the snow had disappeared. I had to do something soon. Our ships were laid up for the winter but already their captains and my shipwright would be preparing them for sea. Someone was a traitor. I could not believe that it was the captain of one of my ships and yet we had heard that a message had been sent to Man. How could that be? I needed help. There was a link back to Man. Old Olaf the Toothless had been the friend of Ragnar the old Viking who had trained me. He had died on Man but we had named the mountain which overlooked the Water after him. His grizzled face seemed to protect us. I would seek his help. I was no galdramenn but I had an affinity with mountains. Snaefell, on Man, had always been somewhere I felt close to Ragnar and the gods. I would go there and seek help.

Viking Dragon

Part 1 The Saxons

Chapter 1

My journey was delayed for before I could leave my wife gave birth to a daughter. My son, Gryffydd, now had a sister. It was Brigid who named her. "We call her Erika in honour of your first wife. From her two children, I know that she was a good woman. And I know that you all believe her spirit protects this land. It is good. This completes the circle."

My wife was a Christian yet even she had seen the power of the spirits. I was happy with the name and I kissed them both. Kara and Aiden came with their daughter, Ylva and my hall felt complete. While the two women fussed over the new baby I took Aiden outside, to the Water.

"I need to find the traitor. We cannot have our enemies knowing our secrets."

"I am sorry, Jarl Dragonheart. I have been distracted of late. I will put my mind to it."

I shook my head, "It is something I must discover. I go to Old Olaf and see if he can give me inspiration. When I lived on Man I often climbed the mountain to be close to the gods. I always found both peace and inspiration there. I have grown lazy of late. I will climb Old Olaf."

"Kara and I have not sensed danger. Perhaps the traitor has died."

"Then I would know who it was. No, he is still here. Perhaps there is more than one; who knows? The isle that is Man may no longer be a threat but if the traitor lives then he can bring harm to my land."

"Will you take someone with you?"

"If I cannot travel to the top of a mountain which I see every morning then my land is, indeed, not safe. I shall go alone."

I waited seven days to ensure that the Norns were not in a malicious mood. Sometimes they allowed a baby to be born only to take them a day or so after their birth. This time they smiled on us and Erika thrived. I left before dawn. Gryffydd begged to come but I needed to be alone and he would struggle to climb the mountain. I promised him that soon I would take him with me. The lower slopes were relatively easy to climb and I wanted the sun to rise and help me crest the peak. It was how I had done it on Man and there was a connection.

It was no longer winter but it was cold. I had wrapped up well and wore my wolf skin. I also had Ragnar's Spirit on my belt. It did not make the climb easy but it was important that I carried it. The sword tied me to the past and to the gods. I carried it always. I paused at the blue water to drink. Aiden had told me that it had powers. I knew not if it was true but it did not hurt to make the connection with the earth. The path was easy to follow for we had mines on the lower slopes and were worn by daily footsteps. As I began to ascend to the top the sun peered over the hill near my first hall and the grave of my wife, Erika. I paused to take it in. I could see the tiny specks that would be the first flowers of the year. Erika had loved flowers. It was going to be a fine day. I allowed the first early rays to bathe my face.

Turning I ascended the last one thousand paces to the peak. The path twisted and turned as it climbed so that the view of my water was hidden from me. By the time I turned the last corner and reached the peak the sun had risen to bathe my water in blue light. Perhaps it was a trick of the sun but the snowdrops on Erika's grave seemed clearer to me and that was good. I sat on the top of Old Olaf and took out Ragnar's Spirit. I plunged it into the ground. I turned from the east and looked south. It was such a clear day that I could see, not only Ulfarrston but also Man. I was meant to be here.

I knew not what I expected but I had all day. I just stared at Man. It was not a threat to us any more but the answer to my dilemma lay there. We had been told that Jarl Erik, my nephew would sail out to meet, at sea, with the traitor. That meant someone sailed from my land. And yet I trusted all of my captains. When Olaf had been the captain of the drekar on which I had sailed he had been free with a knotted piece of rope he constantly carried. If I made a mistake, and I made many, then he would hit me on the back of the head with it. I suddenly felt as though I had been struck from behind. I was a fool! It could not be a drekar captain or the captain of a knarr for the whole crew would have known what they were about. I actually laughed out loud at my own stupidity.

I suddenly saw them clearly both literally and metaphorically; I saw the fishing boats as they left Ulfarrston. Some had crews of one or two but others just had a single fisherman. They would be out all day seeking the shoals of fish in the rich waters which lay south of us. I shook my head, "Thank you, Olaf. I still learn from you."

I pulled my sword from the ground and, sheathing it, headed down the path. Something still nagged in my head. Then I had it. Was the traitor in Ulfarrston working alone or did they have a confederate? I would keep my own counsel until I knew more. As the raiding season was upon us I would have good reason to visit Coen ap Pasgen in Ulfarrston. I found myself smiling as I headed down the path. My sleepless nights had been for nothing. I had feared that someone I had trusted in Cyninges-tūn, had betrayed me. I was wrong. There was a traitor or a spy in my land but they were not of my people and I would find them.

When I reached my home Kara and Aiden were there with my wife. They looked at me expectantly. I smiled and Kara said, "Well, father? Do we have to drag it out of you?"

I smiled, "You normally know what goes on in my head."

Aiden nodded, "We know that you have learned something when you were on the mountain but we cannot yet read it."

"We know that the messages were sent by the water to Man. I have worked out that the traitor cannot be the captain of one of my ships and Old Olaf pointed me in the direction of those who leave Úlfarrston to go fishing. I can discover their identity but I fear there may be someone here, on the Water who also aids them."

Kara shook her head, "The spirits have not told us that. Úlfarrston is far from here. They are not of our people. It is hard to see into their minds."

Aiden nodded, "I will come with you, Jarl Dragonheart, when you visit Úlfarrston. I have indulged myself with Ylva long enough. It is time for me to be galdramenn once more."

Now that I had one problem identified I could think about sailing the seas and raiding once more. I sent word to my Ulfheonar that we would be raiding by the middle of Ein-mánuðr. That would give them time to prepare. I also sent riders to my jarls and hersir that if they wished to raid with me then that would be when we would sail. I ordered no man to follow me. Jarl Sigtrygg Thrandson had chosen not to raid the previous season. My son, Wolf Killer, had also missed out two years since. I was no king. I was gratified that, normally, they did accompany me.

When we reached the shipyard above Úlfarrston we could hear the sound of men working. Erik Short Toe, the captain of my drekar, had Thorir Svensson and the others from his crew scraping the weed from the hull. When that was done they would coat it in the liquid Aiden had made. It stopped the worm from eating into the hulls. The other drekar were also being treated in this fashion. We now had a fleet. As I had expected Erik had almost readied my ship, *'Heart of the Dragon'*. He wanted to be ready to sail at a moment's notice. The others would not be long behind him.

I took him to one side, "Erik, you know that we discovered there is a traitor somewhere in our land?"

"I heard, Jarl Dragonheart, and I was disturbed for I could not believe that a fellow captain would be so disloyal."

"And you were right. I have worked out that it must be a fisherman from Úlfarrston. They come and they go. They sail alone; each fisherman guarding the secret of where they fished. It would be easy for a couple of traitors to sail to Man and pass on information. Tell me, is my idea reasonable? Could someone do as I said?"

He nodded, "I had not thought of that but it makes perfect sense. They see us coming and going. They are small and fast. We do not hide the fact that we sail. It takes time to prepare a drekar for sea. They could easily sail the day before and reach Man. Now that you say it then it becomes obvious. How will you catch them?"

"I do not know. I will speak with Coen." I looked at Erik, "Can I trust him?"

He nodded, "He has the most to lose should you not be the Jarl of this land."

"Then I will speak with him. I have said that we will raid in the middle of Ein-mánuðr. My warriors will gather then."

"How many drekar?"

"I know not."

"And where do we raid?"

I smiled, "Lundenwic is a rich city. It is now the jewel in Wessex's crown. Egbert has sent enough assassins north to kill me and I would like to repay the favour."

"It is a rich city. We would need Siggi and his knarr."

"Aye. I hope that our brethren will join us for we would be rich men if we succeeded."

"And Aiden?"

"I come with you," Aiden smiled.

Erik Short Toe looked relieved. "Then I am happy. With a galdramenn, we have more chance of success and he knows how to read maps."

"Keep this to yourself, Erik, and watch out for any you might suspect."

"I will Jarl."

As Aiden and I made our way to the walled settlement I found myself looking at those we met and wondering about their loyalty. They smiled at me but was the smile in their hearts too? The thought of a traitor caused disharmony. We could not have that. Instead of going into the hall Aiden and I walked to the shore where we could see out to sea. It was late afternoon and the fishing boats were returning with their catches. They had all left together but the nature of fishing meant that some arrived home sooner than others. Some were lucky and some were not.

As the first few fishermen landed their catches and bowed as they passed us I searched their faces. Aiden would be using his own particular magic to determine what was in their hearts.

Coen ap Pasgen joined us. "Jarl Dragonheart, what brings you here to the shore?"

I smiled, "Come, my old friend. Let us walk. I need to speak privately with you." When we were away from any who could overhear us I said. "We discovered that someone was taking messages to our enemies. They have been giving information about our ships. It explains why so many have never returned home."

He looked confused, "And who do you think is doing this?"

Aiden said, "Jarl Dragonheart is not certain but we believe there is a chance it is some of the fishermen." He explained my logic.

Coen shook his head in disbelief. "I find it hard to accept that some of my people could do this but it would explain much. We have lost knarr unexpectedly. What do we do?"

"Aiden and I will be here for a few days seeing to our ships. If you would grant us hospitality then Aiden can use his mind and I can use my eyes. I promise that we will speak with you before we accuse anyone."

"You are a fair man, Jarl Dragonheart. You are not used to hasty and rash judgements. Come we will go to my hall and I will have my people make you comfortable."

By the time it was dark all of the fishing boats had returned and the catches were either being sold or the fishermen had taken them to their smokehouses. The ones who had the foresight did not sell their whole catch but preserved some for the times when the sea was against them. I did not see any clues as to the traitor. More annoyingly neither did Aiden. He could not focus on the thoughts of the traitors. They were stopping Aiden, somehow.

We ate, that night, with Coen and his family. We did not mention our true purpose but spoke of our new babies. Coen's wife was keen to visit and we said that she could come back with us. The closer the ties between our people the less likelihood there was of treachery. When Coen's family had retired we went through what we all knew. It was Aiden who had ideas. "I do not think that it will be anyone who has a family. I have no evidence for that but just a feeling. I think it will be someone who sails alone or perhaps with one other. It may well be that they do not come from here but arrived sometime in the last couple of years."

Coen leaned back. "That helps for it narrows it down to a few fishermen. Tomorrow we will watch them as they sail and I will identify them."

"If we could examine their homes when they are fishing then it might help us."

"We will do that."

With that out of the way, Coen pressed us to escort his ships when next we sailed. "We are now used to trade. We are more prosperous. Losing ships to pirates hurts us."

"With whom would you trade?"

He looked a little shamefaced, "I am afraid that they may be your enemies: the men of Corn Walum and Dyfed."

"I do not mind; trade is trade but we will be sailing further east than that. They would either have to wait for our return or risk sailing alone."

"I will speak with them."

The next day the three of us were up before dawn and watched as the keenest fishermen were preparing their boats. Coen gave subtle nods when a suspect or suspects came to their boats. They sailed before the sun had risen. We hurried to the houses of the fishermen whom Coen had identified. There were six suspects. We decided to try these first. We still had a day or two before we needed to return home. I had no idea what we were looking for but we searched them all anyway. The six huts were all similar in construction. There was a double row of stones with willow uprights. Daub filled the gaps and they each had a coned roof. You could see that these six had only recently come for their homes were not weathered and were apart from the rest.

Inside they were all identical but for one. It was the last one we searched and, until we searched it, I was beginning to give up hope. It was Aiden who found it. It was a Thor's Hammer and was laid beneath the bedding of one of the two men who lived there. It was the only evidence we had found. I think Aiden was directed there by the spirits for I knew not how he could have found it otherwise. We took it outside to examine it.

"This is Danish, Jarl Dragonheart."

"Whose hut is this one, Coen? Did you know they were Danes?"

The headman shook his head, "They are two brothers, Thrand and Finni Karlsson. I did not know they were Danish. They have been here for almost two years. They said they had fled Orkneyjar; some sort of blood feud. They said that they were not warriors but fishermen. They are quiet and everyone likes them. They keep to themselves. I think you may be wrong about them, Jarl."

"As I said before, Coen, I will not judge without words first. I will ask them questions and Aiden will listen to their responses. If they are innocent then we will know. But you should know that the men of Orkneyjar are Norse like us and not Danish. There are Danes who visit there and sometimes stay, but Danes like their own people. They are, however, mercenaries. My nephew was cunning. He may have paid the

Danes to spy. If he had used his own people then we might have been suspicious."

Coen left us and we headed upstream to our ships. "They are guilty, Jarl. I felt it when I touched the hammer. They lied to Coen. Only warriors wear the hammer. We know that."

"Perhaps that is why they hid it. But you are right. The fact that they hid the evidence of what they are, condemns them."

When we reached the drekar we found Haaken One Eye, Snorri and Beorn the Scout. Haaken was always keen to sail. His wife, Unn, was lovely but Haaken tired of her after a winter in his hall. She would be with child again and Haaken would profess to pangs of regret when we were at sea. Nonetheless, he was always the first to board and the last to disembark. He rubbed his hands when he saw us. "When we heard that you were here we decided to follow. Where to this time?"

"Lundenwic. It is some years since we have been there."

"That is a mighty morsel! Will King Egbert be there?"

"I know not but I doubt it. Raibeart Ap Pasgen told me that he is in the west of Wessex still putting down rebellions."

Erik Short Toe, more concerned about the traitor and the danger it represented, asked, "Is the problem solved?"

"We hope that when we return this evening it will be."

"Problem?"

We told them what we had been about and the three of them were keen to accompany us. We stayed at the yard long enough to see that the work was almost complete. We would go back to Cyninges-tūn the day and prepare for a month or two of raiding. It was heading towards dark when we reached the shore. The very first boat was already making its way up the estuary. The catch was so large that the three men could barely lift it. "A good catch eh?"

"Aye Jarl Dragonheart. The gods have been kind to us."

"Were all the boats as successful?"

"All the ones who fished close by us." He laughed, "The Karlsson brothers sailed further south. They will return empty handed for the shoals were all close to the shore to the east. They were heading for Man." He shook his head, "They are good boys both of them but they are poor fishermen." He tapped his head, "They are not very clever for they always choose the wrong fishing grounds." He shrugged, "We have tried to tell them but some people are stubborn."

I looked at Aiden. This was further confirmation of their guilt. By the time the last boat had landed, there could be no doubt for they did not return. Had we not been suspicious then I might have worried for them but our presence had alerted them. I was annoyed with myself. We should have been more subtle. We were hunters and we had spooked our prey. Coen said that if they returned he would hold them for us to question.

The next day we returned to Cyninges-tūn escorting Coen's wife and some other ladies from his town. I knew that Brigid and Kara would enjoy the company. The women of Úlfarrston wore clothes which they had bought from traders. Our womenfolk made their own. I knew that we would be given a list of items which we had to bring back from our raid or our trade. I sent for Scanlan the headman and told him of the planned raid. He, more than anyone, knew what we needed and he gave Aiden and me a list. I asked Aiden to speak with Bjorn Bagsecgson; there were items he needed to make fine swords. The blades he could make but warriors liked fine and fancy adornments.

While they were away I sought out Uhtric my servant. "I need my mail oiling and my spare boots waxing."

"You go to sea, Jarl?"

"We go raiding, Uhtric."

"I will polish and sharpen your weapons. Will you be using the steam hut before you go, Jarl?"

"Yes, tomorrow Uhtric. Why?"

"I will put your wolf cloak in while it is heating up. The heat and the smoke will kill any wildlife and cleanse it."

Like all those who lived in my Stad, Uhtric understood the importance of the wolf cloak. It made me who I was, the Wolf Warrior. "Good. I will need my spare cloak too. Nights at sea seem colder these days."

"It is age catching up with you Jarl." He seemed to remember something. He went to the room Brigid had built at the end of the hall and returned with a long piece of stuffed cowhide. "I made this during the long nights. It will make sleeping on the drekar easier, lord. I filled the hide with sheep and goats' wool. It will resist the sea air and water for I have waxed it too."

Uhtric had been with me since Erika. We had grown older together and he felt what I felt. "That is thoughtful, Uhtric."

My jarls and hersir began to arrive. Some had long distances to travel. My son, Wolf Killer, came with his wife and son. I walked with Wolf Killer by the Water and we gazed at his mother's grave. The smoke was rising from the steam hut. It was good that Wolf Killer had arrived first. We would be able to share the steam hut with Haaken.

"It is good that you have named the child Erika, father. Mother would like it."

I nodded, "Your sister agrees. Will you come later this afternoon, to the steam hut?"

"I will. I must have one built close by me."

"We are lucky here for we have the Water. The river close by Elfridaby is not such a good site."

"No, but it is easier to defend. We have spent some time this winter making it even better defended."

"Good for you face the Danes," I told him of the spies.

"We are ever vigilant and my men speak closely with all who pass through our lands. We have been hurt before and we are wary."

My son's caution was justified. The old Roman Town the Saxons called Eoforwic and the Danes called Jorvik was filling up with Danes. Soon there would be more of those warriors than Saxons. It was a threat we took seriously.

That afternoon I sat in the hut with Haaken and Wolf Killer. "Will you raid, Wolf Killer?"

"I think not. My warriors have all begun families. They wish to spend some time making their homes stronger and their farms more productive. We took enough treasure last year to keep us happy for some time." I nodded. Each of my leaders looked after their own clan as best they could. "Besides Elfrida is with child again. It is early days yet but I will see this child into the world. I am young and I have many more years raiding ahead of me."

Haaken laughed, "Meaning your father and I do not."

Wolf Killer took the bone scrapers we kept and began to scrape off the dirt and dead skin, "You two will never stop raiding. It is in your blood. Even though you need nothing that you will take from Lundenwic you will seek that which you do not have."

I was curious, "And what is it that I seek?"

"A link to the past and your ancestor."

"I see that Kara is not the only one who has inherited the gift from your mother."

"There was a time when my mind was closed to you and to Kara; the dark times when Angharad took my family. Then I saw nothing. Since we have become friends again I find myself dreaming of both you and my mother. You seek a link to your own mother's father. The warrior from the west."

"He is right Jarl Dragonheart. Why else would you keep that old sword in your hall? You can never use it and yet it is guarded as well as your family."

"Does everyone see so clearly into my mind?" I did not mind this interrogation. These were, along with Aiden, the men who were closest to me.

"Only those who know you well, father. You will search the seas and the hidden places until you discover whatever it is that tells you more and yet I fear that you will never know the whole story."

He was right. "You mean my Saxon father?"

"I have spoken of this with my sister. We have powers from your mother and our mother. You have them from your mother only. Things are hidden from you that we see."

Haaken laughed, "And I, Haaken One Eye, see only great sagas and stories from these adventures."

I looked at my oldest friend. "And yet, Haaken, we are the last of those who went on those first adventures when the Ulfheonar were young."

"The day you begin to worry, Jarl, is the day you will die. Embrace the adventure."

Chapter 2

We had five drekar in our fleet as we headed south. Siggi had my knarr and we escorted three knarr from Úlfarrston. Nine ships would be too big a mouthful for any of the pirates who frequented this west coast of Britannia. Even Sigtrygg Thrandson had joined us. Ketil Windarsson sailed onboard Olaf Grimmson's ship, **'King's Gift'**. Olaf was not a warrior but one of the best captains I had. Mine was the largest drekar. Only Wolf Killer's **'Wild Boar'**, still in port and being cleaned, was almost as large. The rest were little more than threttanessa. However, between us, we had over a hundred and fifty warriors. There were still many at home to watch our families. Men like my smith, Bjorn Bagsecgson, could fight as well as most warriors. I did not fear for Cyninges-tūn.

Haaken was in good spirits and he led the crew in a chant to speed us through the sea. We led and I hoped that the ones who followed would be able to keep up.

The storm was wild and the gods did roam
The enemy closed on the Prince's home
Two warriors stood on a lonely tower
Watching, waiting for hour on hour.
The storm came hard and Odin spoke
With a lightning bolt the sword he smote
Ragnar's Spirit burned hot that night
It glowed, a beacon shiny and bright
The two they stood against the foe
They were alone, nowhere to go
They fought in blood on a darkened hill
Dragon Heart and Cnut will save us still
Dragon Heart, Cnut and the Ulfheonar
Dragon Heart, Cnut and the Ulfheonar
The storm was wild and the Gods did roam
The enemy closed on the Prince's home
Two warriors stood on a lonely tower
Watching, waiting for hour on hour.
The storm came hard and Odin spoke
With a lightning bolt the sword he smote
Ragnar's Spirit burned hot that night

It glowed, a beacon shiny and bright
The two they stood against the foe
They were alone, nowhere to go
They fought in blood on a darkened hill
Dragon Heart and Cnut will save us still
Dragon Heart, Cnut and the Ulfheonar
Dragon Heart, Cnut and the Ulfheonar

Once we had passed Ynys Môn we took in the oars and let the winds from the west take us down the coast. We pulled in for the night at the island of the puffins; the one the Welsh called Ynys Enlli. It was uninhabited and the birds who nested there made good eating. I gathered the nine captains around me once they had secured their ships.

"Tomorrow we reach the Sabrina. There we leave the knarr from Úlfarrston. We will be away for twenty days at the most. We meet back on the Sabrina." The three captains from Úlfarrston nodded. I did not think they would risk sailing alone through the treacherous waters north of us. The alternative was to head for Dyflin where they would be afforded protection from Gunnstein Berserk Killer. However, that would still leave them with the dangerous passage across the seas around Man. They would wait.

We bade farewell to them at the Sabrina and then we were able to sail faster. Siggi was the best knarr captain I had known. His only equal had been Trygg and he had been killed with his crew close to Olissipo. It had made Siggi a harder man and a better captain. *Wyrd.* The witch at Syllingar let us pass without a message. Aiden was the only one who was disappointed. Although she usually gave us good prophecies my men feared her power. The last time she had spoken to our young recruit Hrolf. He was now sailing with Gunnar Thorfinnson. That had been his destiny and I would not stand in his way.

Aiden pointed to the east as we passed Syllingar. "I wonder how Hrolf is? Gunnar said he would raid Neustria."

"I have a feeling that Hrolf has been chosen by the gods."

"A little like you, Jarl Dragonheart."

"Perhaps, although you have the mark of the Norns upon you. Think back all those years. Think about how many other hostages died and yet you were chosen to live. You too were chosen. It does not do to inspect the Weird Sisters webs too closely."

We spent our second night on a deserted beach at Vectis. This was Wessex and we kept a good watch. The Norns smiled upon us for we had no trouble and were not spotted. We headed for the Tamese. There were many islands in the estuary mouth and our plan was to spend the night hidden among the mud banks and stunted trees. We would step our masts and be invisible. When we sailed up the Tamese we would use just oars. Siggi would bring his knarr sometime later.

We kept well out to sea. King Egbert had recently conquered this land and his thegns would have keen eyes watching to see for just such as we. Erik knew the waters well and we had maps that Aiden kept. Although there was some guesswork involved I was confident that we would find the estuary before dark. We had our ships' boys at the bow and on the crosstree. They peered ahead seeking out other sails. If we saw one then it was likely it would be an enemy.

"Land to the west, captain!" Thorir Svensson's thin voice barely carried to us but Erik heard and he pushed the steering board over as he led our fleet towards the land of the East Angles. We would use the north shore of the Tamese. Lundenwic was well defended but Wessex lay to the south. Since King Eadwald had been killed by King Coenwulf of Mercia it was a weaker kingdom. I had heard that Athelstan, Eadwald's son, was trying to gather warriors but they would not worry us. Wessex and the garrison of Lundenwic was our enemy.

We edged towards the swampy, muddy north bank of the Tamese estuary. The sun was setting in the west and we would be hidden, in the dark of the east. It took some hours to finally reach land. As soon as we touched the banks Snorri and Beorn leapt ashore. They wore no mail but had their wolf skins about their shoulders. They would have to navigate the marshland as best they could. Their job was to make sure there were no enemies close to us. My captains had the masts of their drekar taken down and laid on the mast fish. Siggi's knarr did not but a merchant vessel seeking sanctuary in the reeds would not alarm any. It took time to take down the sail, the crosstree and the mast itself. Dawn was almost upon us by the time we had done so. We ate cold rations and then slept with a good watch.

I did not sleep. I watched with Aiden and Erik. Although my scouts were good I still fretted while they were away. It was with some relief that I saw them returning. They did not come directly towards us. The tide was now in and they had to navigate the small patches of dry land. The last part necessitated them wading towards us through the muddy pools.

We hauled them on board. They were covered in mud. "We found no Saxons nor men of Essex nor the East Angles nor Wessex. The land is too desolate for farming."

Snorri poured a pail of river water over his head to wash off some of the mud, "But we did find a monastery just along the coast. It took us longer to reach it than it will the drekar. It is just around the bend in the river. It is on the only solid land that we found. It may have been an island in the past but now it sits above the river."

"Is there a wall?"

"Aye but not a big one." Beorn grinned, "It will not keep us out!"

"Then we sail there and attack it after dark. We can carry on to Lambehitha. There is another church of the White Christ there and the halls of Lundenwic will be filled with goods."

Aiden added a word of caution. "Do not forget, Jarl Dragonheart, there will be a garrison at Lundenburgh."

"There will but I doubt that there will be enough of them to worry us. My fear is that they try to trap us in the river."

Aiden nodded, "If the monastery is, as I suspect, at Tilaburg, then the river is quite narrow there. They could block it."

"Then we leave Raibeart ap Coen and his men there. We will hold the monks as hostages."

Aiden said, "We could sell them back to the men of Wessex. It would save us selling them at the slave market."

"We will do that. Aiden, go and tell the jarls and hersir what I intend. I shall sleep now that Snorri and Beorn have returned."

Snorri looked surprised, "You were worried, Jarl Dragonheart?"

I smiled, "There are few of us left from the days of Man. I worry about all who are not within sight of Ragnar's Spirit."

I slept and my sleep was untroubled by dreams. I was far from home and surrounded by enemies but I had rarely had such a large number of warriors at my command.

Aiden shook me awake in the late afternoon. "They are ready, Jarl. Siggi will remain here and sail after dawn to Tilaburg. Raibeart can guard him until we have what we need."

"Good." I washed and swallowed some small beer. I donned my mail and applied the beetle juice to my eyes. Haaken ensured that the new warriors who were with us knew what they were to do. My seax and Ragnar's Spirit were sharp enough to shave. Finally, I combed my hair and moustaches before tying them into neat tails. With my shield slung over my back, I was almost ready for war.

As the light faded in the west we began to row silently downstream. Snorri and Beorn replaced the ship's boys. They knew the precise location of the monastery. I waited at the steering board with Erik and Aiden. It was our noses which alerted us to the presence of the monastery first. It was the smell of wood smoke and the hint of perfume. Some monks burned rosemary and thyme to make their churches smell more pleasant. We knew when we were close. The word was passed down from Snorri and finally reached us. "Oars in. Begin to head to shore." I donned my helmet.

Erik was a master sailor. He could feel the water beneath our hull and seemed to have a sixth sense which stopped him from grounding us. We gently nudged the bank. Snorri and Beorn were already ashore and, when my crew had stored their oars, we joined them. The monastery was half a mile away on the top of a low rise. It was well away from the water. I could see the glow of lights within the buildings. I did not wait for the other crews. We could probably take this monastery with just my men. Snorri and Beorn bounded off to cut off any escape from the far side of the monastery. Olaf Leather Neck and Haaken followed close by me.

Although we were quiet our armour would make a noise. No matter how much oil was applied it always creaked slightly. If they had sentries or sharp ears then we would be heard but we were fortunate. The Norns did not place anything in our way. I heard chanting. The monks were at one of their many services. I saw the wall loom up and I waved forward some of the younger warriors. They stood in pairs with their shield held between them. Olaf, Haaken and I ran at the shields, jumped on them and, as we did so, we were hoisted over the top of the wall. When we landed we made a noise. It could not be helped but the three of us were on our feet in an instant and we ran for the door which we saw ahead of us. No one inside the church heard us. They were still chanting and singing.

When I saw light coming from it I knew that it was being opened. I ran hard and the monk who saw us had the time to shout, "Vikings!" before I ran him through and we burst in. Rollo and Rolf had gone around to the rear of the church, leading more of my warriors as we drove the terrified monks towards the far end of the church and their altar. Two older ones stood, bravely brandishing an incense burner and a candle snuffer in their hands. The rest fled.

I spoke in Saxon, "Put them down and you live. Your God would not want you to die for a candlestick."

Perhaps my tone of voice and use of Saxon surprised them for they obeyed.

"Take them to *'Red Snake'*. Olaf, gather the treasures and the books."

By the time the church had been stripped the other crews had taken everything of value from the halls and the outbuildings. We even had some sheep and a cow. The cow would be butchered and we would eat well on the voyage back.

"Raibeart, send word to Snorri and then guard the priests. Do not harm them. They are worth coin to us."

We made our way back to the drekar. So far it was all going well but I knew that the next part might prove to be more difficult. We left our treasure and captives and set sail upriver once more. We led the way but this time we kept well to the middle of the river. We knew that it narrowed before widening again. There were twists and turns in the Tamese. Had we been using sail it might have taken forever but with my crew rowing, we powered through the black waters. The huts and halls along the shore were in darkness. I knew that there were no forts or defences until Lundenburgh.

The huge Roman burgh loomed ominously on our right. It was still pitch black and we saw no one but I knew that our oars would make white water. Perhaps the guards were asleep for no one shouted the alarm. On reflection, we may have been mistaken for barges for we had no sails to mark us as drekar.

Even though we had made good time, dawn was not far away when we rounded the bend in the river. As we neared Lundenwic I waved to Sigtrygg and Asbjorn to head to the monastery at Lambehitha. I led Ketil and his men to the north shore. We had used this before when we had served King Egbert against King Coenwulf. With the King of Wessex away I counted on a weak garrison.

There were ships tied up at the jetty and they gave the alarm as we approached. By then it was too late. Erik and Olaf put our drekar hard over to stop next to the ships and we used them as a bridge to the shore. It also gave us protection from attack. As we leapt over the side of the merchant ship I shouted, "Rolf Horse Killer, take four men and capture this knarr!"

"Aye Jarl."

Already we had booty for I saw that the ship over which we passed was still laden. They must have been waiting for the high tide to sail. The crew were sleeping on the deck and they sensibly cowered away from us as we passed over their deck and onto the stone jetty. Speed was now of the essence. We had to get to the edge of the settlement as soon as we could. I did not mind the people fleeing to Lundenburgh, slaves were not important, but we wanted them to leave their valuables in their homes and halls. When we had been here before we had seen what riches they had in Lundenwic.

Inevitably some foolish men decided that their goods were too valuable to leave. While I led my Ulfheonar to the edge of the houses I heard cries behind me as Ketil and his men went to empty the halls, houses and storage dwellings of all that they had. I stopped when I saw the walls of Lundenburgh just four hundred paces from us. King Egbert had cleared the land after the attack by King Coenwulf. I had no desire to lose warriors attacking its walls. Women, children and a few men ran from back lanes and narrow alleyways to run towards the fort which was now in an uproar.

"Shields!"

The Ulfheonar locked shields and we formed one line across the road from the fort. Other warriors formed a second line. I saw a glow from the fort as the huge gates opened to admit the refugees and to allow some of the garrison to come out. They had no idea how many men they faced and I guessed that the Eorledman, Thegn or Gesith who commanded would bring men to see if he could chase us off. He was in for a shock.

Most Viking raiders use spears. We sometimes did but my Ulfheonar preferred their own weapons of choice. Haaken and I favoured swords while Olaf Leather Neck liked his axe. The Saxons who approached all had spears. I saw the first glow of dawn behind the walls of Lundenburgh and I saw that there were forty men approaching us. We were evenly matched in numbers but I doubted that they had the quality of warriors who stood with me. The leader had a fine full-face helmet with small wings at the side. The rising sun glinted from it. The overlapping scales told me he had good mail as did the five hearthweru behind him.

When they were sixty paces from us they halted and the Saxon shouted, "Wedge!"

Had I chosen we could have charged them and attacked them when they were in the process of forming a wedge but I waited. I shouted, "Lock shields!" My men all moved a little closer so that each shield overlapped the next by a third of its width and I felt the shields behind us push into our backs. If these had been the Welsh, with their fine archers, I might have had the second rank of shields held over us. Saxons made poor archers. We just braced ourselves for the attack. We all stepped forward on our left legs so that we were braced for the moment of impact.

The wedge complete, the leader led his men towards us. The warriors who approached us moved slowly. I guessed they were more used to watching from the walls. We waited patiently. When they were twenty paces from us the Saxon shouted, "Charge!" The sun suddenly flared brightly above the walls and bathed us all in light.

As one we raised our shields so that they covered half of our heads. It left the Saxons with two targets, our eyes or our thighs. Our thighs were covered by long byrnies. Our eyes were a small target. I held my sword above my shield and that of Haaken. I watched as the Saxon leader deliberately aimed his spear at me. He was relying on the weight of the wall to ram their weapons into us. We waited patiently. We knew how to deal with Saxon spears. Our mail, even if they managed to penetrate our shields, would block any blows.

I used the blade of my sword to flick the spearhead harmlessly up into the air. It slid between my head and Haaken's. Then they struck us. The wedge became a line as I held the leader and those behind him flowed around. Once we were beard to beard then the spear became a useless weapon. The second rank tried to stab over the heads of the front rank. The Saxons had made the mistake of putting taller men in the front rank and the spears were ineffective. Our line had held.

The Saxon leader's face was slightly below mine but he was close enough to hiss at me, "Viking dogs, we shall gut you like fish and put your heads on the walls! I am Eorledman Brynoth and I have slain many Vikings!"

I smiled, "But not, I think, an Ulfheonar! Push!" The Saxons had lost all cohesion now and were a swirling mass of warriors. They had not locked their shields and when I pushed, along with all of my men, with our shields the Saxons were forced back. As soon as there was space I stabbed forward with Ragnar's Spirit. The Eorledman's shield came up to block my strike but the edge slid over the bindings on his scale armour. As I withdrew it I saw leather beneath. We did not relent but all stepped forward once more. This time we had enough space to punch with our shields. I heard a cry from my right as Haaken slew one of the hearthweru. There was a second shout as the warrior who came to take his place was also slain by Haaken.

I pulled back my arm and, as we stepped forward again, I lunged at the Saxon's middle. His scale armour held but my punch winded him and he reeled back into the men behind. The weight of the Saxon and his armour knocked down two other Saxons and the Eorledman struggled to keep his feet. There was space before me and I brought Ragnar's Spirit down towards Eorledman Brynoth. Had the blow struck he would have died but one of his men tried to intervene. He took the strike instead and my sword hacked off his arm close to the shoulder. His falling body afforded Eorledman Brynoth the time to regain his balance and shout. "Back to the burgh!"

They turned and ran. I had no intention of following. I turned as I sensed a weapon coming towards me. A shieldless Saxon was thrusting his spear at my right side. I deflected the spearhead with my sword and then smashed him in the face with the boss of my shield. It struck him square on the face. His nose disappeared in a mess of blood and bone and he fell down dead. I was so surprised that I looked down at him. I had never killed a man with my shield before.

Turning around I saw that we had slain fifteen or so of the Saxons. My men were despatching those who were wounded. "Search the bodies and take the mail and the weapons to the ships. Olaf, take six men and stop them leaving by the north gate. I will send a messenger to you when it is time to leave."

Haaken joined me, "They were poor warriors."

I nodded, "Egbert will have his better men in Corn Walum. Did we lose many?"

"None. Some of the newer warriors were wounded. Arne Sheep Head now has a long scar across his face. Aiden will need to sew it."

"Let us see what we have and then return downstream."

Ketil's men were carrying boxes, chests and jars back to the ships. They were in good spirits, "We have a fine haul, Jarl Dragonheart!"

"You know what they say, Sven Thrallson, do not count your treasure until you are safely in your home. The Weird Sisters might be listening."

The warrior clutched the amulet around his neck, "Sorry Jarl! You are right!"

When I reached the river I saw that we had managed to capture four knarr. I did not have enough crew for all of them. We would crew two and sink two. I took off my helmet and walked down the river bank so that I could see Lambehitha. My drekar were still tied up but the men I saw, in the distance, did not look to be in any danger. I returned and climbed aboard the first knarr we had captured. Aiden was there organising the storage of the captured items.

"I think this knarr and the one at the end are the best two, Jarl. They have the largest holds. I am filling them first."

"Good. We will burn the others before we leave. Is it rich pickings?"

"Kara and the women will be happy. There are chests of fine pots from Frankia as well as spices. The other knarr we will take has a cargo of wine."

"Why were they not unloaded?"

"It was the festival of Easter. It is a holy day for the Christians and they do not work."

That explained much. I crossed to "**Heart of the Dragon**". Erik was still refitting the mast. He smiled, "A successful raid, Jarl. When do we leave?"

"I have Olaf watching the north gate. We will leave when Sigtrygg and Asbjorn are done. I need two men to captain the two knarr I will take. The men from Cyninges-tūn can guard the crew. We can row back to Tilaburg with just the Ulfheonar."

"I have two captains in mind. Thorir Svensson is one and Cnut Cnutson the other."

Cnut was the son of one of my dead Ulfheonar. He was now a warrior but he had been a ship's boy. He knew how to sail.

"Jarl! The other drekar come!"

I looked upstream and saw the sails of my two drekar as they sailed towards us. I shouted, "Snorri, fetch Olaf and his men. We leave." I crossed the knarr to the jetty. "Rollo Thin Skin, we take this knarr and the last one at the end, the one with the wine. Have the men from Cyninges-tūn crew them."

"Aye Jarl."

"Aiden, we fire the other two ships, see to it."

"Aye Jarl!"

It was mid-morning as we let the sails and the current take us back to Tilaburg. The smoke from the burning knarr obscured Lundenwic but I knew that some of the houses closest to them had also caught fire. Even as we passed Lundenburgh I saw Eorledman Brynoth leading his men out to try to save them. As we headed downstream I saw warriors on the south bank close to Suthriganaworc. They were pointing at us. I saw a rider heading upstream. Soon they would summon the fyrd.

I saw Erik looking back at the knarr. "What do you think of them, Erik?"

"They will slow us down but we can take more goods. What will we do when we return home? We cannot row *'Heart'* with just the Ulfheonar."

"I will put my mind to that when we reach Tilaburg."

"You intend to stay?"

"I have seen nothing yet to frighten us off. We have fourteen days before we need to think about heading back to the Sabrina. With one good raid now we can enjoy the whole of summer back in our home."

Aiden had joined us, "I, for one, would rather spend more time with my family. I do not feel the need for as many adventures as once I did."

We reached Tilaburg at noon. Raibeart came to greet us. I saw Siggi with the knarr. I stepped ashore and pointed to the two newly captured ships. "Empty the first of the knarr on to yours Siggi. I would not crew her unless I had to."

"The treasure from the monastery did not take up much hold space. What is the cargo?"

"The second has wine. We will leave that aboard as the knarr is full. The first has a variety of goods but the women will like the pots!"

Siggi rubbed his hands, "And more profit for us!"

I headed up the hill towards the monastery. Raibeart met me halfway up, "A successful raid, Jarl?"

"Aye Raibeart. We lost no men and the Saxons fled to their fort. We will raid along the river. Take your men, on the morrow and cross to the southern bank. We will rest here today and I will take men north. Are there any horses close by?"

"The monks have four."

"Good, then I will send Snorri and Beorn to scout."

"I put the monks to work preparing food. They have a plentiful supply of food and ale here."

"That is excellent, for I am hungry."

I went to the hall where the monks ate. There were ten of them and Raibeart's men were at the doors to prevent them from escaping. I took off my helmet. A young priest saw my red eyes and made the sign of the cross. I smiled, "Fetch me food and ale."

I laid my wolf cloak down and slumped at the table. I was tired. Time was I would have thought nothing of raiding all night and all day too. My Ulfheonar entered. Haaken was animated as he told the others of his two blows which killed two men in quick succession. They took their helmets off when they entered the hall and then sat down.

Haaken sat next to me. "And what of you, Jarl Dragonheart? You killed a man with your shield. Who has heard of such a thing?" He put his hand around my left arm. "This must be like an oak tree."

"It was just lucky. Perhaps he had a thin skull."

Haaken tapped his own head. We had fitted a small piece of metal into his skull when he had been laid low the previous year. "You cannot say that of me. I am Haaken One Eye, Iron Head!"

The food was brought over and the ale. The monks were terrified of us. We had been raiding the north and the west for many years but I think this was the first time that the Tamese had been raided. It was a rude awakening for them. I waited until we had eaten and drunk before I spoke with my Ulfheonar and my jarls.

"Tomorrow we leave a guard on the monks and ships then we head north. Raibeart will search the southern shore and we will see what Essex has to offer. We will not range far. I have no doubt that the Eorledman will send for help and we will have to face Saxons in the field. Rest today. I want one man in five as a sentry. Arrange for the changes yourselves."

Olaf Leather Neck banged the table with his seax handle, "Jarl Dragonheart! You have led us to success again! May the Allfather watch over you!" They all began banging the tables, making the pots and beakers rattle. I was lucky to have such men to lead.

When I awoke it was late afternoon. Aiden had done little during the night and had not bothered sleeping. He had been examining the books and the parchments we had captured. Knowledge was Aiden's treasure. "Well Aiden, are you pleased?"

"There is much here which we can use and some that we can sell. I have given thought to the knarr we emptied. If we fill it with the goods we wish to trade we can sail to the land of the Franks. They will buy the Holy books and the items from the churches. We have no need for such things. Siggi could come with us and then we could even sell the knarr too. You are right we cannot crew two such knarr. This way we make a profit and do not have to waste such a fine ship."

That made sense to me. "Good, then see Siggi and sail tomorrow. Choose your crew."

The two knarr sailed before dawn and I led my warband north. We went as three boat crews. We had left enough guards to closely watch the monks although they were so frightened that we would kill them that they seemed quite submissive. Snorri and Beorn had taken horses and they rode north before dawn. They met us on the Roman Road not far from Tilaburg. "We have found a hall. It is unguarded and looks to belong to an Eorledman or the like. It is on a hill. There is a farm and they have animals."

"How far is it?"

"Six Roman miles."

I had thirty men with me and I was confident that we could reach the hall and return unharmed. We began to run along the road. We reached the small stream which was a mile or so from the hall and we watched from the trees. "Snorri, take Beorn, Rolf Horse Killer and Rollo Thin Face. Make sure no one flees north."

We gave them a start and then spread out in a long line to ascend the slopes to the hill. It was a rich farm. There were sheep, cattle and horses grazing in the fields. I saw thralls with yokes around their necks labouring. It looked like the owner was building a second wing to the house. We approached unseen. The land lay in such a way that we were hidden from those who were toiling around the buildings. I had time to wonder why the thegn had not built a palisade around his home. The slope was such that a palisade and a ditch would have ensured he was safe from attack.

As we emerged from the dell, just fifty paces from the hall, we were seen. There were screams from the women and the men ran for their arms. I needed to give no commands to my men and ran as quickly as we could to those with weapons. I recognised the thegn from his fine clothes. He grabbed his sword and axe and stood before his door. I ran straight at him. He held his sword before him. I just raised my shield and hurled myself at the entrance. I knocked him to the ground. He slashed at my leg with his sword but I moved my foot out of the way.

"Surrender and you live! You are a brave man but you will die if you fight."

In answer, he swung his sword at my leg again. I brought my sword over and he managed to block it with his shield before rolling away. That was a mistake for he bared his back and Ragnar's Spirit hacked through his neck. The women and children who cowered in the corner of the room screamed and began to weep.

"Do not try to escape and you will not be harmed." I needed them to be as calm as possible. I turned, "Finni The Dreamer, watch these."

I went out of the hall. My men were finishing off those who had resisted and herding those who had surrendered towards the hall. "Ulf Olafsson, take some men and begin to drive the animals back to the ships. We will only need ten men for the prisoners."

"Aye Jarl. We will eat well this night."

I went to the other side of the hall and saw my four men walking towards me. They were driving four captives. When they neared me they said. "We killed the man. He resisted but we captured these."

"Have them load all of the food and valuables into carts. They can pull them. I would leave as soon as we can."

It was mid-afternoon by the time we crossed the stream and headed south. In the distance, I saw smoke spiralling into the sky and I wondered if that was one of my other jarls. I rode one of the captured horses and I went to speak with the woman who looked to have been the thegn's wife. I spoke in Saxon and, as always, it seemed to surprise the Saxon woman. "Your husband was a brave man. What was his name?"

She looked up at me and I could see the contempt on her face. She contemplated insulting me but she must have been a pragmatic woman for she answered, "Wulfric of Belesduna."

I nodded and rode in silence. That name would be useful. Aiden would put his red dot on his parchment and add another name. His maps were useful. It was how we had known of Lambehitha. The treasure from the two monasteries and their churches had almost filled the captured knarr. Even if the Franks paid us a fraction of their value we would still be rich.

"What will happen to us, Viking?"

"My name is Jarl Dragonheart."

She crossed herself, "You are the one who can become a wolf!"

I laughed, "It is a legend. Do not believe all the stories you hear. I wear a wolf skin and I carry a wolf charm. That is all."

"You did not answer me. What will happen to us?"

I liked her. She was afraid of me and yet she did not show it. She was willing to stand up to me. "To be truthful I know not yet. However, I never lie and I say to you that it may be you become slaves. I will promise you this; if you are to be a slave it will be in my home and you will not be ill-treated."

She gave a scornful laugh, "And that is supposed to make me feel better? We will still be slaves."

I pointed to the thralls who pulled the cart just ahead of us. "They were free once, lady. They are slaves. Did you treat them well?"

She looked nonplussed, "They are thralls!"

I shook my head, "As are you. If your husband had given you a wall and armed men instead of another building you might still be free. Those are the choices he made and you pay for them with slavery."

I urged my horse on. I had been taken as a slave. It was not the end of your life. It depended upon your attitude. Scanlan and Seara his wife had been slaves and I had freed them. Now they were happy. Deidra and Macha had been nuns and yet they were now free and held in high regard by my people. Slavery was not the end of life unless you chose to make it so.

My other bands had returned to the monastery with varying degrees of success. We had many sheep and cattle as well as enough horses to mount one warband if we chose. Raibeart returned with more treasure from a church. It was not as great as that from either Tilaburg or Lambehitha but there were precious metals and fine linen. He told me that they had destroyed the ferry which crossed the river at that point. We had cut off Tilaburg. We placed the captives, all of them, in the church. The priests comforted the wife and family of Thegn Wulfric. I guessed he had been an important man.

Rather than raid the next day we consolidated what we had. We slaughtered the older animals we had captured and salted the meat. We had found a great quantity of salt at Belesduna. I did, however, send riders to spy out any other sources of treasure. They brought the news that the fyrd had been raised and warriors were heading for us. It was not unexpected.

"When will they get here, Snorri?"

"If it was us then tonight but the Saxons move slower than a snail. It will be the morning before they reach us. They are heading first for Lundenwic."

My jarls and captains gathered around me. "Do we stay and fight or leave, Jarl Dragonheart?"

I smiled, Olaf Grimsson was the youngest of my captains. "We stay and fight, Olaf. Firstly we have to wait for the return of Aiden and Siggi and secondly, the Saxon fyrd is not a reason to flee. We will, however, be prudent. The ships will anchor in the river. It will stop the Saxons using ships to attack us and prevent reinforcements from joining from across the river."

The afternoon and evening were spent in sharpening weapons, oiling mail and preparing defences. I knew we would be outnumbered. I intended to use the land to help us. I would make them attack up the slope. I had Snorri gather fifteen warriors to use bows. We still needed men to guard the captives and so I was left with a hundred and twenty men to face the enemy. Twenty-five of us had full byrnies but all my warriors had a helmet, a shield and either a short byrnie or leather armour. We would be better armed than the fyrd.

We rose before dawn. Snorri had said it was unlikely they would attack before morning but it paid to be prepared. We had cooked half a dozen old sheep the night before and we ate well. The monks brewed good ale and we were as prepared for battle as any. Each warrior went through his own ritual. Mine was the same each time. I donned cochineal and then groomed myself. I took out Ragnar's Spirit and asked for the help of my old mentor and I touched the pommel stone which had come from deep within the earth. It was a link to the Mother. That done I was ready.

I went outside to join the sentries who watched to the west. Snorri had seen the fyrd approaching Lundenwic from the west. They would join the remains of the garrison. The warriors of the garrison were the real warriors. There would be other thegns who would bring their hearthweru. The Saxons found courage in numbers. The Saxons made good swords; some said the best but they did not handle them as well as we did. They used them like an iron bar. We had Beorn put a sharp tip on our swords so that we could stab. We had discovered that you could open up mail that way.

My men wandered out as they were ready. If I had given the alarm then they would have rushed but there was little point until the Saxons were in sight. One of the sentries shouted, "I see the banners and the crosses, Jarl. They come."

The Saxons always liked to have their priests with their crosses in their armies. They also carried boxes with pieces of the dead holy men with them. It rarely seemed to help them. I saw them as they rose along the Roman Road to Lundenwic. It looked to be a large number but there was little order. I saw the standard of Eorledman Brynoth and he rode with five or six other fully mailed men. I took them to be other thegns or Eorledmen. The hearthweru looked to be small in number, perhaps forty of them and only half were mailed. They looked to have brought a fyrd all of whom had a shield and a spear. Lundenwic was indeed a rich city.

They halted at the bottom of the hill upon which the monastery stood. It was neither a large nor a steep hill but we would have the advantage of height and that was always an advantage. Eorledman Brynoth rode forward a little way ahead of the throng of warriors behind him. He took off his helmet and held his hands open.

Haaken said, "It looks like he wishes to talk. Do you think he comes to surrender Essex to us?"

My Ulfheonar laughed.

"Possibly, Haaken. or maybe he has heard the stories about you and wishes to know the truth!"

That brought an even bigger laugh. It showed my men were comfortable but, more importantly, the Saxons shifted uncomfortably. They outnumbered us and yet we could still laugh. That was always disconcerting. Our ships were on the river and yet we had not fled.

"I will go and speak with him." I took off my helmet and handed it to Leif the Banner. My shield was behind my back and I kept my hands from my sword. I stopped twenty paces from him and waited.

"I come to ask you to surrender the captives you took, Jarl Dragonheart."

"And why should I do that?"

"Because if you do then you shall leave and live. If you do not then you stay and die."

I shook my head. "The last I saw of you, Eorledman, was when you were running back to Lundenburgh's walls. I do not think we have anything to fear from you."

"You are outnumbered and the men of Kent are coming."

"We stay until I am ready to go. We have many more animals to eat and there are churches all over this land. They yield much treasure and your women... well they are not as comely as ours but they will fetch a good price in the slave markets of Dyflin."

"This is your last chance."

"And we reject it."

He smiled, "Very well, then let battle commence."

There was something disquieting about his demeanour. He was up to something but I could not work out much.

"What did he want, Jarl?"

"He wanted us to leave!"

They all laughed. I had just donned my helmet and turned when I heard a roar from the bottom of the slope. The fyrd opened ranks and thirty mailed warriors, Danes, began to march towards us in a boar's head wedge.

I shook my head, "He has hired mercenaries!"

Olaf laughed, "At least we will get some decent armour from their corpses." He spat on his hands and prepared for battle.

Chapter 3

As the Danes marched up the slope with their double point the rest of Eorledman Brynoth's army fell in behind. The odds were now most definitely stacked against us. "Sigtrygg, extend to the right. Spears!"

The two ranks behind us pressed closer to us and their spears were jabbed over our heads. We all had a spear in the front rank. The main purpose of the double row of spears was to slow down their advance. We all had our swords in the earth just behind us. They would be the weapons we used to kill. We would be able to draw them easier from the ground than from a scabbard.

I did not recognise the Danes, just their helmets, armour and battle rings. There were many such mercenaries. They were happy to fight for anyone so long as they were paid. The Danish mail was as long as ours but I saw that some did not have sleeves. The front ten all wielded long two handed axes. My Ulfheonar knew how to deal with them but some of the newer warriors might not. Our front rank was composed of our best warriors. My jarls all stood with their oathsworn. We would have to withstand the hammer that would be the Danish attack.

"Snorri, you know what you must do."

"Aye, Jarl Dragonheart. These Danes are in for a shock."

He and the archers would send arrows over our heads. A Dane could wield an axe or hold a shield. He could not do both! Snorri and the archers were twenty paces behind us and were standing on the monastery wall. They had a clear line of vision to the Danes and mail could be pierced at fifty paces. The Danes were chanting. It took some moments for me to realise what and then I heard it, "Halfdan the Black! Halfdan the Black! Halfdan the Black!" It was the name of their leader. I saw why he had the name. His beard and his hair were as black as my wolf cloak. I saw many scars on his bare arms, testimony to his battles.

We waited patiently and when they were thirty paces from us Snorri and his archers began to release their arrows. It was a controlled shower. I saw the Dane next to Halfdan fall back with three arrows in his chest. Although he struggled to rise he was trampled by those behind. He was the first to fall but seven more fell before they were close enough to us to swing their axes. Only Halfdan and a second axe bearing Dane reached us and Halfdan had two arrows in his forearm. They did not appear to bother him. I left Snorri to thin out the ones who were following and I waited for Halfdan. I knew he would come for me. Leif the Banner stood behind me with my wolf standard. I did not hide from my enemies.

He ran the last two paces, leaving most of his wedge behind. He and his fellow swung their axes at Haaken and me in a double circle. It was almost mesmerizing. I knew that if it hit my spear it would shatter it. I wanted to strike a blow with it and so I timed my thrust so that the axe head was on its way up. It caught in his mail and I twisted and pushed. It made him slow and I pushed again. I heard a crack next to me as Haaken's spear was shattered. Above my shoulder were two spears but they would only help if Halfdan closed with me. A warrior standing behind Halfdan grabbed my spear and pulled it from me. I anticipated it and let go. He overbalanced and, as he did so, an arrow struck him in the throat. By my reckoning, more than a third of the Danes lay dead.

As the axe of Halfdan the Black came at me again I dropped to one knee and held the shield over my head. I reached for Ragnar's Spirit and as the axe smashed into the shield, numbing my arm, I thrust forward and stood up. Halfdan had good armour but my sword and my movement was too much for his mail. My sword went into his stomach and emerged at his shoulder. He roared and tried to bring his axe at me but he was too close and the spears from behind me darted forward and struck him in the mouth and the cheek. He now had four wounds and that was too much. I watched the light go from his eyes and he started to fall back.

This was our chance, "Push!" Spears, swords and axes fell upon the disorganized Danes.

Haaken had killed the other axeman and Sigtrygg and his men had slain the other Danes. We moved down the hill towards the Saxons. We now faced Saxons who did not wear mail. They were not in a tight shield wall and we were. They were downhill from us and when I brought Ragnar's Spirit over my head it split the Saxon thegn's helmet and skull in two. Blood and bone splattered on those behind. Olaf's axe took the head of the standard bearer and Haaken gutted a second thegn. With their leaders and hired swords gone, the Saxons began to fall back.

I shouted, "Second and third rank, pass!"

It was a manoeuvre we had practised and, as our front rank turned the next ranks stepped forward; a fresh line with unbroken spears. They hit the disordered Saxons while I formed my shield wall once more. We moved down the hill, following my men. They began to spread out before us into a large half-circle. If Eorledman Brynoth had had any sense he would have formed his reserves into a shield wall behind which the others could shelter but all he did was to feed more and more men, piecemeal, into the fray. It failed!

As we came up behind my men, who were tiring now, I shouted, "Break left and right!" I was proud of our men for they did it in one motion. I raised my sword for my elite warriors, "Charge!"

We began to move quickly down the slope and I led my thirty warriors directly for the Eorledman and his banner. The other thegns and leaders were mounted and gathered around him. We were just twenty paces from him when his nerve broke and he turned and fled. The other thegns followed a heartbeat later. The ones who had no horses, the ordinary warriors were struck by a solid wall of Ulfheonar. Their braver warriors stood but they were slain. The others were no match for my wolf warriors. All resistance ended and the Saxons left the field. We were too tired to follow but not too tired to cheer. We had won! Or, at least, the Saxons had retreated and were no longer a threat.

I turned to Haaken. "It seems we can stay a little longer in this land." I headed back up the slope stepping over the Saxon dead.

"Then we can go home as the richest Viking raiders ever."

I turned over the body of the warrior I had taken to be Halfdan. I looked at his many wounds. The spear I had thrust through him would have killed a normal man. "Perhaps he was a berserker."

Olaf said, "I remember being told of potions and plants which warriors can eat before a battle so that they feel neither pain nor wounds. This one should have succumbed to his wounds when you struck him with the spear."

"*Wyrd*. Have the bodies stripped. You were right Olaf. We have a fine haul."

Our warriors had suffered wounds and deaths. Some of the men of Cyninges-tūn would not be returning home. Arne Sheep Head was now missing a piece of his distinctive hair. He would live but he had taken a fierce blow.

I took off my helmet and wandered down to the river to bathe. It was not the clean water of home but it would have to do. I felt better with the blood and the gore cleansed from my body. I longed for the steam hut. I shook my head. Old Ragnar would be appalled. I was becoming soft. I was almost a Roman. I washed the blood from my sword and my seax. I cleaned the cochineal from my face and then trudged back to the monastery.

Some of my warriors were coming the opposite way and we exchanged greetings. Those, like Sigtrygg, Ulf and Asbjorn, who had fought with me many times, paused to clasp my hand and nod. It was the bond of the warrior. We had emerged victorious but we had all lost enough friends to know that there might come a day when we would not.

I went into the hall where the captives were held. I could hear wailing as I entered. Audun Karlsson had commanded the guards. I went over to him. "Why the wailing?"

He laughed. I had chosen him because he could speak Saxon. "The old priest told them that God was on their side and he would give strength to their warriors' arms and they would be victorious. They were all on their knees praying throughout the battle. When they heard that we had won then they began to weep."

I shook my head and shouted, "Listen to me. Those who came to rescue you are dead or fled. You will be treated well but you are my captives. Cease this wailing for it offends my ears. I was a slave once and I now lead men. Your salvation lies not with this White Christ but within yourselves!"

I saw the priests crossing themselves as I uttered the blasphemy. As I left I wondered if I should have sent them to Frankia with Aiden.

The next day I sent out three large warbands to the east. We had not raided there. Although the land was marshy they did have farms and churches. For two days they scoured the land and returned with more candlesticks, linen, animals and slaves. We could have left then but I wished to wait for Siggi and Aiden to return. We still had many days before we had to meet Coen's knarr on the Sabrina. Despite my words, the captives still wept and prayed. It was getting on my nerves. My ships in the river were a large enough deterrent to ensure that no one moved up or down the river. They were a dam of ships.

"Snorri, how many horses do we have?"

"Thirty, Jarl."

"We take the Ulfheonar and Sigtrygg and his men. We will ride to Lundenburgh. I think I will speak with this Eorledman Brynoth."

The horses were not the largest I had ever seen and my feet almost touched the ground but it saved walking and cut the journey by half. We were seen long before we reached the Saxon stronghold. The gates were barred and the walls were manned. I dismounted and, with Leif the Banner and Haaken One Eye, I approached the walls. I stood a hundred paces from them. It was a contemptuous act for if they had any decent archers they could have easily hit me but I knew that they would not even try. My guards at the monastery had told me that the Saxons regarded me as some sort of mythical monster. I think they believed I was a half-human form of Grendel!

The Eorledman shouted down, "What do you wish now?"

"If I wanted your town I would take it for I have seen little to stop me. Even when you hire savages from the east we defeat you. You have no honour, Saxon. I did not see you in the shield wall. You did not trade blows with us. King Egbert will not be happy when he returns."

I had hit home with my last barb for he jabbed an accusing finger at me, "And he is returning, Dragonheart! We have sent riders to him!"

I laughed. It would take almost half a month to reach him and as long for him to return. Even if a message had been sent to the King of Wessex, Egbert was too clever a general to come back for one Viking raid.

"Then I should go, should I not, before he returns? Perhaps I shall go now and sell my captives in Dyflin's slave market. And yet I stay here. You have much yet which I can take and no one to stop me. Your men of Kent failed to arrive, did they not? Who is left? Perhaps the Mercians will come to aid me? We change our allies these days. I fought for Egbert against Coenwulf and the Danes and now you bring Danes to fight me. Strange bedfellows!"

He was silent and Haaken said quietly, "You have him confused now, Jarl. He knows not what to do."

"And I have not finished yet, Haaken." I raised my voice, "Perhaps I should bring my men and ships from Tilaburg. We could camp here around your burgh. What say you to that?"

He had not seen that possibility. I doubted that there would be enough supplies in the burgh to feed the ones who had fled there and I knew that we had hurt their trade and Lundenwic prospered on trade.

After a short silence, the Eorledman shouted, "What will it take for you to leave?" Before I could answer I saw a priest next to him say something. "And to leave all the captives here too?"

"Gold and silver!"

"How much?"

"Bring all that you have in three days to Tilaburg. If it is enough I will leave. If you have brought all that you can then I will let you have the captives."

"But how do I know how much is enough?"

"You tell me. How much is the prosperity of Lundenwic and how much do you wish the captives returned?"

He spoke to those around him and said, "And how much would you pay if the situation was reversed?"

I laughed, "You do not know me Eorledman; any who touches what is mine pays with his life. Ask the Danes Egbert sent to hurt me. They enjoyed the blood eagle. Do not make the same mistake King Egbert made. I inflict this upon Lundenwic because your King Egbert sends assassins, warbands and killers into my land. So the answer is, I would pay in blood! I would pay in death!"

Even from a hundred paces, I saw his shoulders slump as he said, "Very well we will come but do you give your word that you will not raid while we gather the gold?"

"If you want me to stop raiding then come sooner!"

I sent Asbjorn and Ketil south of the river, the next day and they scoured the lands of Kent. The men of Wessex had taken much but we still managed to bring pots, treasure and weapons.

Siggi and Aiden returned the day before my deadline. I noticed that the knarr rode higher in the water. They had managed to trade. Aiden and Siggi's faces confirmed the success of the voyage.

"We have many chests of gold, Jarl. The King of Wessex is not popular in Frankia. They may not like Vikings but they despise the men of Wessex."

"Did they know you were Vikings?"

"They suspected but, like Haaken here, they turned a blind eye to it for they wanted the knarr and the treasure we took."

"Good. We can begin loading the knarr with the best of the animals and the rest of the treasure. The Saxons come tomorrow with gold to buy us off. I intend to sell the captives back to them. We will not have the bother of selling them in Dyflin. Siggi, we will need someone from your knarr to steer the captured knarr."

"I will see to it, Jarl. I have one who could be a captain." He looked sad, "Since Trygg was slain I have missed the company of another captain. Einar Blue Eye has served me well. I would, with your permission, give him the knarr."

"Of course."

That last day was hectic as the animals we would not be taking were slaughtered. We took the skins and hides. They would be treated back in Cyninges-tūn. Tanned hides and skins were both valuable and useful. The meat we salted and put in some of the empty beer barrels. We had drunk many of the barrels of beer and ale the monks had had and they made the perfect container for the salted meat. The captives knew that something was going on and I was approached by Hilda, the wife of Wulfric, the slain thegn. She had learned to defer to me and she gave a slight bow, "Lord, you are leaving?"

"We are leaving!"

"And us?"

"You will leave too unless Eorledman Brynoth brings enough gold to satisfy us."

She looked upset, "My fate is in his hands? Then we are doomed for he has coveted my husband's lands for years. If my son is sold as a slave then he will have the land for himself!"

I had thought that the man was cunning. "Do not worry. They want the churchmen so much that he will pay. You have shown courage, lady and I would spite this Eorledman. You will not be sold in Dyflin but say nothing to the priests."

"But why?"

"I have my reasons." I smiled, "Do not judge all Vikings by the actions of a few. If the priests know what I have just said then I will sell you and your family to the Irish and that I swear!"

"Then I swear I will say nothing." As she held the cross which was around her neck I believed her.

My scouts reported the arrival of the Saxon host. There was a large number but I could see that they came not for war. They had priests with them and wagons carrying chests. I went to meet them with my jarls.

"Let us get this over with I either have a tide to catch or Saxons to slaughter. First, where is the gold to make us leave?"

The Eorledman snapped his fingers, imperiously, and ten chests were brought forward. I nodded to Haaken who opened each one and sifted through them to make sure that they had not filled the bottom with rocks and salted the top with a few coins. "It is good, Jarl Dragonheart."

"And now for the captives."

The priest who had the most regal robes waved forward two slaves who carried two boxes and laid them before us. Haaken, check them again and nodded. I turned, "Bring forward the captives."

Aiden led Hilda and her family and the farmers and their families. The priests and monks, all twenty of them, were guarded.

"Here are your captives." Hilda gave me a grateful nod as she passed me.

Eorledman Brynoth and the priest became almost apoplectic, "This was for the monks and priests!"

I smiled, "I am the seller here. If you wish the monks then I want another three boxes of gold and coins."

I was gambling but I had seen more wagons lower down the hill. The priest nodded and waved them forward. They unpacked three chests and brought them to us. They were filled to the brim. I had seen one more box chest there.

"Very well you have paid my money and we will leave." I turned and shouted, "Fetch the priests and burn the monastery!"

The priest in the regal robes shouted, "No! We have paid you!"

"And I have given you that for which you paid. We said nothing about leaving the church and the monastery standing!"

"Here, one chest of gold to leave the church alone." A final chest, smaller than the rest appeared as if by magic.

I smiled, "Very well. Do not fire the church!"

The Saxons did not leave but watched as we loaded our drekar and knarr with our booty. We had achieved far more than I would have dreamed possible. As we headed out to sea Haaken said, "When others hear of this raid, Jarl, they will visit this land in even greater numbers."

"I know, Haaken, but next time they will defend better and pay less. This is *wyrd*. It is weregeld for all that King Egbert has done to us."

We were watched from the banks as we left. The skies were dark and foreboding. It seemed ominous. My drekar led the other ships. We had used a couple of men from each drekar to crew the new knarr which we had named "***Weregeld***". With Siggi abeam of her and Asbjorn behind she would be as well protected as any. Sigtrygg and Olaf sailed on the flanks.

Aiden seemed disturbed as we headed out to sea. "What troubles you, my galdramenn?"

"The Danish mercenaries worry me. They came within a short time. You say there were about thirty and that is not enough for a boat crew. Where are the rest? Had I been there when the battle was fought I might have detected their thoughts."

I looked astern. "Let us assume you are right," I smiled, "and you are rarely wrong, then there may be more Danes and they have to be north of us." I turned to Erik, "Where is the wind from?"

"The northeast Jarl. It carries us home quickly."

"Aiden thinks that there may be Danes around. Aiden, when did the feeling come upon you?"

"When we passed the island where first we sheltered."

Erik nodded, "There are many channels on the north side. You could hide a fleet there. What do we do, Jarl?"

"We have to sail at the speed of the knarr. Slow down and I will speak with Siggi. When we begin to turn around the coast I will let him and the other knarr lead. We will be a wall of wood behind them. The Danes will have to come through us."

The coast of Kent turned south and, as we slowed, Siggi came abeam of us. I had Erik get us as close as he could but, even so, I still had to shout. "Aiden fears Danish pirates. You lead, "***Weregeld***". If trouble comes then sail for the Sabrina and we will catch you up."

"Aye Jarl."

We used Leif and the banner to signal the other drekar into a line. I needed not tell them anything. I merely pointed astern and held my sword up. They knew the signal. There was danger. As soon as we made the turn to steerboard the wind pushed us along at a far faster rate. If there were Danish pirates they would be able to close with us quickly. One fear I had was that they might be ahead of us but then I realised that Eorledman Brynoth would have waited until he had the priests before telling his erstwhile allies. We had a little time. We could have rowed but that would have tired my warriors and would have done us little good.

We had to keep the knarr in sight and they sailed at the speed of the wind. The advantage would be that the Danes if they caught us, would have rowed and they would be tired. We were on the left of the line with the two smaller drekar between us and *'Odin's Breath'*. We were the biggest by some way but Asbjorn's drekar was bigger than most. Sigtrygg's *'Crow'*, was the least of my worries for he was an experienced captain and warrior. He would keep his drekar out of trouble.

"Snorri, break out the bows and have the archers gather here in the stern. We will keep them at a distance for as long as possible."

"We will be releasing into the wind, Jarl."

"I know but we do what we can. A couple of lucky strikes can make all the difference."

I was not certain I believed it but Ragnar had told me that a true warrior never gave up until he saw Odin's face.

Erik shouted, "Thorir, keep a good watch astern!"

"Aye Captain."

The ship's boy had his legs wrapped around the mast as he sat on the crosstree. He had young eyes and he would see the enemy first. We began to edge around the southern coast of Kent and were heading due west. Hope sprang in my heart. I began to believe that Aiden might have been wrong when Thorir's voice rang out. "Jarl Dragonheart, there are six Danish drekar astern."

"Prepare for war!"

I had not yet taken off my mail and I picked up my helmet. I would delay putting it on until the last moment. Haaken and Olaf joined me. "They will catch us and we must somehow defeat them."

"*'Red Snake'* and *'King's Gift'* are both threttanessa, Jarl. They have small crews."

"I know Olaf."

"And their captains have never fought at sea."

"Thank you, Haaken. Is there something you wish to tell me that I do not know?"

Haaken was silent. Aiden said, "Is it too risky to use fire?"

"The wind is wrong, Aiden. Fire arrows do not have the range of normal arrows and we would be releasing them into the wind. No, I am afraid this will be an old-fashioned battle. We must use the skills of the Ulfheonar and Asbjorn."

"*'Crow'* has Sigtrygg and his men on board. He has fought at sea."

"But not for some time." This was all my fault. I had been so confident that I could defeat the Saxons I had forgotten about sea battles. We had not prepared. I promised myself that, if we survived this, then we would work out tactics should such a situation occur. Had Wolf Killer been with us we would have had a second drekar which was as big as mine. I glanced astern and I could now see them. They were catching us. I was tempted to row but that would not help my knarr. If anything we needed to go slowly. I put my hand on my sword and stared up at the skies as though they might give me inspiration.

And then the idea came to me just as suddenly as the lightning had struck the tower back on Man all those years ago. "Aiden and Snorri have fire and fire arrows prepared."

Erik said, "But Jarl that is risky and they will not reach the enemy!"

"They will if we are behind them."

"But how ..." He smiled, "You have the cunning of a fox."

Olaf looked confused, "Then explain it to me Jarl for I know not what we do!"

"We turn and sail across their bows and then into the wind. They are using oars and they will go beyond us. They will pass close enough for our arrows to do them damage and then when we are turned the wind will be with us and carry our arrows further."

"But what of the others? They will not know the plan."

"I have three experienced jarls aboard those ships. They will work it out quickly enough besides, we are the largest drekar and we can do this alone."

Haaken burst out laughing, "Each time I think I have the saga in my head, Jarl Dragonheart excels himself!"

I turned to Erik, "I leave the turn to you, Erik. You know how to judge these things."

"We need them close enough so that they are still rowing. They will stop when they are within three boat lengths. I will wait until they are four lengths away. If we shorten sail a little now it will slow us down and, perhaps, tell the other captains what we plan."

"Good idea. Olaf, you keep watch on the Danes."

Now that I had a plan I felt better about the way the events were turning out. Firstly it would ensure that the knarr escaped. Our people would benefit even if we were dead. Secondly, it gave us a fighting chance. If they held the wind gauge then they could dictate the battle and thirdly they would now not only be tired but confused and those two conditions made men make mistakes.

"Five lengths, Jarl."

Erik said, "Then it is time!" he shouted, "Prepare to come about!"

I had to help him, along with Olaf, to push the steering board hard over. We began to head south and we kept the wood of the steering board hard over as we turned to face east. Snorri, Aiden and the archers were now in the bows with the small brazier and the fire arrows. They would not release yet. As we began to turn east I saw the bows of the Danish dragon ship hurtling towards us. The captain had not managed to get all of his oars in and, as we turned and my archers released arrows at his stern, our drekar smashed across half of the oars. I had seen the effect before at first hand and not only would the oars be broken and therefore useless, but the splinters could severely wound and even kill a rower.

"Haaken, what of the other drekar?"

"They have all turned, Jarl and they are passing between the Danes." Asbjorn would have two drekar to contend with; one on each side. I hoped that my others were as lucky as I had been and that they would also break some oars and that their arrows would inflict casualties.

We were close enough to see the faces of our foes. Some shook their fists. I saw others lifting wounded warriors and all the time Snorri and his ten archers were loosing arrows at the crew around the steering board. We were going so slowly now, heading into the wind, that we were barely making any way. Had our sail not been partially shortened then we would have stopped. Erik continued, with the help of Olaf, to turn us so that we could sail along the sterns of the Danes.

As we passed the stern I saw that we could almost touch it and that the helmsmen and the others had been slain. I grabbed the torch which we kept at the stern to signal the other drekar and hurled it as high as I could. The wind caught it and carried it to the stern. There was no one to douse it. Ship's timbers are notoriously dry and as we began to move, more quickly north, flames leapt up and the ropes and sheets began to burn. One Danish drekar would not be able to fight.

None of my other ships had thought of using fire arrows but they all had archers ready and as they sailed, now ahead of us, they showered arrows on the Danes. The four remaining Danes were trying to turn to mirror our course. As they turned into the wind their full sails caused them to slow to a stop. We now had the wind and we sped along their line.

Snorri and Aiden worked as a team and their arrows struck the second drekar. This time there were crew ready to douse the flames but the Norns aided us and two arrows struck the sail, which could not be doused. And then we had passed that and the third drekar loomed up. Fortunately for the Danish captain, he had not turned as quickly as his fellows and only two arrows struck him but he was too far away to be a danger. A fourth had become becalmed as its captain miscalculated and I saw him as they used their oars to turn the lumbering drekar around.

That left the last two and they had closed with each other to provide mutual help. Although stronger they had no manoeuvrability. The two threttanessa danced around them like hounds around a bear. They were irritating more than deadly but it kept the attention of the Danes on them. I saw as we neared them that the last ship had managed to grapple **'Odin's Breath'**. That would not do.

"Ulfheonar. We go to the aid of Jarl Asbjorn. Prepare to board the last drekar."

They all went to the side.

"Erik, we will board at the stern and cross to Asbjorn's drekar. Go alongside him."

"Aye Jarl."

It was not as risky as one might have thought. I would lead twelve warriors and attack the most vulnerable part of the ship. All attention would be on Asbjorn's drekar and we would have surprise; I hoped. Erik judged it well. Our sturdy side struck the stern and Olaf and Ulf led my Ulfheonar onto the deck of the Danish ship. It was smaller than ours and lower in the water. I was the fourth one on board. My men had slain the five who had been there. The steering board was next to me and I took the axe from the dead warrior's hand and hacked through the rudder boss. The drekar could not steer until it was repaired.

There was just Rolf Horse Killer behind me with his two handed axe as I ran to follow my men. Olaf, Haaken and Ulf were carving a path through the Danes to get to **'Odin's Breath'**. The ship was rolling as it was beam onto the wind and the waves. Keeping your footing was difficult. Had I not done this many times before I would have fallen but I kept my balance. A Dane tried to swing his axe over his head and he overbalanced. I slashed across his neck with Ragnar's Spirit.

Rolf was young and he was able to adapt. He had his shield over his back and he held his axe at the end and in the middle. He would not overbalance. He jabbed it forward and caught a Danish sailor in the middle. As he pulled it to one side he tore open the Dane's stomach.

Ahead of us, the Danish warriors had realised that we were aboard and our progress was halted. What they did not know was that we were Ulfheonar. Ridiculous odds do not matter. I heard a roar as Olaf launched himself at the three Danes who blocked our way. Haaken's sword darted out swiftly to hamstring one of them and Ulf used the fallen body to jump high into the air and crash down on the warriors pressing to get at Olaf. My Ulfheonar spread out and Danes were pushed over the side to be dragged down by their mail into the icy waters.

I was almost knocked against the mast by a blow from a Danish axe. My shield took the blow and I stabbed at his head. Using an axe two handed meant you had no shield. Ragnar's Spirit went into his mouth and came out at the back of his neck. Asbjorn and his crew were given heart by our sudden attack and they fell upon the other side of the Danes. Rolf and I were suddenly without foes. "Rolf, hack a hole in the hull!"

He grinned, "Aye Jarl."

I shouted, "Back to *'Odin's Breath'*!" Olaf and the others redoubled their efforts and soon joined up with Asbjorn. His archers picked off any Dane who looked likely to follow. I felt water at my feet. Rolf had succeeded. The drekar was sinking. "Back to the ship."

I punched a warrior in the face with my shield as I swung Ragnar's Spirit sideways. I cleared a path and followed Rolf Horse Killer. The Dane was filling with water faster than I intended and I wondered if I would make the side of Asbjorn's drekar. Its deck was higher than the Dane's. I sheathed my sword and looked for a way off the doomed vessel. I saw a Danish body and I ran at it. I pushed off and leapt up. It was a leap of faith but it was rewarded as my Ulfheonar pulled me to safety. By the time I had turned around the Dane was almost sunk and we had beaten off the Danish attack.

Chapter 4

We caught up with the knarr the next morning. I only knew of Asbjorn's losses but I suspected that he had suffered the most. Eight of his men had gone to Valhalla. They had had a glorious death and we would honour them when we reached home. My Ulfheonar had suffered slight wounds but nothing to prevent them from rowing. Haaken spent the whole of the next day composing his saga. He felt that our victory was so great that men would speak of it for years to come. "Three of those Danish ships will have survived. Think of how they will tell it."

For Haaken it was all about the glory. I was not Norse born and for me, it was the survival of as many of my men as possible and we had been lucky. We hove to close to Vectis. I was anxious to find out about our other losses. It turned out that Asbjorn had been unlucky. Our plan was a good one but the Norns had intervened. Two Danish drekar had closed with him and he had been attacked before he could escape. We did not go ashore for Vectis was Wessex but just rested on our ships. We had plenty of food; thanks to our raid.

The winds abated and, when we left, it was a gentle voyage around the edge of Corn Walum. We had time to talk of the raid. "It was so successful Jarl Dragonheart that, perhaps, we could do it each year." Erik Ulfsson was keen for more riches.

"It was successful because no one had done it before. King Egbert has almost conquered Corn Walum. He will build burghs. Besides they will be watching for us. We need to find places which have not been raided before. They are hard to find. For myself, I am happy not to raid. If any of my Ulfheonar or other warriors wish to use my drekar to raid then they are welcome to do so but I have a daughter. I would like to see her grow."

I could see that I had disappointed my younger warriors but my older ones had tales enough to tell their children. I listened while the young warriors planned further raids. I hoped that they were not letting success go to their heads. That could be fatal. Coen Ap Pasgen's knarrs were heavily laden and waiting for us in the Sabrina. They joined our two knarr and my drekar were like sheepdogs patrolling the flock. We saw some Irish pirates as we neared Ynys Môn. The winds had taken us close and speeded our journey. We could not avoid contact. There were three of them and they headed west as soon as they saw our drekar. They had learned that these dragonships had teeth.

Sigtrygg left us south of Úlfarrston. We would send his share of the profits by packhorse. He was keen to return to his land. Sigtrygg had fewer warriors than most of my jarls and it had been his sons who had stayed to guard his home with the older warriors. He would return with mail, pots, swords and spices. His people would prosper. Rather than dock at Úlfarrston, the three drekar sailed up to the shipyard. There was damage to our two larger drekar and both Asbjorn and Erik were desperate for Bolli to repair them.

Aiden took the younger warriors and they escorted him and his precious maps, parchments and the ingredients for his spells back to his hall. The rest of my crew marched down to Úlfarrston. The knarr would take some unloading and my warriors liked me to divide the spoils of war.

As we walked Olaf Leather Neck reflected, "It is a pity we could not have taken the mail from those Danes on the ship we sank. It was fine mail. My blunted axe is a testament to that."

Ulf Olafsson said, "I like not battles at sea. A good warrior can be defeated by a lucky one. We were fortunate that the Norns were sleeping."

He could mention them now for we were on solid ground and had returned home. A warrior never mentioned them when we were at sea. Haaken said, "But were they? When we left Tilaburg I thought the adventure was over. We were lucky to have a galdramenn with us. Had Jarl Dragonheart not adopted the formation he did we might have lost a drekar."

Erik Ulfsson shook his head, "Danes are becoming a problem, Jarl Dragonheart. When they just settled in the east that was one thing but hiring their axes out to Saxons is something else."

He was right and he had voiced my thoughts. "You are right, Erik. Eoforwic is almost more Dane than Saxon. I am just grateful that the gods put the high mountains between us and Northumbria."

The five knarr were already being unloaded at the jetty in Úlfarrston. The hundred men I brought would make short work of the unloading but the division would be hard. I smiled to myself. Aiden normally did that for me but he had been eager to return to Kara and Ylva. He had changed.

I spoke with Coen as the goods were taken off and placed into five piles while the animals were gathered in five herds. I had told Haaken how I wanted them divided. I told Coen of our raid and the attack. "It is lucky then that my knarr waited for you, Jarl. Those Irish pirates would have made short work of my three ships."

"My jarls all wish to raid again. I will ask them to escort your ships to the Sabrina if that is where they go."

"I think they would trade with your brethren in Ljoðhús. They are made welcome there and the seal oil is a valuable commodity as are the seal skins." He pointed at the pots and cloths his men were unloading. "They are desperate for such fine goods."

I nodded, "Then I will see which of them wish to raid the monasteries on the west coast of Hibernia and the men of Strathclyde although I am reluctant to poke that wasp's nest. They can be defeated but there is little treasure to be had from them. Tell me, did the Danish spies return?"

"No, Jarl, although some of my fishermen saw the wreckage of a fishing boat a week after you left. There was a violent storm. Perhaps it was they who perished."

"Perhaps." I was not certain. I did not like such unanswered questions. "Have your men watch for them and if there is any sign then let me know."

"I will."

"Jarl Dragonheart we are done."

I went over to join my jarls. The five piles were impressive. "Are you happy with the division? Does any man wish me to make changes?"

The jarls and the hersir all shouted as one, "No, Jarl Dragonheart!"

"Good," I turned to Coen. "I would have you watch over Jarl Sigtrygg's goods. He and his men will fetch horses tomorrow."

"I will have my men guard it. It will be safe."

I turned to Erik Ulfsson, "Have the horses loaded. I picked up one box of coins. It was not the largest but it was substantial. "Come Haaken, we will return to Erik."

Each drekar had some of the captured goods in their holds. We had made one division when in Tilaburg. It was dark when we reached the shipyard but Erik had been busy. The hull had been emptied and they were already removing the mast so that they could repair the damage to the side where we had hit the stern of the Danish drekar.

"Erik, here is your share."

I handed him the chest, "Jarl, it is too much! I have never seen such a chest of treasure."

"You earned it and I do not think that *'Heart of the Dragon'* will raid again this year; not unless my men wish it."

"Good, for I have some improvements to make and this coin will please Bolli."

I shook my head, "It is my drekar and I will pay for the improvements." I took out a purse of coins. This was treasure I had taken from dead Saxons when we had first defeated them in Lundenwic. "Here, use this and if it is not enough then send to Scanlan and I will send more. It is not right for a captain to pay for work on the ship of another."

"Thank you, Jarl. Then my wife will be even happier!"

Despite the lateness of the hour, we made our way up the Water to Cyninges-tūn. We had been away long enough and all my men wished to see their families and their homes. They would become restless again but not for a month or two. When the summer waned they would seek the sea and they would raid but, for the next few months, they would enjoy their farms and their families.

My men were noisy as we marched along the water and my sentries in my town roused the families. We were greeted like heroes by grateful wives and sleepy children. Aiden and his escort had warned them of our imminent arrival. Brigid had food ready for me when I entered my hall. She held a sleeping Erika in her arms and I kissed first my wife and then my daughter. Brigid wrinkled her nose, "You smell of the sea! And sweat!"

I grinned and shook my head, "I am sorry my pungent smells offend you. I shall bathe before I return next time."

She smiled, "No, but I am just saying that I will have Uhtric light the fire in the steam hut in the morning and then I will have a husband who does not smell like a fish!"

"And I will happily enjoy the pleasures of the hut believe me."

"The raid went well. Aiden told me. Does that mean you stay within these walls for a time? Will you see our daughter grow?"

"I will not go to sea for a while and I will be in the hall but not for the whole summer. I must see my son and visit the Stad on the Itouna. You could come with me if you wish."

She laughed, "You will forgive me if I say no. I know how you and your men are happy to sleep on the ground and suffer horses' backs for days. Just so long as you are away for days and not months then I am happy."

Uhtric had brought in a bowl of hot food and some freshly brewed ale. While Brigid nursed the babe I ate. After the food had gone and the ale was drunk I had a second horn. It was a good ale. Brigid was a fine alewife. "Have you heard from my son?"

A frown crossed her face, "I am such a goose! You have a new grandson, Garth."

My face must have lit into a smile for Brigid's frown disappeared. "He named him after me?"

"Aye, for he came out kicking and screaming. He fought for life and Elfrida said he was just like his grandfather. They said it was *wyrd*." She shook her head and crossed herself; it felt blasphemous for her to say such things.

My wife was a Christian and said that she did not believe in superstition. Secretly I think she did but would never admit to it. That is the way of women. They like to have the last word. Old Ragnar has said that they liked the first word, the last word and as many others in between. He was afraid of no one but he would have rather faced a dozen warriors than a woman's sharp tongue. I went to bed happy. I had a new grandson, my wife was happy and we had had a good raid. The world of Cyninges-tūn was in harmony.

We had work to do the next day as my people waited for me to divide up the animals, treasure and goods we had brought back with us. Haaken and my men were always disappointed when I did not take a greater share. I did not need it and they could not understand that. I think that was the blood of my mother's people. My family would not suffer but why did I need extra gold and silver? I had plenty. I had never been defeated in battle and every time I slew a great warrior I was the richer. I took a ram and an ewe for I had an idea to crossbreed the animals. My own flock, which my thralls watched for me, were hardy but they had little meat and their wool was not high quality. The two I had taken were. I would have Scanlan begin to breed them.

When they had all departed I sought out Bjorn Bagsecgson. I had gold for him but it was for a purchase I wished to make. "A good raid, Jarl. I shall do well for already every young warrior has been with gold and asked for a byrnie of mail! Some have even enough gold for a good sword. Some of the mail you brought can be repaired but much of it will need to be melted down and reused."

"The Saxons and their churches are well endowed, Bjorn." I handed him my helmet. "I would have you attach mail around the bottom of my helmet."

He frowned. He had made the helmet. "Is there a problem with the helmet, Jarl? Is it unsatisfactory?"

"No, Bjorn, but I have seen warriors who have had their throats slashed in battle. It is too vulnerable a place. The weight will not be much."

"No, and it is a good idea." He smiled, "Of course as soon as you have it then Haaken and the others will all come in to copy the idea."

"I know!"

Once Scanlan knew what I intended for my sheep he was happy. "I have hired some shepherds, Jarl. They are building a hut on the fells close by Old Olaf."

He was not asking permission but he had been a slave once and he was still deferential to me. He had yet to make a bad decision. "That is good. You have my permission to give them one lamb in four for themselves."

"A wise decision Jarl. If we did not then they might take them anyway."

"Scanlan, there were Danish spies at Úlfarrston. They have fled but I want all newcomers watched carefully until we know that we can trust them."

"These shepherds are not from outside our land, Jarl. They lived up close to the Stad by the Itouna and they feared the raids from Strathclyde. They lost their flock last winter; some to the wolves and some to raiders."

"Then, when my men are rested, I will take a warband and we will scour the land north of the Itouna. It is time they learned to go elsewhere for their animals."

Finally, I went to see my daughter and granddaughter. Ylva would be a great volva one day; her mother and her grandmother had both been volvas and her father was a galdramenn. But to me, she was just my first granddaughter. She giggled when she saw me. I took that as a good sign but my daughter assured me that it was just wind. We spoke of the treasures we had captured and how they would improve the lives of our people. Already those who lived in our town by the Water had better homes than any other in the land for they had much stone in their construction.

"We have to do something about the cattle and sheep raids from north of the river. Arne Thorirson is a good hersir but he is not a warrior." Raids and wars had taken my jarls from the northern borders. I needed to put a warrior there who would be an effective leader.

My son and daughter had a way of knowing what I thought. Aiden said, "Ulf and Erik are both good warriors. They have recently taken a wife each. Perhaps one of them might like to rule the northlands for you. Ketil has kept the east quiet. He was a good choice. Which one would you choose?"

"I think Ulf for he is older and Erik is close to Rollo and Rolf. He has taken them under his wing. I do think it would be good for the Ulfheonar to separate them."

"Then make him Jarl. Arne will appreciate that. He is a good farmer and a stout man in a shield wall. You need an Ulfheonar to guard the frontier." It was an easy decision to make. I knew why I had delayed in making it. Ulf Olafsson was one of the most reliable warriors I had. He would now be many leagues north if he accepted my offer.

Macha and Deidra came through with freshly made bread and cheese along with a horn of ale. Although they had both been nuns of the White

Christ and Christians, they had adapted well to our way of life. I doubted that they would admit it but both seemed content in my land. If they chose to leave then we would not stop them. Since my wife arrived, they had a small community of Christians. They found comfort in each other's company.

"Try this, Jarl we have flavoured the cheese with thyme and wild garlic."

Both were expert makers of cheese. I tasted it and it was delicious. "I shall have some of this for my hall if you would. My wife would enjoy it."

"It was she who suggested it. You have a good wife there, Jarl."

"I know." I wondered if it was her religion which made it so in their eyes.

Kara nodded, "And you have raided well, Father. Those fine pots are better than any our potters can make."

"That is because we do not have clay hereabouts. The gods gave us slate, iron and copper. North of the Dunum, Jarl, close to where the Roman fort and bridge lie, there is fine clay. Perhaps those who live there make pots."

"If not we could take the clay. It is something to consider." There were always ways of improving the lives of our people.

After I had eaten and drunk I left and went back to my hall for my horse. Ulf Olafsson lived close to the tarns. He had a few sheep, although it was hardly a flock. It was something he could do when he came home and wanted to be the farmer. In his heart, he was a warrior. He liked the privacy and that was something he would not enjoy at my stronghold to the north. I would have to see if he was amenable to my offer.

It was a pleasant ride and gentle enough for my horse. The trail wound up through the trees towards the muddy bottomed tarns. I smelled the smoke from his home. As I dropped down from the rise I saw him smoking some venison. His wife, Anya, who was with child, was seated on a log watching him. She was much younger than Ulf and I had wondered before he had married her if he would ever take a wife. She stood as I approached. "Keep your seat, Anya Olafsson. I need words with your husband."

"It is a poor wife who cannot entertain the Jarl of this land. I have some freshly brewed ale."

She went inside as I dismounted. My horse wandered over to the small tarn by which Ulf had built his home. "She is a good woman Ulf. You are lucky."

"I know, Jarl Dragonheart. I wonder how I managed without her for so many years."

She returned with the ale and some pickled pike for the two of us. "Here, Jarl. These are just ready for eating."

Ulf and I tried them. They had the sharpness I liked. She turned to leave us alone, "No, lady, please stay. I have something to ask your husband and it will save him seeking your opinion when I have gone."

I could see that I had them both intrigued. She sat on the log again.

"I need a leader to be jarl in my northern stronghold, Ulf. Thorkell's Stad has been the subject of raids from the north and it needs a good warrior to command. Aiden and I believe that you would be the best warrior we could choose. What say you?"

He looked surprised, "Me, a jarl? I am honoured. Do you think I could lead?"

"I would not have asked you otherwise. It would mean, of course, moving and you would not have the privacy you enjoy now. You would, however, have stone walls, good kitchens and men to protect your wife when you were away."

Anya's face had already given me the answer I desired. She beamed and grasped her husband's hand. She nodded at him. "I would be honoured to accept, Jarl, but I am sad that I will no longer be Ulfheonar."

"Wolf Killer and Sigtrygg are both Ulfheonar and jarls. We have a bond which is not troubled by distance. You will always be Ulfheonar. I trust you to act in my name but I should warn you that you will need to keep the sheep and cattle thieves at bay."

"I can do that."

"Are there any you might take as oathsworn?"

"Anya has two brothers. They came on the raid to Lundenwic and now have mail, helmet and sword. They do not wish to farm but would be warriors. I would like to train them. They would be the start of my garrison."

"Good, then we leave in six days. Come to my hall and get carts for your goods."

He clasped my arm, "Thank you Jarl Dragonheart. I will not let you down."

"You are Ulfheonar. You could not even if you tried!"

We returned to the town. I set about organising my trip. Uhtric had already cleaned my mail and sword. Brigid understood the need for my journey and she helped to prepare my clothes. Hunting the cattle thieves was not a quick task. We would need to find them first. Some of my men came by when they saw me preparing. Haaken, Erik, Rollo and Rolf all wished to come with me. The others, however, wished to stay with their families. The barbarians we would be hunting were not worth much gold. The three who came with me did so because they felt obligated. They could not let their jarl risk his life without some of his oathsworn. For Haaken it went beyond duty. We were the last of the original band. Neither of us would be happy fighting without the other at his side.

Rolf said, "I owe everything to you, Jarl Dragonheart, I am only a warrior because you saw that I had potential."

"And you have fulfilled it, Rolf Horse Killer."

"Will this be enough men, Jarl Dragonheart?"

"Of course, we are only fighting barbarians. The Jarl and I could manage that alone," laughed Haaken.

Ulf and his wife brought her two brothers and their goods to Cyninges-tūn. Sven and Einar were young. Sven had seen just fifteen summers and Einar two more but I could see that they could both become good warriors. They had broad chests and they had muscles. Both would be tall. It would be expensive to make them mail but if they were trained well then it would be worth it. They had Saxon swords and that meant they had taken them in battle. That was always the best way.

Anya was not close to childbirth but, as we rode north towards the Rye Dale I worried about her. Kara had told me that there would not be a problem with the journey for she was a healthy woman but that did not stop me worrying. I smiled at the concern Ulf showed. He was a fierce warrior and as ruthless as Olaf Leather Neck but Anya brought out a different side in him. Erik rode on the other side of Anya and she was as safe as though she was guarded by the bodyguard of the Emperor.

Einar and Sven had not ridden before and Rolf and Rollo laughed as the two young warriors fell as we climbed the col close to the Scar of Nab. It was not that long since they had been as poor. Now they rode easily. We had learned that riding to battle was easier than walking.

"Instead of laughing why do you two not give them advice on how to stay on the horse's back."

"Yes, Jarl Dragonheart." Chastened they went to offer some help to the two young brothers.

I nudged my horse closer to Haaken and I rode at the front with him. "They seem good boys, Jarl. I am pleased you have rewarded Ulf Olafsson. He has been one of the most loyal of your warriors."

"I know and we need a strong hand in the north. It is lonely there."

"Did not Snorri wish to come?"

"I sent Snorri and Beorn to escort Wolf Killer's share to him. They would have come otherwise."

"I know. I was thinking of scouts."

"Rollo and Rolf are both Ulfheonar. They can scout. Perhaps they are not as good as Snorri or Beorn but we will need others one day. None of us are getting any younger."

He was right but then I remembered old Ragnar and Olaf the Toothless. They had been ancient and yet they had still wielded a sword and defended their land. We were neither Saxons nor barbarians. We were Vikings!

As we had travelled slower than normal we did not reach the old Roman fort until evening. I liked the fort. It was solid and had baths. They needed some work but I could bathe and feel clean. It even had a fish pond which always made me sit by it and look at the water. I had no idea why but when I was there I felt at peace. I doubted that I would have any peace on this visit but I had a haven to visit should I need it.

Arne Thorirson greeted us as we entered. "Jarl, I was not expecting this visit."

I put my arm around him and took him to one side. Haaken knew me well enough to shepherd Ulf and his people inside the fort. "Arne, I have asked Ulf Olafsson to be jarl here."

"An Ulfheonar as our jarl? We are honoured."

"You are not annoyed? He will be taking over the fine quarters here."

He shook his head. "To be honest, Jarl Dragonheart, I spend more time on my farm. I am a hersir and not a jarl. I can fight but you know well enough, that this fort needs a leader. I am just sorry that I have let you down. I have not stopped the raids from across the river."

I shook my head, "That is my fault. I should have rid the land of this problem myself." I turned him to lead him into the hall. "Tell me how are the men? Are they busy on their farms or can they fight?"

"We are all keen to rid ourselves of this problem. The crops are in the ground and the animals are grazing. We will fight and then Jarl Ulf Olafsson will teach us how to protect ourselves."

"Good, for I wanted no ill-feeling between the two of you."

"And there will be none Jarl."

Arne and his family still lived on the farm which was within sight of the fort. I had chosen Arne because of that. I saw now that I had made a mistake. He was a good man but I had given him too difficult a task.

Our late and sudden arrival had meant there was no grand feast but we ate well enough. I was just happy that Ulf and his family got on with Arne and his. They were two sides of the same coin.

"Tell me, Arne, where are these raiders coming from?"

"The Itouna can be forded in many places but the old river cannot be forded save far upstream. They cross the Irthing close to the place it meets the Itouna. From there they spread along the valley. They take the cattle there. Sometimes, if they are bold enough, they raid the sheep farms further south."

I looked to Ulf, "Then we know what we must do, We ride, tomorrow to this confluence of the rivers and we cross and head north. We will not wait for them to come again. We go to war and we teach them the price of stealing from our people. It is expensive for the penalty is death!"

Chapter 5

The force I led north was not the largest nor the best armed. Excluding the men, I had brought we had no men with mail. Only two had horses but they all had a shield, a helmet, a seax or sword and a spear. It would have to do. There were just twenty-five of us. I decided that I would demand that every warrior in my land have a sword and a bow. That was the only good news about the warriors I led. The men of the north each had a bow and knew how to use it for they were hunters. Seventeen bowmen could make a difference. I would have to use my eight mailed warriors to best effect.

We crossed the river into enemy territory and I saw just how easy it was for the barbarians to head south. Even the men on foot waded across. This was no barrier. I had Rollo and Rolf as scouts. They were not invisible like Snorri but he was unique. None could disappear quite like Snorri. Five miles north of the river they returned, "Jarl, we have found a village. They have many sheep and cattle."

I knew that this might not be the ones who had raided us but the odds were that they were. I waved Ulf over. He was now my second in command and I needed to teach him how to win. I halted the men. As well as the twenty-five warriors I had four boys. They would guard our horses. We dismounted and I had the boys take our horses to the nearby stream. With Haaken at my side, I took Ulf to one side. "What is your plan, Ulf?"

"Jarl Dragonheart, I will do whatever you wish."

Haaken shook his head, "Ulf, when you are Jarl of the North then it will be you who has to decide. The Jarl and I are here to advise and to fight alongside you!"

He nodded. He smiled at me, "I will copy you, Jarl. I will send Rolf and Rollo with two of my men to the far side of the village and then we will attack from this side."

The smile on my face told him that I agreed, "Good. Remember, Ulf you do not lead the Ulfheonar. These are farmers with swords. Your men will only be as good as the man who trains them. Your wife's brothers will have to be your lieutenants and your rocks."

"I can see that now." He waved over Rollo and Rolf. When he had given them their instructions they loped off. The two young warriors knew what to do and they knew where the village was as well. He turned to the rest. "Today I will lead with my kin and my brothers from the Ulfheonar. All that I ask today is that you follow close behind. The next time we fight you shall be with me in the front rank. Watch these warriors for they are the best that you will ever see."

The formation was too loose and the instructions too vague but it was a good beginning for his men saw Ulf take charge. As we moved forward I made sure that I was next to one of Ulf's kin. They had fought in Lundenwic but there they could hide amongst the mass of warriors. Here they could not. We were seen when we were four hundred paces away from the village. The boys watching the sheep fled from us screaming and shouting. It meant that the men of the village had some time to prepare. It would not be enough.

The men of the village looked to have grabbed their helmets and shields quickly. Barely half had a shield and a third did not have a helmet. They had a variety of weapons from swords and axes to billhooks. Ulf roared like a berserker and he ran so fast that he outstripped all of us. I was more concerned about Sven and Einar than myself. I had no need to worry. As the chief of the village lunged with his spear at Sven the young warrior dropped his shoulder and raised his shield to fend off the blow and then he eviscerated the man. It was as good a strike as I had seen. Ulf and his men were ruthless. They were paying these barbarians back for years of raids and they showed no mercy. I have to confess that it was my mailed men who did the most damage. The ones who tried to flee ran into Rollo and Rolf. They cut them down to a man. There were no prisoners.

Ulf looked around and said, "Is anyone hurt?"

"Oleg and Olaf have cuts."

"Harald is lying on the ground."

"He tripped and knocked himself out!"

"Sven, secure the animals. Einar, secure the villagers." He pointed to three men. He did not know their names yet. "You three search the huts. Look for loose soil. It is where they will bury their treasure. Arne, take some men and search the dead. They look piss poor to me but who knows, they may have a coin or two." He could not help but look to Haaken who nodded his approval. I had chosen a good jarl.

Even so, I could see him debating what to do with the captives. He looked at me but I kept my face like a stone and gave nothing away. Eventually, he said, "Go! Flee! If I see you here again then you will be taken as slaves!"

Of course, they did not understand a word. His gestures were obvious and so he grabbed a brand and lit the roof of a hut, "Fire them all!"

As soon as the village was ablaze he walked up to the women and roared, "Go!" He pointed north. This time they understood and they fled.

He turned to me for approval. "Well done, Ulf, but if you are to talk to your neighbours, you had best learn their language!" He had the good grace to smile.

We herded the animals and set off for the boys who were guarding the horses. Arne and the men from the Stad were animated as they each described what they had done. Ulf shook his head, "They are getting quite excited about killing a few farmers! You and I could have dealt with them all on our own, Jarl Dragonheart."

"We could but your men have made a start. Had you not been here would Arne have led them?" Ulf shook his head. "And yet now he talks as though he can take on the world. Take small steps, Ulf. The men you lead are poorly armed and armoured. The men I sent up here had mail and it now lies with them in their graves or adorns the back of some barbarian. This is the beginning; it is small enough but you can build upon it."

The boys with the horses greeted us noisily and they took over the herding of the animals. As we mounted Ulf said, "I can see that I have much to learn about being a leader."

"Anya's brothers did well. They obeyed orders and they did not lose their heads. They may be younger than the others you lead but they show the benefit of our raid in Lundenwic and the mail. When a man wears mail and a helmet he feels more like a warrior."

It was getting towards dark when we neared the fort. "When will you leave Jarl Dragonheart?"

"We will stay with you for seven days. We can ride north again, tomorrow. If we do that for three or four days then your neighbours will realise that you mean what you say."

He laughed, "Even though they did not understand a word of what I said?"

"Your actions spoke for you."

The animals were divided up amongst the victorious warriors. It was not much of a haul but as it was the first time they had taken from the nearby raiders it was a start. Although the men from north of the river had not been mailed some had swords and axes. I recognised the quality of some of the weapons. They had been taken in battle. There was even a decent Saxon sword amongst them. The arms of Ulf's men also improved.

We left the next day and crossed the ford. Rollo and Rolf led us towards the river they called the Esk in these parts. We saw the town which guarded the crossing from a mile away for we had the higher ground. We were, of course, seen and this time the men of the north had time to prepare. We rode closer to them this time before we dismounted.

We would have to fight the enemy in battle lines. This would be a sterner test of Ulf's new warband.

As I handed my reins to the boy I asked him, "Can you use a sling?" He grinned and took one out. "And you others?"

They nodded eagerly and the eldest said, "Aye Jarl."

"Then hobble the horses for today you will get to kill your first enemy."

Once again I had to leave the orders to Ulf. I owed him as much. I smiled when I saw Haaken speak into his ear. Haaken could never keep his mouth shut. He had often done that with me. I watched the men of Strathclyde as they formed up. This time there were two warriors who had mail. I suspected they had been taken from Vikings; perhaps even my men. Some of the helmets they wore certainly had. We were evenly matched in numbers. They might have actually outnumbered us. I hoped that Ulf would use a wedge formation so that the Ulfheonar could bear the brunt of the enemy weapons.

Ulf turned, "We fight in a wedge. I will be the tip." He frowned when he saw the five boys who held slings.

"I thought the boys might be blooded, Ulf Olafsson."

He nodded, "Aye for we are a warband this day."

We formed up and the front six were Ulfheonar. Sven and Einar were in the fourth rank at the end of the left and right. They had proved that they were reliable. Ulf gambled that our weight of mail and our skill would win the day.

The men of Strathclyde formed a shield wall. I saw that it was just one rank deep and that the shields were all of different sizes. They could not lock them. We could not run as we might if this was a wedge of veteran warriors. We would approach at the walk. We did not have spears at the front. My Ulfheonar preferred their swords except for Rolf Horse Killer who wielded his axe. He was behind me on the right and his shield was slung behind his back. The men from the village would have a shock when he swung that deadly Danish weapon.

I saw the mailed leader in the centre of their line as he shouted orders and they tightened their line as stones flew over our heads. Ulf shouted, "Right boys, let's see if you can do better!"

Stones clattered off my mail. I would have bruises but no more. Ulf's boys, in contrast, were hitting farmers and warriors without mail. I saw one struck on the hand and he dropped his spear. Even though he picked it up again he was wounded. And then we hit. Ulf had aimed our wedge directly at the one who had shouted the orders. I concentrated on the man to his left and I swung my sword over as his spear struck my shield. I was aware of a movement behind me as Rolf swung his axe and the man to the left of the mailed warrior I fought was hacked across the middle by a double-handed axe swung with all the force of an Ulfheonar. It ripped him in two and he fell, leaving a hole in the line. Rolf stepped next to me.

My sword had been stopped by my enemy's shield but the blood from the man next to him has spattered his face and I could see that he was shaken. We were too close for him to use his spear. If Rolf had not stepped next to me then I would have been able to swing my sword but I could not and so I stepped forward and head-butted the man. He reeled back and, as I moved into the gap I was able to bring my sword over and the blade caught him on the helmet and face. Ragnar's Spirit sliced through both and into his skull. I saw that the leader of the men of the village had been slain by Ulf and his shield wall was in disarray. Rolf swung the axe with the freedom of a warrior who knows the enemy has no mail. The boys with the slings continued to rain them on the enemy. Sven and Einar fought with wild abandon and, in the centre, the Ulfheonar carved our way through the heart of the enemy line.

The survivors broke. It was then the men from Ulf's Stad wreaked revenge on their former tormentors. Without mail, they hurtled after the survivors and they found unguarded backs. The boys with slings grabbed knives from the dead and hurried after to slit throats and despatch the wounded. That day they went from boys to warriors. Their lives would never be the same again.

The Ulfheonar had borne the brunt of the fighting and we stopped and took off our helmets. Ulf was grinning. "That went better than I thought."

I nodded and turned to Rolf, "A fine stroke with the axe."

"Thank you, Jarl Dragonheart."

"Next time do not break the wedge. You stopped my swing and if the enemy had been better then you might have fallen. A wedge is only as strong as each individual part."

"I am sorry Jarl. I felt the joy of battle in my hands."

Haaken said, "That is but a step away from a berserker! The Jarl himself is not immune from such reckless acts but a good warrior controls his blood."

We moved into the village. The women and children had fled and this time they had managed to drive some of the animals with them. But it was a larger village and we were able to collect more that Ulf and his people could use.

Arne and the others were euphoric when they returned. All were blood-spattered but, apart from minor cuts, unharmed. "We could conquer the whole of this valley if we chose."

I was about to speak when Ulf snapped, "Fool! You have six Ulfheonar who destroyed the enemy! You would have lasted two strokes against those two mailed warriors. They had fought before. When the Jarl and my brothers return to Cyninges-tūn it will be we who have to fight! Now gather the weapons and the mail. We have made a start and I am pleased but it is only a start. When each of you wears mail and knows how to fight then we might think of conquering this valley!"

Arne nodded, "Aye Jarl. You are right. Come let us do as our Jarl says!"

I turned to Haaken and said quietly, "Ulf was a good choice."

"He was and he led well." Both of us had picked up on Arne's words, *'our Jarl'*. He was now their leader

As we rode home I said, "We will not need to ride tomorrow Ulf. We will stay for another three days and then return home. What think you?"

"I think you are right. The farmers have work in the fields and I need to organise my defences. I had yet to look at my walls."

"And you have potential in those boys. They were the difference today. Their shower of stones discomfited the enemy."

Haaken said, "And I am ready for a rest. I would try out the baths in the fort. I wish to see if they are good as the Jarl's steam hut."

"We have baths?"

I nodded, "I think they need work but we will look tomorrow and see."

Once again we feasted well on Strathclyde animals. Arne and the others seemed almost reluctant to return to their farms but Ulf was insistent. He wanted the opportunity to explore his new stronghold. I took the Ulfheonar down to the baths. There was some damage and Erik looked disappointed, "I thought that the Romans built to last. This looks ruined." I could see what he meant. Half of the roof had fallen in.

I shook my head. I had seen these in Miklagård and had an idea of how they worked. "There are three things we must repair. First the water supply." I pointed to a broken pipe. Water was coming from a pond but it could not use the channel it was intended for. The ground was wet and muddy. "Erik, you take Rolf and Rollo, find another pipe and repair it." He nodded. He now had something to do. "Haaken and I will see if the furnace can be mended. If that is broken beyond repair then we have baths but they will be cold ones! When that is done we will look at the roof."

The roof was the least of our worries. We went down to the furnace. It was below the baths and it looked to be intact. "This is good, Jarl. I cannot see anything wrong with this!"

I took a long stick and poked it down the flue which led to the hot room. I found an obstruction. "There is the problem. Something has fallen down. We must repair it."

We scrabbled around and found what we needed and after much strenuous work cleared the detritus of centuries. When we went into the so-called hot room we found a couple of broken stones. We went to the paved area outside and took a couple of suitable ones. It was soon finished. By noon Erik had repaired the water supply and the furnace was mended. "We will let the water fill up and light the fire."

"What about the roof, Jarl?"

"Is it raining Erik?"

"No, Jarl."

"Then we repair that tomorrow. I would like a reward this night for our hard work."

It was late afternoon when the water was hot enough and we enjoyed a pleasant couple of hours in the baths. The hard work had been worth it. The baths leaked a little but I told the others that I would have Aiden read and discover how to repair it. Ulf was happy. "I am the only jarl with a bathhouse."

It was such small luxuries which appealed to my men.

The next day, refreshed, we began the equipping and training of Arne and the others. All the boys from the neighbouring farms turned up. The ones we had taken with us to raid had told them of the glory of war. Ulf would have a larger warband. Success bred confidence and that bred even more success.

Anya was happy too. Every woman likes a clean home and the Roman quarters were easier to keep clean. Sometimes we made choices and decisions and they were perfect. This had been one such decision. Perhaps I should not have been surprised for it had been Aiden who had planted the seed in my mind.

Before we could take the warband to practice a shield wall, men and their families from the outlying farms began to pour towards us.

"Raiders from the north Jarl!" We rang the bell which would summon all the workers into the stronghold.

This would be a test of the defences and of the men who manned the walls. As the last refugee entered the fort we slammed shut the gates. I stood on the gatehouse and peered north. There was a warband of fifty or more warriors. Eight were in mail and they arrayed themselves beyond bow range. Had we had more men I would have met them beard to beard but there was little point in risking all. We had to defeat them and that meant using the Roman defences.

Ulf looked at me and I could see that he was worried. "It seems our raids north have brought us trouble."

"It would have happened anyway. Better now while we have six Ulfheonar here." I patted the wall. "We have taken places with walls but never such walls as this I think. How would you attack these walls, Ulf?"

"If I did not have ladders I would attack the gate. I would use axe men to break through the timbers."

I pointed, "And unless they use all of their mailed men then our archers and even your boys with slings can hurt them. What we do need is rocks. I would have your men fetch rocks. We can rain them down on the mailed warriors."

Haaken said, "Then the problems will begin for they will leave here and raid your lands. We must be ready to fight them beyond the walls when they have bled enough. These barbarians are brave to the point of madness."

He nodded, "I will get my archers and slingers ready!"

I went down to the quarters I was using to don my mail and prepare for war. It had been some time since I had fought from a wall. Normally it was we who would be doing the attacking. By the time I had reached the walls again the men of Strathclyde were preparing to advance to the walls. They were not fools and they had assembled a shield wall two shields high. My Ulfheonar joined me on the walls. I saw Sven and Einar waiting for orders.

"Sven go to the east tower. The men there will need a leader. Einar, do the same on the west."

They hurried off, eager to be doing something. Erik laughed, "They will be safe enough there. This is where they will attack."

I nodded, "But this way they will see mailed warriors at the two towers and assume that we have more men than we actually do."

The enemy came towards us. The leader had committed half of his men to this first attack. He had divided his mailed men between his two groups.

Ulf led some of those who were not warriors to deposit rocks and stones on the wall above the gate. He looked down the length of the two walls. There were not enough of the enemy to attack more than one wall. We had plenty of men and boys. The men of the north would not be able to simply walk into the fort. The shield wall was now within range. Ulf shouted, "Archers, slingers, release!"

There was a whirring and a series of twangs followed by cracks as arrows and stone struck the shields. While they remained tightly locked the shields would provide protection but once they reached the gates they would have to lay down their shields and use two hands to wield their axes. Some of the shields now had the added weight of arrows. I wished that we had javelins. They would have weighed down the shields even more. The stones cracked against the shields. Behind them, the men must have wondered if their shields would hold. Ulf was a strong warrior and, as the shield wall stepped onto the bridge over the ditch he picked up a rock and hurled it down. It struck the middle of the shields and the weight must have stunned the bearer for a hole appeared and stones and arrows hit flesh as archers and slingers saw targets. Two men fell into the ditch before the shields became a protective cover once more.

My Ulfheonar each picked up a stone and they threw it down. I chose one and I managed to throw it and strike the leading shield and the warrior beneath. One of the boys managed to hit the warrior on the side of his helmet and he fell to the ground. An archer pinned his leg to the bridge. They were brave but they were now doomed to failure. As men hefted their axes and attempted to hack the gate, stones and arrows struck them. They began to pull back. In the time it took them to rejoin the other half they lost a further two warriors. Ten lay wounded or dead. They would be an obstacle for the next attack.

The next attack did not materialize. The leader, mounted on his horse, took off his helmet and approached the gates with his hands out, palms uppermost. They wish to talk. Ulf looked at me, "This is your fort, Ulf Olafsson. It is for you to speak."

He took off his helmet. His eyes, red with cochineal made him look even more frightening. He sheathed his sword and leaned against the wall. The northerner halted at the bridge. I saw his eyes glance down at the dead and the dying. He spoke our language, badly, but better than Ulf could speak his.

"We have come to punish you for attacking our people."

Ulf nodded, "And now that we are punished you can go back home!"

The man frowned, "You are not yet punished!"

"You have attacked my walls. Let us call that punishment."

"You must pay us for the men you killed and the animals you took!"

Ulf laughed, "Are all your people as stupid as you? We have taken back merely that which your people stole from us. I am here to tell you that if you raid again then we will make war on you and make your land a place of bones."

It was the barbarian's turn to laugh. "With such a small number of men? I think not!"

I took off my helmet. I had enough of their language to speak to him, "No, friend, Jarl Ulf will have the support of Jarl Dragonheart, the Wolf Warrior and we will feast on the flesh of your animals!"

I could see that he expected neither to be addressed in his own tongue nor for it to be me who did so. He pointed to Ulf, "Let you and I settle this! We will fight man to man here!"

Ulf said, "And when I win, what then?"

"My men will return home and there will be peace. The gods will decide this."

"Very well."

As he turned I said, "You do not need to do this."

Ulf smiled, "You and I know that I do Jarl."

I nodded, "Make sure you win."

He tightened his wolf skin about his shoulders. He was Ulfheonar. He would win. It mattered not how strong the other warrior was. Ulf would keep fighting until life left him. Others stopped long before death!

The barbarian took off his cloak. I saw that his mail was just a chest and back protector. His arms were bare and it did not reach past his knees. His shield was slightly smaller than Ulf's. All of this was important. I could not tell who had made his sword. Bjorn had made Ulf's and his would be true and strong. Ulf would wear his cloak. He had killed the wolf he wore and eaten of its heart. It gave him the protection of the wolf and would not impede him when he fought.

Erik, Rolf and Rollo accompanied him to watch for any treachery. I did not think that there would be. The warriors from north of the border were, generally, honourable. There was little preamble. Any words which needed to be said had been spoken already. Ulf was marginally shorter than the chief and that would give his opponent a slight advantage but Ulf was fighting for more than the chief from Strathclyde, he was fighting for his own land.

The chief swung his sword and Ulf blocked it with his shield. When Ulf tried a swashing blow at the chief he countered it with his own shield. I saw the disparity in the size of shield. Ulf's, like mine, was so big that it virtually just rested upon his arm and shoulder, held there by a long leather strap as well as the grip. The barbarian's was much smaller and he had to expend energy raising it. The blow from Ulf also had more direction and the bigger man reeled a little.

Each man fights his own way. I always liked to move quickly and go on the offensive. Ulf was different and he liked to weigh up the strengths and weaknesses of his enemy. The first blows exchanged they warily circled each other. One false move could result in death. This time, when the chief struck, Ulf blocked with his sword. There were two reasons for that. He wished to test the blade of his enemy and it left his shield free to be used offensively.

As the blades rang together it was Ulf's which sounded clearer. Sparks flew from them. Ulf had the quickest reactions and he swung at the chief's head. The chief was forced to block with his sword. The barbarian was forced back a little by the force of the blow and Ulf punched hard with the boss of his shield. He hit the chief's face and his nose erupted in a mess of blood and bone. The men on the walls cheered; first blood. The chief stepped back and wiped his face with the back of his bare arm. He looked at the blood as though he could not believe it.

Ulf swung again and the blow was blocked but I thought I detected a slight bend in Ulf's opponent's weapon. As he raised it to strike it did not look as straight as it had. Bjorn Bagsecgson always made swords with a point so that we could stab. Most of our enemies just used the edge of the blade. Ulf lunged. It was clean and it was swift. It was not a blow that the chief was expecting. That, allied to his small shield meant that the strike found flesh and we all saw blood spurt from the man's arm. His shield, which hung from it, dropped a little.

He was a brave warrior and he went on the offensive. Ulf had been expecting that and he took the flurry of blows first on his sword and then on his shield. The chief weakened with each strike as blood seeped from his arm and his nose. Ulf trained every day and he would not tire in single combat. I saw Ulf steady himself as he prepared to go in for the kill. He feinted with his shield and, as the chief raised his shield to counter, Ulf swung sideways at the warrior's left side. It was a good blow and the blade was sharp enough to break some of the mail links. It also caught the warrior off balance and he lurched to the side. Ulf then used a manoeuvre many of my warriors used. He spun away and then around the man. To the chief, it was as though he had disappeared. Ulf Olafsson brought his shield and boss into the back of the barbarian. Disorientated the chief overbalanced and fell to the ground. As he tried to rise Ulf brought his sword down on the back of his neck and decapitated him. He stuck his sword in the ground, reached down and lifted the head to turn and face the warband.

Two of the oathsworn of the chief, who were mounted galloped towards Ulf. My three Ulfheonar raced to form a shield wall in front of the triumphant Ulf. As the two horses swerved to avoid the human wall Rollo and Rolf swung their weapons. Rolf's axe cut the body of one of the warriors in two while Rollo's strike took the second warrior's leg at the thigh.

I shouted, "Your chief gave his word! The gods will be angry at any more treachery!" There was tension which was almost visible and the warband just stared at me. I heard the horses' hooves as they slowed to a walk and then there was silence. "Go home now or I will visit such disaster upon you, that the land north of the river will be fit only for carrion. I will leave no one alive!"

Three of the warriors spoke together. One looked at Ulf and said, "It was a fair fight and our chief gave his word. We will return home." They walked up to the body and picked it up. Ulf kept the head. It was a trophy and would adorn his gate. They turned and headed northeast towards the ford. They were beaten. We descended to congratulate Ulf. He had trounced his foes and gained two horses and three sets of mail. More importantly, his people had seen him and knew they had a warrior to lead them.

Chapter 6

We returned home after a further four days. We made sure that the warband had gone by trailing them to the river. We burned their bodies and Ulf improved his defences. "A worthwhile journey Jarl. I am glad I came."

"And I am too. I feel happier about our northern borders. When Jarl Thorkell the Tall ruled I did not worry but since Sven White Hair was killed it has always troubled me. Ulf Olafsson is the equal of our old comrade."

"He is, indeed. And now I can spend some time with my family. Who knows I might even increase its size!"

My young warriors, Rollo and Rolf laughed. They had yet to start families although there were many maidens in Cyninges-tūn who would have happily taken them to their beds.

Erik said, "Aye I will tend to my fields and thrash my lazy thralls. My son will soon be old enough to hold a seax. His training cannot start too soon."

Haaken's face darkened a little. He had two daughters and desperately wanted a son. That was the real reason he would make Unn pregnant once more.

"Jarl Dragonheart, when did you begin to train as a warrior?" Rollo was the youngest Ulfheonar.

Haaken answered for me. "He did not. While the rest of us in the village were fighting with each other and wielding weapons Jarl Dragonheart was in the mountains with Old Ragnar. He hewed wood and watched over the old man. He learned to use a bow but it was not until he killed his first wolf that Old Ragnar showed him how to use a sword. The gods favoured the Jarl for the first time he had to fight," he gestured to his empty orb, "the day I lost my eye, he used his sword for the first time in anger and we all knew that he had a natural gift."

I said, "I was lucky. You are right Erik to begin training your son as soon as you can. I did with Wolf Killer and he was Ulfheonar earlier than most."

I saw my two young warriors taking all of this in. They just accepted my skills and there were many legends and stories of what I had done since I had become a warrior but few knew how I became one. Only Haaken now remained from the old days and only he knew the truth of the story. At my request, he had not written a saga about it. There were enough stories of my deeds. The story of the sword alone was told from Miklagård to Dyflin, wherever Vikings gathered to tell tales.

As we rode through the gates we were greeted as though we had been away for years rather than half a month. My son Gryffydd ran over to see me. He was growing so quickly now that I could barely keep up with his spurts of growth. He shouted, "Dragonheart!" I was away so much that he saw me as the jarl rather than a father. After Erik's words, I felt guilty. I should be making him a warrior.

"My fine young warrior; soon you will come to war with your father!"

Brigid, nursing Erika, tutted, "There will be time enough for that. Let him grow first!"

"Three more years and then he shall have his first sword. Prepare yourself, wife. He is a Viking and he will defend this land when I am dead and buried."

She shook her head," I hope that will be a long time in the future. Come, enough talk of war. Let us eat and you can talk to your son."

I hoisted him up and noticed just how much he was growing. Times past he would have felt like a feather. Now I could feel his strength as he gripped my arm.

Aiden and Kara came, with Ylva to see me when I had greeted my wife and baby. I smiled when I saw them, "You dreamed?"

"We did, father. The spirits are pleased. Our home and our land are safer."

"You were right about Ulf, Aiden. He is the right leader. When you have time we made repairs on the baths there but there is a leak and our stonework left much to be desired. Have you the knowledge to see what is wrong?"

"I can find out. I am still searching through the papers you brought last time. It would be useful to do so. When the rains come it makes the heart of Cyninges-tūn a muddy morass. The Romans built good drains. I will see what I can discover."

"Have Wolf Killer and Elfrida made a visit yet?"

"No, husband, but he asked for you to let him know when you returned."

"Good, I will send to him for it is almost half a year since I have seen my grandson. He will be growing."

Kara laughed, "Father, we all grow!"

"I know but when you are young you grow the most. Even Ylva looks different from fourteen nights ago. Besides I have yet to see Garth, my new grandson."

The two women fussed over their children. I left with Aiden to walk by the Water. Gryffydd followed. I was about to send him back when

Aiden said, "Children learn, Jarl, by watching elders. The more he is around you the more like you he will become."

I held my hand out and my son grasped it. "But he will not understand that of which we speak."

"When I looked in Haaken's head I saw his mind. It is a strange thing. Since then, when on the battlefield, I have oft times looked inside the heads of the dead. There is more inside our skulls than we know. Where do Kara and I get our power from? The spirits. And how do the spirits speak with us? Through our minds. Let your son listen to us and the words will dance around in his head." I must have looked dubious for he smiled, "It cannot hurt and you want no secrets from your son do you?"

He was right. Aiden was always right, "Come then, son, and when you become bored you can skim stones across the water!"

Surprisingly he did not. When we sat on the large stones he sat on my knee and cuddled in to me. Soon I forgot he was there but he remained awake and alert. "There are many young men who are restless, Jarl. Your success in Lundenwic has fuelled their desire for gold and for glory."

"We both know, Aiden, that it would be a mistake to raid Lundenwic again so soon. We raided Wintan-ceastre last year. Where else is there?"

"Neustria. Gunnar Thorfinnson was going to raid there. He thought that it was a place filled with riches."

"But who would lead them?"

"Perhaps your son, Wolf Killer. I am guessing that he will be envious of your success. We sent him gold but gold earned is always more valuable than gold given."

"I am not unhappy about our warriors raiding but we have lost enough brethren for me to baulk at losing more."

"You and I are not Norse-born, lord. It is in their blood and they are happy to die in battle. You know that."

"You are right and I should be used to the idea."

We were silent for a while and I noticed that Gryffydd was asleep. It was a dreamless sleep for he moved not. Aiden looked at my son. "Perhaps, Jarl, it is time that you dreamed."

There was more to Aiden's words than an idle comment. "Why, what do you know?"

"The spirits have words for you, Jarl. Both your mother and Erika have visited our dreams of late and there is something else. There is a figure who hovers on the periphery of the spirit world. He will not approach us. We think he wishes to speak with you. It is an old man."

"Ragnar?"

"We never saw him so I do not know. It might be. You should dream."

"I do dream, each night."

Aiden shook his head, "You know what I mean. You need to lie alone in the steam hut and you should take one of Kara's potions. It will open the door to the spirit world. Now that you have a new daughter the time is right."

"That is why the two of you came to speak with me."

He nodded, "Since you have been away we have been visited each night. We cannot use all of our powers until he has spoken with you." He laughed, "Your daughter needs her sleep!"

I carried my sleeping son back to my hall. Uhtric took him from me. It was obvious that Kara and Brigid had been speaking about me. Brigid had that frown which meant she was not happy about something. She did not approve of my communication with the dead. It went against her religion. Kara, however, had a way of making Brigid less angry. We could not rid her of what I called her *'pagan frown'*.

Kara smiled, "I have sent a messenger to my brother to tell him that you are home."

Brigid recovered her composure. "And Asbjorn would speak with you about raiding. I told him to join us this evening. We have pike."

"Good." Pike was one of my favourite dishes.

When our company had gone she asked, "Do you have to dream? I like it not."

"The dead will not hurt me for they are my ancestors."

"It is not seemly and..."

"And your priests do not like it either. Yet you believe that the White Christ did not die. He lives in your heaven, does he not?"

She shifted uncomfortably, "We do not talk of such things."

"But you do. At Easter, you celebrate his death and then his ascent into the skies. Does his spirit not live?"

"It is not the same."

I smiled for I had her now, "When you die you will go to heaven?"

"I believe so."

"And your spirit will live there?" She nodded. "What is the difference?"

She stood and laid Erika in her cradle. "It is not the same and I have too much to do than sit here and argue with a pagan!" She was flushed as she went to the kitchen. I heard her bark at the thralls. When she was herself again she would apologise. It was their lot to suffer the sharp edge of her tongue.

When Gryffydd awoke I spent the rest of the day with him. We wrestled and had a play fight. Soon he would leave my hall and play outside with the other youngsters of Cyninges-tūn. It would not matter then that his father was Jarl. He would be treated as roughly as any. Bloody noses and bruises would toughen him up and prepare him for war.

Asbjorn and Einstein arrived at my hall. They had brought a gift for Brigid. It was a pair of bone combs. They had both made them and one was carved with a wolf design while the other had a dragon. The two warriors had great skills and for such fierce men could be quite delicate. Brigid was touched. She was no longer cross; she was the hostess and the wife of the Jarl. She knew how to behave. She had been brought up in a Welsh court. She knew how such things were managed.

After we had eaten she left us before my fire with a fine black ale. "Your wife keeps a fine table, Jarl."

"You two should think of taking a wife. Cyninges-tūn needs young warriors and the ones from your loins would be most welcome."

"That is the reason we have come this night. We would raid again. We made much on the last trip but when we are wed we will journey less often. We would both be comfortable."

"Good. Then you have my permission."

They looked at each other, "We would like to take *'The King's Gift'* too, Jarl. There are many warriors who wish to go A-Viking with us. We need two drekar."

"Are you happy about young Olaf as the captain?"

"He has proved himself. I am more than happy."

Einstein was normally the second in command to Asbjorn. I could see that he had his own warriors now. It was *wyrd*. "Then, I am content. I have to tell you that I think my son may wish to join you. The *'Wild Boar'* has not sailed for some time."

"That is even better for it increases the places we could raid."

"And where would you raid?" I held up my hand, "I advise only and it will be your decision but I would suggest that you avoid Wessex. We have visited that well too often and I think that King Egbert may well be waiting."

"We were thinking of Olissipo."

"We lost Trygg there and we laid it to waste."

"They may have rebuilt it."

I quaffed my ale, "Aiden has given thought to your dilemma."

"How did he..." Asbjorn smiled, "a galdramenn! What was I thinking?"

"He suggested Neustria. It is close enough and untouched. Gunnar Thorfinnson may have raided but he is but one drekar."

They brightened, "That sounds like a good idea and if it comes from Aiden..."

"He will have the charts for your captains. My son will be here soon. We will find out if he wishes to join you."

Wolf Killer arrived three days later. He left his family at home. With young children, Elfrida did not relish such long journeys. As he and his oathsworn rode up I could see a difference in my son. He had now filled out and become a huge warrior. He had always been tall but it had taken until now for him to become a warrior almost as big as Olaf Leather Neck. He strode over and clasped my arm, "Thank you for the treasure, Father, but you had no need. I am more than capable of providing for my own family."

I put my arm around his shoulder and led him into my hall, "You forget, Wolf Killer, that you are my family too. Indulge me!"

He nodded, "Thank you."

"Your new son, Garth, prospers?"

"He has a pair of lungs on him that is for certain. Aye, he prospers but he tires Elfrida."

"And Ragnar?"

"He is desperate to be a warrior. Two more summers and he may well be ready to come with us."

"You should have brought your whole family. Kara and her women have a way with children."

Some years Kara and Wolf Killer had been estranged. Even though they were now closer Wolf Killer still preferred to keep their lives separate. I knew I had spoken out of turn when he said nothing.

"And what brings you from Elfridaby?"

"I would go A-Viking. I should have come with you to Lundenwic but my new son demanded my attention."

"This is *wyrd* for Asbjorn and Eystein wish to raid. They talk two drekar."

"Wessex?"

"No, for Aiden and I counselled against that. We suggested Neustria."

He smiled, "Aiden is rarely wrong on these matters but you never are. I will do as you suggest. When do they wish to leave?"

"They were waiting for your arrival."

"You knew what was in my mind?"

"Let us just say that I thought you might wish to raid."

When Wolf Killer left to speak with Asbjorn I visited Kara. "When Wolf Killer sails with Asbjorn I will take your potion and dream."

"That is good. The old man visits often. I saw him not far from here."

"Saw him?"

"In my dream. He was in the cave of the Lough Rigg, close to the Rye Dale. The place Wolf Killer killed his wolf."

"*Wyrd*!"

"Truly."

After Wolf Killer had seen Asbjorn and Eystein he left. "I would stay but both jarls wish to sail as soon as they can. They leave for Úlfarrston today. I must return and fetch my men."

"Do you wish your wife and family to be here?"

"I would not mind you keeping an eye on them but I will leave enough men to guard my home There are many warriors who wish to raid with me and I can choose the best."

"When you return then bring your family here. I do not see enough of you."

"I know and I have been at fault. I promise that I will bring them here."

After he had gone I had Uhtric saddle my horse and I rode to the cave. I had not been here since the time of the wolf hunt. Not only had my son killed his first wolf, but Beorn Three Fingers had also been bitten by a wolf as had Karl. That day had been one we all remembered and now a spirit haunted it. I was never one to run away from spirits. I would visit the cave and see if he spoke with me.

I rode up through the Rye Dale and, after speaking with Audun Thin Face, took the path through the forest which led up to the strange cave. The last time I had come I had been prepared and well-armed and we had left our horses in the forest. Now I rode up and onto the rock ledge. I dismounted and tried to lead my horse inside but he would not move. I tethered him to a stunted tree close to a large pool of rainwater.

I walked in and, as I did so, realised what a huge cavern it was. The roof was so high that I could barely see it. There was another pool just inside the entrance but it could not be rainwater. Even as I looked at it I heard a plop as water fell from the roof. I moved further in and saw that it turned a little to the right. I followed it and it became darker. I stopped. I did not wish to fall down a hole or trip on a rock. I had told no one where I was going. Suddenly I felt a shiver down my neck. There was someone or something in the cave with me. The air became oppressively heavy and my eyes felt like they wanted to close. I could almost feel the breath of something there with me. I was in the presence of a spirit. I was frozen to the spot. I closed my eyes and found myself I had no idea how long I had been in this cave. This was not meant to be. When the dream came I was not supposed to be here. I was supposed to be close to my daughter. Who knew if this was a good or an evil spirit? I remembered the witch Angharad.

I forced my hand to the hilt of Ragnar's Spirit. As soon as I did so the air became lighter and I could move my feet. I headed back to the entrance. When I reached the entrance I found that it was now dark outside. The sun had set. How long had I been in the cave? I mounted my horse and made my way through the forest. When I saw the glow from the hut of Audun Thin Face I breathed a sigh of relief. I was back in my world.

Scanlan had organised a search party and they found me not far from the tarns. Since Ulf had moved north this was a deserted part of my land. "Jarl, Aiden and the Lady Kara told us to find you. We thought we had lost you."

"No Scanlan but I was foolish. I have learned my lesson."

Brigid and Kara both wore the worried faces of someone whose child has gone missing. I knew that I would have to endure their sharp tongues. Surprisingly Aiden came to my aid, "Jarl Dragonheart is unharmed. He needed to do this. He will now dream here where we can protect him."

Kara nodded, "You are right husband. I will prepare the potion tonight and tomorrow you can dream." Brigid looked as though she was going to object. "Would you rather he wandered off again? Here he will be watched over by Erika, his mother and us. We know not who lives in the cave. Trust me in this."

Brigid nodded.

Uhtric lit the fire in the steam hut. Scanlan arranged for some of my men to guard the hut until I entered. My people were taking no chances. Brigid was tearful all day. When the time came for me to leave she hugged me so tightly that I thought that she would crush me. Aiden came with me across the Water. He had the potion. Once we were across we laid Ragnar's Spirit in the centre. Its hilt faced east and its tip the west. Once I was prepared he handed me the potion. "We will dream as well, Jarl. You will be safe but I know not what you will see. The old man could be good or he could be evil. Until you speak with him we cannot use our powers."

I smiled, "I will visit this world."

He clasped my arm and then he and the guards left me alone on the eastern shore of the Water. I drank the potion and then sat. The heat from the steam hut and the smell of thyme and rosemary filled my sanctuary. I felt my body begin to become cleansed. I took the bone strigils we had and scraped my arms and then my chest. I found myself becoming drowsy and I lay on the rush mat and closed my eyes. One moment I was awake and in my world and the next...

I was back in the cave but this time there was a glow from the far end. Gripping Ragnar's Spirit I moved towards it. I heard a snuffling and felt the ground beneath my feet begin to rumble. I pressed forward. I owed this to Kara and to Aiden. The glow grew brighter and, as I turned the corner, I saw a huge dragon sleeping. Covered in golden scales it was curled around itself. It filled the far end of the cave and I felt like an insect next to it. I heard its measured breathing. It slept. There was heat from its nostrils and I saw a spiral of smoke rising slowly to the roof of the cave. Suddenly one eye opened. I leapt back and all went black.

I heard Aiden. He was calling for me. I ran back into the cave but there was no glow and it was empty. I ran into the far recesses but he was not there. He called me still. I found myself flying. I crossed the Dunum and saw the river bank where I had been taken as a slave and I flew north. I saw the fort where I had hidden beneath the sea and then I saw the Roman Wall. I heard Aiden calling once more and I found myself tumbling towards the earth. I thought that I would crash into the ground but I found that my fall was arrested. I looked around and saw that the dragon had cushioned my fall with his wings. As he laid me on the ground he changed before my eyes and became an old man. It was not Ragnar and it was not Olaf yet I knew him.

I saw that we were on a pile of bones. Old rusted weapons surrounded us. The old man spoke, "I am Myrddyn. The people of this land now call me Merlin but my name is Myrddyn. I have waited for generations for you. You have been chosen. Your ancestors protected this land from those who would destroy it. It is your task to do so now. The spirit of the wolf is with you and today, the spirit of the dragon. You have the heart of the dragon and now you must have the power of the dragon. Do not fear death for, so long as you wield your sword, then none can defeat you. Keep it safe and your land is safe. The dragon fire will consume your enemies. You need to find this place when you leave the dream world. This is your destiny! This is your future. You will be the Dragon Warrior!"

I opened my mouth to speak but no words came out and the old man turned into a dragon again. I was in the air once more but this time there was a strange wailing like a spirit in torment. I found it hard to breathe and I began to cough.

I opened my eyes and found that the hut was wreathed in smoke and the hut itself was on fire. I grabbed Ragnar's Spirit and ran out in to the morning air. As I moved the curtain from the door a sudden gust of air took the flames and engulfed me. I was on fire. I ran to the Water and threw myself in. It felt cool and I found myself at peace. I lifted my head and bobbed up out of the Water. I saw a boat coming towards me. Scanlan, Aiden and Karl One Leg were on board. I turned and saw that the steam hut was now a pyre. The smoke rose high into the air and the flames greedily consumed the walls and the roof. I would use the hut no more.

"Jarl, you were on fire!"

As Scanlan and Karl hauled me on board I smiled and said, "I thought I was supposed to be safe, galdramenn?"

"I am sorry, Jarl. I saw the fire but I thought it was the dragon."

"You dreamed too?"

"Aye, I did."

Scanlan said, "Lord I have never seen anything like it! I was certain we would pull a charred corpse from the Water and yet you live and you breathe. It is a wonder!"

I lay back in the boat and closed my eyes. "You had best get to Ulf's Stad, Aiden, and work your magic there. If I want to use a hot room you will need to repair the baths!"

Part 2 The Danes

Chapter 7

Aiden left for the fort a week after Asbjorn and the others had sailed for Neustria. I had four young warriors escort Aiden. He did not wish an escort but I pointed out that he might need them to labour on the baths. Since we had defeated those from north of the river the border would be safe enough. It was Kara who first alerted us to danger. Aiden had been gone half a day when she ran to my hall. "My husband is in danger! His spirit cried out to me!" She looked terrified and her words filled me with dread. Why had Aiden not seen the danger?

With any other, I would have been sceptical but Kara was not given to flights of fancy. "Send for the Ulfheonar!" Although many did not live in my settlement I had half a dozen who did. "Uhtric, my armour!"

By the time I had donned my armour and mounted my horse eight of my Ulfheonar were ready to join me. Haaken was still on his farm with his wife but I had Olaf, Snorri, Erik, Rollo, Rolf, Finni, Vermund and Leif. Those eight would have to do. We were about to leave when a horse galloped in. The saddle and its haunches were bloody. Karl One Leg said, "It is Oleg's horse. He was one of Aiden's escorts."

I nodded, "Keep the gates barred until I return. I like this not. This may be a trick by our enemies."

We found Oleg close to the village of Thirl. He had obviously been wounded and was trying to get back to us. He had bled to death. We could not yet do him honour. We had to find the living. My daughter had said that Aiden called to her. That meant he was still alive. We found the site of the ambush close to the dale of Mungo. Where the trail headed north-west to Ulf's Stad a party had waited for them. There were three dead warriors from Cyninges-tūn but, thankfully, Aiden was not amongst them.

Snorri leapt from his mount and searched the ground. "They took the horses and they headed north and east."

"The men of Strathclyde?"

Snorri shook his head and held up a Danish bracelet which had fallen. "These were Danes, Jarl!"

Olaf Leather Neck said, "What are we waiting for? They have Aiden."

I shook my head, "Why take him? This makes no sense. If they had killed him then I would understand but why Aiden?"

Snorri was not only the best scout I had, but he was also the most thoughtful Ulfheonar. "Perhaps they did not come for him but recognised him for what he is. You do not kill a wizard lightly. They may have been on a raid and this has changed their plans." He pointed to the tracks. "This was a large warband. It explains why they killed our men and lost none of their own."

I had a sudden chill run down my spine. "Olaf, return to Cyningestūn. Karl will need help. If this is a trick to draw us out I need you to protect my family. Send for the Ulfheonar and their families. Until our drekar are back we defend our land."

"Will you have enough warriors, Jarl?"

I laughed, "I have Ulfheonar! We can take on the world if we have to!"

Olaf was a loss but he was the most dependable of my men and he would ensure that my family was safe. After he had gone I said, "Snorri, find them!" As we rode I gave thought to the two Danish spies. Perhaps their boat had not sunk. It now occurred to me that they might have faked their own death to remain in my land. There were many places where men could hide and observe. I wished that I could remember what they had looked like but it had been a brief view as they sailed away to fish.

My scout led us east. The Danes had used the Roman Road. This was not the one which ran the length of the wall; this was another which ran south. It crossed a higher peak and it led to the Dunum. The Norns had been quiet for too long and they were taking me home. I was returning to the place I had been enslaved. As we rode east I begged the spirits that the Danes had not harmed Aiden. He was resourceful but the Danes had no love for me and they could do him harm just to spite me. As we ate up the miles I wondered why this had been hidden from both him and Kara. Why had this Myrddyn not warned me? There was too much I did not understand. Lundenwic had seen us at our most successful; now we were in danger of losing someone who was vital to my land.

They were on horses. That helped us for Snorri was following the trail of animal droppings. And they kept going. Even when the sun dipped behind us they kept moving north and east. They reached the Dunum and there, close by the old, deserted hill fort, we were forced to stop. Snorri pointed to the hard ground. "The road splits here, Jarl. There is one road which follows the Dunum and the other heads towards the north and east. We could follow one or the other but we would gamble. We need daylight now."

Erik said, "Jarl they must rest too. If they do not then we will see their dead horses and then we will catch them. I know you worry about Aiden but I would take heart from the fact that we have not found him. If they have carried him this far then they will not harm him. At least not until they get where they are going."

"Erik is right, Jarl. Even if they have a drekar then the two rivers they are heading for are more than half a day's journey away. We rise at dawn and we ride hard. We are Ulfheonar and we will not stop."

Finni was right and I dismounted. We unsaddled our horses and my men had a fire going. We had water but no food. For my part, I could eat nothing anyway. I sat and looked east. We were fortunate that it was summer. The night would not last long. I knew that sleep would not come and I stood watch while my men slept. Aiden was now more than just my wizard; he was the father of my granddaughter. He was family. What I could not work out was the reason for his abduction. Was it deliberate or an accident?

I watched the false dawn and went to make water. I shook my men awake and then watered my horse. He was saddled and I was ready as I watched the thin light of dawn appear in the east. Snorri mounted and rode next to me. "You did not sleep?"

"No, Snorri. Find him!"

He nodded and trotted off. I waited until all of my men were ready. We had to wait until Snorri found which of the two roads they had taken. Snorri was soon back and he waved us to the north-eastern road. He pointed behind him and I saw a thin tendril of smoke rising in the air. We trotted along the road. Five miles down the road we found where they had camped. We dismounted for if Aiden had lain here then there would be clues. It was Rolf who found the answer although he did not understand it.

"Jarl!"

I went over and saw what looked like a series of squiggles in the soil. There were random pieces of wood there too.

Rollo stood next to Rolf. "I know not what it means, Rolf."

"Neither do I but it is not natural is it?"

I recognised it. I had watched Aiden make his scratches on parchment. It directions; my galdramenn was talking to us. "It is a map. Aiden was skilled in such things and I have seen this. That is Dun Holme and that has a river. They are taking him to the Wear. They can sail drekar up as far as the hill fort."

Snorri said, "Then we can catch them! It is a day's hard ride. I doubt that they will think we are close by. They would not have lit this fire else. They are less than five miles ahead of us."

That was all the incentive we needed. We knew where they were going and we rode hard. They did not stop at the old hill fort. Those who lived there hid as we galloped past. Both we and the Danes were the enemies of those who lived here. I began to worry. Where was the drekar? I knew now, for certain, that they would be heading for a boat. I knew not the reason but we had to hurry. The river could be navigated not far from Dun Holme.

We were just a mile or so beyond the hill fort when Snorri suddenly reined in and pointed right towards the river. There were freshly broken branches and tracks in the mud. They had left the road and that meant that the drekar was close by. We saw them less than a hundred paces ahead. The trail twisted down a steep bank and one of the Danes had been thrown from his horse. The others were gathered around as he began to stagger to his feet. We saw each other at the same time.

I drew my sword as we galloped up. I cared not how many we faced. The Danes, like us, did not fight on horses and they all dismounted to form a shield wall. Snorri leapt from his own horse and drew his sword. I kicked my horse in the flanks. One of the Danes realised that I had no intention of stopping and he swung his axe at my horse. I was ready to slip from his back. I let go of the reins and brought my shield around. As the axe bit into the chest of my horse, which was already trying to turn, I brought my shield up. I flew from my horse's back. The dying horse took out two of the Danes and my shield hit a third in the head. He fell to the ground stunned.

After rolling I quickly stood and fended off the blow from the sword which had been aimed at my back. The Dane I had stunned began to rise and, as I turned to face my new opponent I stamped hard across his throat. He lay still. The second Dane threw himself at me and I blocked his savage strike with my shield. I brought Ragnar's Spirit around in a wide sweep and struck below the shield of the Dane. It was a powerful blow and it smashed into his left leg. It buckled and I punched with my shield as he dropped. I caught the off-balance Dane square in the middle of his helmet and he fell. I stabbed him through his mouth and turned to see off the others.

My Ulfheonar had slain almost all of the Danes but there were three left. One held Aiden and had a seax to his throat. The other two stood on either side. Aiden looked calm. He smiled, "I told these Danes that you would come."

The Dane holding him pulled tighter and snapped, "This galdramenn comes with us! One step closer and he dies!"

I knew that was a bluff. If they wanted him dead then why did they need to bring him all the way across the country? He would not kill him. I took a step forward and said, "Snorri!"

The Danes took a step backwards. "We will kill him!"

"And if you do then we will give you the blood eagle." As I took another step forward there was a twang as Snorri released the arrow. I had the Dane's attention and he did not see the arrow which pierced his left eye. He fell to the floor and before the other two could react I had savagely brought my sword around to hack through the neck of one while Rolf's axe had struck the other. The noise of the conflict had attracted the attention of the other Danes who were below us by the river. The trees prevented us from seeing the drekar but I heard their shouts.

"Grab the horses. We must flee."

Aiden smiled and took my hand in his, "Thank you Jarl. Even though I knew you would come I did not know if you would reach me before we reached the drekar."

"We will talk later."

I mounted one of the Danish horses just as the Danes appeared. They were spread out in a long line and they had cut off our escape south. We would have to ride north. Rollo, Erik and Leif had the spare Danish horses with us. We might need them and they would be denied by our enemies. "Finni, watch Aiden. Snorri, find us a way out."

I slipped my shield around my back as I urged the Danish horse up the slope. He was struggling. It was with some relief that he made the trail at the top. Snorri pointed north. "Here Jarl, there is a well-worn path!"

We galloped down the trail. I heard the shouts from the Danes behind. They were following. Our horses were not the biggest. They would not be able to move much faster than the Danes. I relied on the fact that the Danes would tire. When the horses succumbed and could go no further then we would turn and fight.

Snorri had a wonderful sense of direction. A mile from the fight he found the Roman Road which headed up towards the Wall. We could not use our former route. The Danes could cut us off. We would have to find a different way home. Once on the road, we could move faster and, gradually, we lost the Danes. I suspected they were still following but we could afford to slow down a little and save the horses.

Aiden turned to me and said, "Jarl they were after either you or me when they came. They are the brothers of Halfdan the Black. Those two brothers, Thrand and Finni Karlsson were with them. It was Thrand whom Snorri slew. They had been waiting in the woods north of the Rye Dale and were waiting for either you hunting or me seeking herbs. The brothers knew us both by sight. They took great pleasure in telling me how they had fooled me by wrecking their own boat. I am sorry Jarl. I should have dreamt them and I didn't. Perhaps my powers are fading."

"No Aidan, it is the Norns. They are toying with me and with those who are close to me. We will have to deal with these Danes but not just yet. First, we must get you back to Cyninges-tūn. My daughter will be worried."

Rolf shouted, "Jarl, I can see them. They are a couple of hundred paces behind us."

"It is time to push on again. We will ride hard for a mile. Let us see if we can lose them."

I tried to estimate how far we might have to run to escape the Danes. Aiden shouted, "I think it is thirty miles to the Roman Wall."

"Then we will reach there by dark." I wondered just how much Halfdan's brothers wanted me. Would they pursue us all day and all night? This was a blood feud now. They would not rest until I was dead. I urged my horse next to Aiden's. "Why did they take you? What was their intention?"

"They wanted you but they recognised me. Their leader had been at Tilaburg and, like the two brothers Karlsson, he knew me. He said they would take me to Ragnar and Harald, Halfdan's brothers. He thought they could use me as a hostage. I think they wanted to bargain with me."

I laughed, "Then they do not know me."

"No, Jarl. I tried to tell them but they would have none of it. They were also afraid of me. They took from me anything I might use which was magical. They threw away my leather pouch with my herbs and my amulet. It is why I had to leave the clues in the mud and with twigs."

"It worked." We rode in silence and I wondered how best to deal with these Danes. There could be no reasoning with them. We would have to fight them. With just a handful of Ulfheonar, I could not hope to defeat them now. I had to get back to Cyninges-tūn. I would need a large warband. I had to draw them back across the country.

"Rolf, are they in sight?"

"No Jarl."

"Then stop and gather round."

If they thought me mad they said nothing. "We need to draw them back across the divide and then we can bring a warband to defeat them. Leif, ride to Cyninges-tūn. Fetch a warband to the wall. You can ride across country and be there in a day of hard riding. As soon as you are on our land you can get a mount from one of our farmers. We will draw them across the country."

Erik said, "Is that not a risk, Jarl?"

"Would you rather we reach home and then keep watching over our shoulders for a warband of Danes to descend upon our valley and slaughter our people?" He shook his head. "This way we get it over with.

We pull them west. Let them think we are weaker than we are. Leif, ride!" Leif smacked his horse in the rump and took off.

"I see them, Jarl." Rolf was our rearguard. He had good eyes.

"Then we ride but make it look as though our horses are struggling."

As the day wore on we rode and stopped. We let them get within two hundred paces and then we moved. It was exhausting work. Snorri reined in when we approached the Roman fort on the Tinea. "We will need to find somewhere to rest, Jarl. We could stay here. It is defensible."

"No, Snorri, I want to be further northwest and closer to home. Leif still has hours to go before he reaches our people. It will be late tomorrow at the earliest before a warband could reach us." Even as I said it I knew that I should have sent him to Ulf Olafsson first. Ulf and his warriors were the closest to us.

"Jarl we need food and we need to rest the horses."

"We ride to the fort and then dismount and walk. That will rest the horses. We will still be within sight of the Danes but we will have a good lead over them."

As we rode Aiden said, "You are gambling, Jarl."

"I am. If we keep on this road then they cannot get ahead of us. We have drawn them away from their drekar. They may cut their losses and return to their boat but if they see us walking and not riding then they will renew their efforts. It will tire them out. If we are hungry then so are they. If we are tired then they are even more so."

He nodded and said, "There is another fort just eight miles ahead. We will have to stop there."

We descended towards the Roman bridge. When we reached it I dismounted and looked up the hill. The Danish warband was strung out. It was a large warband. I wondered how many drekar they had. The warriors I could see wore no mail. They would be the ones keeping us in sight. Even as we stopped I saw one of them halt and turn. He would be shouting to the brothers. We walked across the bridge and we passed the old fort. We kept walking while we were within sight of the Danes. The road was straight for some way beyond the fort and the Danes could still see us but as it passed through a wood we were hidden.

"Mount and we ride for the next fort. Let us hide there."

It was a five-mile ride to the fort. The Danes were too far from their drekar. They would have to camp. I wondered if they would camp at the fort we had just passed or would they pursue us? They would now know our destination. If they were determined then they would rest for a short time and then try to catch us as we slept.

Evening had fallen as we dropped down into the river valley. We dismounted when we saw the bridge over the river and the deserted

Roman fort. "Rollo and Rolf, stay on this side of the bridge and watch for the Danes. We will take your horses."

We unsaddled the horses and led them to the river to drink. "Snorri, we need food!"

"Aye Jarl. I could eat a horse and not bother to skin it!"

I had not slept the night before and now exhaustion was setting in. When the first drops of rain fell on me I felt grateful for they refreshed me but as the raindrops turned to a downpour I became less happy. We took shelter under the roof of the crumbling bathhouse. Aiden managed to get a fire going and then he said, "I will fetch Rollo and Rolf. We have no need for them to watch. I will make an alarm. We will be warned of the Danes but I do not think that they will venture out in the rain."

Aiden was away for some time. Rollo and Rolf returned, "Aiden said to come into the dry, Jarl!"

"He knows what he is doing. "

Snorri came back with a young lamb. Within a few moments, it was skinned and butchered and the joints speared on the ends of seaxes and thrust in the fire. It would take some time to cook through but we would eat each part as it cooked.

Aiden returned. "If they come then we will hear them."

I nodded. "We must take it in turns to sleep. They will come before dawn."

Snorri said, "Jarl you have not slept the longest; you will sleep. We have Aiden now."

He looked at Aiden who said, "He is right, Jarl. You will make bad decisions if you are tired."

I nodded. My eyes were closing. I curled up in a ball and pulled my wolf cloak over my head and I dreamed...

I was on Halvelyn and I was alone. I was naked with no sword to protect me. The creatures of the night crept up on me and they surrounded me. I looked around for a weapon and spied a broken branch. I held it, determined to sell my life dearly. I swung it around as the foxes and rats leapt at me. I felt their teeth as they nipped at me and I began to bleed and then there was such a roaring that I thought my head would burst and flames danced all around me. A huge dragon, the one I had seen in my dreams, landed and it picked me up in its talons. We flew high into the air. We flew so high that we left the earth far behind. We flew over Ulf Olafsson at Thorkell's Stad and he waved as I passed over. Circling the dragon began to descend and I was dropped on the top of Old Olaf. As I turned, the dragon ascended and disappeared. I reached up to touch the beast and it was gone.

"Jarl!" I looked up and saw Snorri. "It is almost dawn Jarl." The rain was still relentlessly pouring down.

"We must send to Ulf Olafsson for help. Let Rollo go. Give him a spare horse. Tell him to get there as quickly as he can."

"You dreamed?"

Aiden said, "He dreamed."

"Rollo! Ride to Ulf and have him bring his men along the wall to meet with us." He leapt on his horse and galloped off.

Just then we heard a cry from the river. "They have tripped my trap, Jarl."

"Then we ride. Let us mount."

As I mounted Finni stuck a lamb shank in my hand. "We saved this for you. You cannot kill Danes if you are hungry."

I mounted the horse and felt every bone in my body aching. It was some years since I had ridden so hard and slept on the ground. I was getting old. We began to trot down the road. I tore hunks of meat from the shank as we rode. Suddenly Snorri said, "There are Danes on the road!"

"Rollo?"

Snorri shook his head. "They have come from the south and I can see no sign of him."

"Then head north, towards the wall. We can cross the wall. We will be slower but the wall will give us some protection and it will hide us for a while."

We heard more shouts from behind as more of Aiden's traps were set off. They would incapacitate and not kill. Their purpose was to warn us. It was rough ground over which we travelled and we headed for the wood and the high scars. The rain was so hard that, if we could make the woods then they would find it hard to see us. If they had to search then we could buy time for our men to reach us.

I bit another chunk out of the cold lamb. I had never tasted anything so fine in my life. I barely chewed I was so hungry. As we reached the woods we halted. I turned and, still eating, looked at the Danes. They were trotting towards the woods. They had been refreshed by the halt. I turned and followed Snorri through the woods. We emerged on the other side and I saw a pile of rocks. "We will hide behind them. When they come through the woods they will waste time searching for us." There was something familiar about this landscape but I could not remember being here. Perhaps the teeming rain made it look like somewhere I had been before.

It was when we disappeared behind the rocks that I spied them. It was a pile of bones. There were pieces of rusted metal too. It was a grave, an old barrow, and the rain had washed away the soil. I saw Aiden and he had a look on his face which I had rarely seen. It was as though he was awake and yet dreaming. He dismounted. Snorri shouted, "Aiden!"

"Leave him!"

He wandered over to the pile of bones and reached down. I had no idea what he sought but his hand seemed drawn to something. He lifted a piece of cloth. It looked to have been golden but in the rain and with the detritus of an age it was hard to tell. There looked to be metal at one end. To me, it looked like the sleeve of a giant's kyrtle. I moved closer and it was the second object which had a greater effect. It was a golden dragon with a metal chain. It was the dragon of my dreams. This was the place that Myrddyn had shown me.

Aiden turned and, still looking dazed, brought them over to me. He handed me the chain and the dragon. "Jarl, this is what the old man wished you to have. They are both from the times of the Romans. They are links to your ancestor."

I lifted it up and saw that it was the same dragon which had carried me to Old Olaf. I put it around my neck. Suddenly a Dane appeared and shouted, "I have them!"

"Mount!"

Snorri knocked an arrow and sent it in the direction of the Danish scout but he had already gone to ground. Holding the long sleeve Aiden mounted and we galloped west. As we did so I heard a weird wailing as air passed through the dragon sleeve. Finni shouted, "What is that? Is it the dead, Jarl? Have we done wrong?"

"No," shouted Aiden, "This is *wyrd*! This is the fulfilment of the Jarl's dream. The dragon cries. The dragon is born again!"

I had to put the thoughts of the dragon beyond me for the Danes were flooding across the rough ground towards us. The rocks and spongy, muddy turf were not good for the horses and we could not extend our lead. We rode in a rough line. There was little to be gained from travelling one behind the other. I risked a glance over my shoulder. Some of the Danes, the ones with mail, were falling further behind us.

"Head for the wall! There is a gap up ahead at the fort!"

There was an old Roman fort which rose above the valley. We would be able to make it before the Danes and once through we would be able to reach the road. The leading Danes were less than forty paces behind us. As Snorri led us towards it I glanced over my shoulder and saw that the Danes were even more spread out. Our manoeuvre had taken them by surprise. Disaster struck when we were just sixty paces from the ruined gatehouse. Aiden's horse slipped and stumbled. He was never the best rider and he flew from its back. Vermund had the last spare horse.

"Rolf and Finni, come with me."

I reined my horse in and slipped from his back. The Danes redoubled their efforts to reach me as Snorri and Vermund helped a groggy Aiden to the back of his horse. Rolf and Finni flanked me. I slipped my shield around and drew Saxon Slayer. I stabbed directly at the middle of the leading Dane whose spear was already lunging towards my head. Without taking my eyes from the Dane I flicked my head out of the way of the spear. The Dane impaled himself on my sword. Finni's sword struck a second Dane so hard on the side of his helmet that he fell stunned and Rolf's two handed axe took the head of the third. There was a gap to the nearest Danes and I shouted, "Mount. We have done enough."

Our horses were so tired that they had not moved far and we quickly remounted. Snorri's arrow made the closest Dane duck behind his shield and we lumbered up the slope to the gatehouse. The gates had long ago fallen and the rain, which still poured down had weakened the stones. "Rolf smash the gate's support with the back of your axe."

While Finni held his horse Rolf leapt from his back and giving a mighty swing the powerful young man's axe thundered and cracked into the left-hand gate support. The ancient wood crumbled. The stones were loose and they tumbled down the slope filling the gate and falling down towards the Danes. It would give us a lead. It would be a short one but it would have to do. As soon as he had mounted I shouted, "Ride along the wall."

The Roman wall had a turf top and was wide enough for two horses. It was less slippery than the cobbles inside the fort. I turned and saw that they had yet to clear the gate. Trees had grown over part of the wall and, as we headed west, we were hidden from view.

The rain began, thankfully, to ease off and the skies cleared from the north. To our right was a sheer drop and the dark waters of a large tarn. Snorri shouted, "Jarl we had best be off the wall here. There is a cliff ahead."

"Find us a path!"

After a hundred paces or so he leapt from the wall with his horse to the soft ground south of it. Most of the others managed to do so as well but Aiden was still shaken from his fall and he had to gingerly lead his horse. We galloped south towards the road. We had travelled almost twenty miles since dawn and we were exhausted. The Danes would be too. We reached the road and we stopped. Two of the horses were lame or would be soon and I had a feeling that the Danes were up to something.

"Aiden, the Danes who waited for you, were they alone?"

He still looked shaken but my question made him become more alert. "They may have been but then again the men who took me spoke of large numbers of Danes."

Erik said, "If there were two brothers might that not mean two or even three drekar? Remember that Halfdan the Black had over forty men with him. That is not a small drekar. There could be seventy or eighty Danes out there."

Aiden's shoulders slumped, "I have let them make me panic and I should not have done so. I knew you were coming, Jarl and I should have used my head. Of course, there were two drekar. They had me. It makes sense that they would have other men waiting to ambush you. It was just luck that you evaded them."

"Or the Norns!"

"Aye, the Norns."

"Then we should stop running. We are dancing to their tune. Ulf will be on his way soon. Leif and the men from Cyninges-tūn will be here tomorrow. There is another warband. They are driving us towards it."

Aiden nodded, "That explains why there were Danes on the road close to the fort."

"We dismount. Aiden, take the horses to the woods and hide. Tonight we become Ulfheonar. We will teach them to be wary of the darkness." We dismounted and hefted our shields around. We helped Aiden to lead the horses to the dell between the wall and the road and we tied them to the trees. Aiden drew his short sword. He pointed to the dragon around my neck. "The spirits would not give you that in order for you to die here on the wall. The Norns have plans for you. What you do is right. I feel it in my bones."

I led the Ulfheonar half a mile to the east and the edge of the woods. I was now down to a handful of men: Snorri, Rolf, Erik, Vermund and Finni. There were six of us to stop a warband. To many, that would have seemed impossible but these were Ulfheonar. Snorri pointed to the east. "They have been driving us and I see now why they did so. Have you noticed Jarl that it has been the men without armour we have seen? They are saving the others for the battle. They will come across this open ground and then enter this wood."

"Then we wait here!"

We spaced ourselves out so that any who entered the wood would have to pass us. The sun was setting early this night. The clouds still filled the sky and it was dark. That suited the men who wore wolf skins.

I stood behind a tree which masked my profile. With my black cloak, black helmet and mail I was invisible. The only thing which reflected light was my sword. Ragnar's Spirit seemed to glow in the dark and I kept it hidden behind the tree.

I heard the Danes. They were talking as they approached. "Why we have to do the chasing and Ragnar's crew just wait is beyond me!"

"He is the elder. Besides we get to kill the Dragonheart and gain his sword."

"I will not risk that. No man has fought him and lived."

"But the glory!"

Another voice shouted, "Shut up or I will cut your tongues out!"

"They are far ahead of us, Hersir! We would smell their horses."

"Spread out. We have the chance to close with them. No more talking."

The last voices were just paces away and I held Ragnar's Spirit ready to strike. I watched as a warrior holding a spear and a shield passed the tree. He paused and sniffed. Had he smelled me? Then he walked on. I put my left hand around his mouth and pulled Ragnar's Spirit across his throat. His warm blood gushed over my hand and I lowered him gently to the ground. I could not see my other men but I knew they would have slain those who had passed them.

I turned to the other side of the tree. The Hersir had said to spread out. Sure enough, I heard the Dane walking towards me. He too paused and sniffed the air. Could he smell blood? As he passed me I took no chances. He was not wearing mail and I rammed my sword up through his ribs and into his heart. I lowered his body to the ground too.

There was silence and then I heard a voice. It came from the east. "Sven, where are you? Are they close?"

I risked looking around the tree. It was the mailed warriors. There were thirty of them and they had halted short of the wood. I guessed that we had slain all of their scouts. The warband halted and closed ranks. Good warriors could smell trouble. I knew that they were listening. They would hear us when we moved. No matter how quietly we shifted our position there would be some sound. I silently sheathed my sword. The sheepskin in my scabbard ensured silence. Then, cupping my hands together, I howled. The other Ulfheonar howled too. And then, as one we stopped and I turned away to head through the woods. The effect of the howling of the wolf was always the same. The warband tightened their ranks and drew together. Those who had never heard it before asked others what it was and the leaders would try to determine how many Ulfheonar lay in wait in the woods. The noise of their questions masked any noise we might make.

I made my way back to Aiden and the others all joined me. We had bought some time and delayed the inevitable but sometime in the next few hours the warband we had seen and the one we had not would meet up and we would be in the middle. Our only hope lay in Ulf and Haaken One Eye. I knew, in my heart, that the Ulfheonar would move heaven and earth to get to me. We were brothers and our spirits called to one another.

Chapter 8

Aiden was smiling as he greeted us. "The wolves howled."

Snorri snorted, "And the Danes filled their breeks!"

Just then we heard their feet, in the distance, as they ran along the road. We did not have the luxury of time. We could not congratulate ourselves. Our horses were now a little more rested. It was possible to risk riding them again. We clambered into the saddles and burst out onto the road. Up ahead, on the road were the warriors. I should have known they would take to the road; it was less risky for them. They gave a shout of triumph as they saw us. Perhaps their leaders were angry that there were so few of us. Until this moment they had only seen us in the distance and true numbers could not be ascertained. Now they knew our paucity of numbers. We turned and rode hard to the west. The Danes left the road to pursue us.

Aiden rode at the front with Snorri and our one spare horse. I rode at the rear with Erik. We kept up a steady pace. The horses we rode would be ruined after this. They were used to short journeys with grass and frequent rests. We had asked them to do the impossible and they had almost managed to do so. Our salvation came close to the river. Figures loomed up out of the dark and I feared, at first, that it was the second warband.

Jarl Ketil Windarson's voice gave me hope, "Jarl Dragonheart! There is a warband to the south of us!"

I reined in as his men appeared from the sides of the road. "And there is one behind us. Aiden, take the horses, and we will form a shield wall."

Dawn was not too far off and we would be exposed by the sun but we could not run with two warbands hunting us.

"How many men are there with you?"

"Twenty. One of my riders met Rollo and he told us of your dilemma. He continued on to Ulf. I sounded the alarm and my people are inside my fort. I brought my oathsworn."

Just then the Danes who had been pursuing us appeared at the top of the rise. We must have come as a surprise to them for they halted. In the dark, our numbers would be hard to gauge. What was obvious was that there were more of us than there had been. A warrior stepped forward and shouted, "I am Harald Halfdansson. I am here with my warriors to collect weregeld for my brother Halfdan the Black!"

"Your brother hired out his sword and he perished in battle. He had his sword in his hand! There is no weregeld to pay."

"That is not the way the Eorledman told the tale but it matters not. We will kill you and then I will wield the sword touched by the gods!"

"You will have to prise it from my dead hands first."

"I will do so."

They stood in silence. Snorri said, quietly, "I like this not, Jarl. Why do they not attack? They have the slope and they have numbers."

"You are right. Ketil, have you archers with you?"

"Aye Jarl."

"Have them prepare their arrows. On my command I want them to release a couple of arrows each at the warband and then we will run towards the wall. This road is a trap. At least there are towers on the wall where we can hold out until Ulf and Haaken arrive. Aiden, send the horses down the road. We are done with them now and it may fool the Danes."

"Aye Jarl. Bagsecg and Karl, organize the archers."

A moment or two later they said, "Ready!"

I shouted, "Release!" There were only seven arrows in each flight but they had the desired effect. The Danes hid behind a tight shield wall. We were already running north towards the wall. We would have a ditch to negotiate. We knew where that would be but the Danes might not. There was a fort but that was more than a mile along the wall. I doubted that we would have the time to reach it. Dawn began to break in the east and the Danes saw that we had not continued down the road and they began their pursuit.

"Ditch!"

The ditch was not the same as when the Romans had built it and the sides were not as steep. However, if you ran and did not know it was there then a fall could still break an ankle. We scrambled out of the other side and made our way to the wall. I spied a small tower; the Romans called them mile castles. This one looked to be largely whole and we could use it for defence. The gate had long gone but the wall still ran around the top.

"Ketil, have your seven archers climb to the tower. Aiden, join them. Place your men on the wall above the gate. The Ulfheonar will hold the gate."

Ketil knew me well enough not to object. We were the best and the gate was just wide enough for six warriors. Ketil's men would have to keep the Danes from pressing too closely.

The ditch did indeed slow them up. We had just formed up in the gate when the warband appeared over the rise and rampart before the ditch. Three warriors, eager to get at us failed to notice the ditch and they tumbled into the bottom. I heard their cries of pain. Suddenly Aiden shouted, "Jarl Dragonheart! The second warband approaches!"

I turned to Snorri, "So both brothers are united!"

"Do not fear Jarl, Haaken One Eye will not let us down."

"He has far to come and Leif may have run into this warband."

Snorri laughed, "He is Ulfheonar. He only runs into that which he intends!"

When they had climbed from the ditch Harald Halfdansson began to organize his men. This would not be a wild attack. Dawn and daylight were his allies. He had his brother to join him and we could run no more. If we left the mile castle then they would surround us. He knew that we had to stay where we were. The second warband was more numerous than the first. Their scouts had not been decimated by Ulfheonar. I saw the warrior I assumed was Ragnar Halfdansson. Like his brother, he had a four-legged symbol painted on his shield. Both brothers had long Danish axes.

I shouted, "Aiden, how many do we face?"

"There look to be over sixty, Jarl but the ones at the back are milling around. There are at least twenty in mail byrnies."

One of Ketil's men shouted, "Good! I tire of my leather one!" Others laughed and that gave me hope for they were in good spirits. We had chosen the one-mile castle which could not be attacked from the west. There was a cliff and a quarry there but that also meant we had no escape that way.

The Danes made a wedge. They did not use all of their men. It just had thirty men but the front half were all mailed. The two brothers would use that to force us from the gate and then unleash the rest of the warband. Aiden commanded the archers. Ketil's men knew that they had a galdramenn with them and would obey him. By using the tower we had increased the range of the arrows and when the first flight flew over I knew that Aiden had judged it well. He did not have the archers target the ones with mail at the font. Instead, they struck the ones at the rear. Two were too slow to raise their shields and they fell. The wedge was already weaker. More importantly, the ones at the rear now had to have their shields held over their heads. They would not add their weight to the attack.

Ketil's men above us used some of the loose stones and they hurled them at the Danes. One mailed warrior fell when a large stone struck his helmet and the rest were forced to raise their shields to give themselves some protection. As they did so I shouted, "Charge!"

It was a surprise move and it took them by surprise. Only the Ulfheonar could have done what I intended. With their shields above them, they had no protection and my sword rammed into the middle of the surprised warrior at the fore. Rolf's axe took out a second and Vermund the head of a third. "Back!"

We raced back to the gate and Ketil's men continued to hurl stones. I heard a horn and saw that the brothers had decided to withdraw their wedge. They had lost four of their best men; two in mail and two others. It had been costly and they would have to reorganize.

"Search the bodies of the dead. We can use their weapons." We would take the mail later but their axes, swords, spears and seaxes would come in handy. We passed the weapons up to Ketil's men. They could throw the spears down when next the Danes attacked. I kept a throwing axe. It was more of a hatchet than a true throwing axe but it would have to do. Then we made a small barrier of bodies. They would either have to halt and clear them or climb over them. Either way, we would take advantage of their disarray.

Aiden shouted, "Jarl Dragonheart, there are more Danes coming from the east."

Snorri said, "They would be the ones who could not keep up. The odds are lengthening."

"So long as we are above ground then there is hope."

Ketil's men brought around skins with ale around to us and some dried venison. I kept watching the Danes as they organised another wedge. This time it was made up completely of mailed warriors. There were thirty of them. Some were still in reserve but the brothers were counting on breaking us with these warriors.

We pulled our shields around as they approached. They came steadily. They were not risking slipping on the mud. The previous wedge had churned it up. When they struck us then it would be at a walk. Aiden held the archers. Not one arrow was wasted. The Danes, however, had the shields of the ones at the back raised in case we did. They came so slowly that we had time to assess the warriors we would face in ten paces. The front three all held spears. They had learned from their first attack. The ones at the side held axes.

"Ketil! Have the men ready with the stones." During the lull, they had gathered more stones from the northern wall. The Romans had used them to make a cobbled surface and they made perfect missiles.

Ketil and his men waited until the Danes were climbing over their dead warriors. The bodies were slick with blood and gore and, as they stepped across them, they were pelted with stones. It is hard enough to fend off stones but it was doubly difficult while trying to climb across a slippery pile of bodies. As they flailed around trying to keep their balance my men threw spears and arrows at them. One of the Danes lost his balance and fell towards me. I rammed my sword under his byrnie and into his gut. I twisted as I pulled it out. The first five men were all either wounded or slain before they could get to us.

Holding Ragnar's Spirit in my left hand I threw the throwing axe. It embedded itself in the face of a Dane. He fell with the others. All order was gone in the wedge but the Danes were now angry and desperate to get to grips with us. They were wild with fury. We, in contrast, were calm. Rolf swung his axe and it scythed across the weapons the Danes held before them. The rest of us stabbed and slashed at the wall of mailed warriors who tried to force us from the gate. Had they had a proper wedge with men pushing from behind then it would have been easy. As it was it was almost impossible.

A spear was thrust at my head and I raised my shield to block it. I chopped at the shaft of the spear with my sword and the head fell at my feet. Vermund lunged forward and took the warrior in the gut. A throwing axe was hurled at me. I only saw it at the last moment and I did not manage to get out of the way. It glanced off the side of my helmet. Bjorn had made my helmet strong. It was merely dented. And then the horn sounded again and the Danes pulled back.

I turned, "Is anyone wounded?"

Finni wiped some blood from his cheek; he had been cut by a spear. "A nick, that is all, Jarl."

Rolf had not fought in such a battle before and he said, "We could stay here all day!"

Erik shook his head, "They will realise that the gate is not the weak point. It is the walls which are. They have enough numbers. The next attack will be on the walls."

Erik was right. "Ketil, Aiden, prepare for an attack on the walls."

Once again, we saw the Danish brothers gesticulating as they decided what to do. They had the numbers to surround the mile castle and overwhelm our men. They could use their shields to climb the walls; we had done so ourselves before now.

The whole of the Danish line moved forward. The mailed warriors were spread out amongst those without mail. This time the attack would break us. Aiden and the archers now had more targets and they used their arrows well. The warriors who came towards the gate were not in a wedge and they had time to step over the bodies of the dead. It was a measured approach. When they were just five paces from us they threw their spears. It was not difficult to block them but, in doing so, we were unable to attack them and they used the opportunity to climb safely over the bodies. One or two stones were thrown at them but the majority of

Ketil's men were defending the walls from the advancing Danes. I saw one of Ketil's men pitched from the wall as he was hit by a spear.

I reached around and pulled the spear from my shield and rammed it into the ground so that I could use it later. Then they hit us. Our shields were already before us and we braced ourselves for the swinging axes. Even as I took the blow from the two-handed weapon, I jabbed upwards with my sword. The Dane's shield came up to catch the tip but he just forced it up to his helmet. It rammed his head back and, as he was overbalancing, I punched with my shield. He was using his axe one-handed and he did not have the strength to swing it. He began to totter backwards and I ripped my sword across his throat. The warrior next to him saw his chance and he tried the same blow. I was wearing the dragon around my neck and the sword rasped along it. I brought my own sword down and hacked into his right arm. Blood spurted and the sword fell from his fingers.

The gate was now free of attackers. We had been faced by seven men and now five lay dead and two more would not last an hour. "Erik and Snorri, take Rolf and clear the wall to the west. Vermund and Finni we will take these on the east."

I picked up the spear and, as we reached the pyramid of warriors trying to climb the walls I stabbed it into the side of one of the shield bearers. As he fell so the whole pile of warriors above him followed. They tumbled to the ground. We hacked and we chopped as they struggled to rise to their feet. It was like sending a stone down a mountain. Soon the Danes were fleeing as we pushed out and Ketil's men rained death. Once again the horn recalled the Danes to lick their wounds. It was gone noon and I knew that they must be tiring.

"Despatch their wounded and gather any spears." I turned to Erik, "We must use the spears to make a barrier around us. I want four of you on the walls. When they attack again they will concentrate their efforts on Ketil's men."

Ketil and Aiden joined me. "That last attack almost succeeded. The next one surely will, Jarl. My men are brave but we are outnumbered."

"I know Ketil. I will give you four Ulfheonar. You can have two on each wall. I will defend the gate with Rolf and Finni." I smiled at Aiden, "The dragon has saved me. Look."

I held out the dragon hanging from the chain. The line scored by the sword could be clearly seen.

Ketil ran his fingers along it. "Is this new, Jarl?"

"We found it on the wall as the wizard Myrddyn told me I would."

"Myrddyn? Is he alive?"

"He came to me in my dream."

"*Wyrd.*"

"Jarl, they come again!"

"Then we will repel them again!" I raised Ragnar's Spirit as Ketil and Aiden raced back to their posts, "Ulfheonar!"

My Ulfheonar took up the chant as the Danes advanced once more. As I faced our foes I began to think my ears were playing tricks for I could hear the chant still and it was to the south of us. Suddenly Aiden's voice rang out, "It is Ulf and Haaken! They are attacking the rear of the Danish line!"

"Then let us join them and end this!"

We were the closest to the Danes and we ran directly at them. The oathsworn of the brothers faced us but they could hear their comrades being slaughtered by Ulfheonar and the men from Thorkell's Stad. I ducked under a wildly swinging axe and rammed my sword into the middle of the Dane. He had good mail and my sword slid down the links. As I pulled back some of the links caught on the hilt of my sword and it dragged him towards me. He could not keep his balance and I hit him with the boss of my shield as I disentangled the sword hilt. When he fell backwards I hit him again on the weakened mail links and this time the sword tore through them and ripped into his side. I pulled out Ragnar's Spirit and thrust it through his mouth, pinning his skull to the ground.

Harald Halfdansson stood glaring at me. Rolf and Erik had hewn two of his bodyguards already and were dealing with the other two. I walked towards him. "Before I slay you, Dane, are there any other brothers I should watch out for? Do I need to take my drekar to your homeland and kill every member of your clan?"

He shook his head and looked like a dog drying itself. "You have no need, shapeshifter! My family lives in Jorvik and they will come for you soon enough!"

He swung his axe at my shield. Although I blocked it, I felt my arm shiver. I moved my right arm behind me. I wished to disguise my strike. He took that as weakness and swung again. This time I did not block the blow but used my feet to step backwards and, as the axe head flew past me, stepped in and brought my sword backhand against his shield arm. It bit deeply into his flesh. I pulled my blade back and felt it grate against bone. He was too close for a swing with his axe and he had to step back to free his arm. I saw the blood dripping from his left arm and I brought my sword around to smash into his shield. He tried to swing at my head, one-handed with his axe. As I ducked beneath it I lunged up with my sword. It went into his jaw and then into his skull. As I withdrew my blade he fell at my feet.

Rolf swung his axe and took the head. He stood holding the Dane's blood skull and began chanting, "Dragonheart! Dragonheart! Dragonheart!"

That appeared to be the signal for our enemies to flee. Ragnar Halfdansson and his oathsworn began to run east. The Danes who managed to disengage followed him. I saw Haaken as he and my Ulfheonar despatched the last of the Danes. We had won! Against the odds, my Ulfheonar and Ketil's men had succeeded. It had been impossible but we had done it. I looked around and saw, to my horror, that Vermund Thorirson lay dead. I had lost another Ulfheonar. The dead Danes around him were a testament to his courage and he would be in Valhalla now. Each time an Ulfheonar fell it was like a marker for the future. They were preparing my way to the Otherworld!

Haaken and my Ulfheonar left the task of ending the lives of the Danes to Ulf's men. "How did you escape this trap, Jarl?"

"Trap?"

Beorn the Scout nodded, "I found the trail of the second warband, Jarl. They had been heading for Cyninges-tūn. I am guessing that they received word that you were here and they came north to join the others. As soon as I discovered it I told Haaken."

"We came as fast as we could, Jarl, but the heavy rains made travel almost impossible."

I shook my head. I saw the guilt on all of their faces. "This was *wyrd*." I held the dragon symbol. "Had I not been pursued I would not have discovered this. My dream told me I would find it."

Rolf could not contain himself, "And we found the voice of the dragon!"

My men stared at him as though he had lost his mind. Aiden said, "It is true. We found the site of an ancient battle. It looked to me as though the two things came from the times of the Romans. The Jarl is Dragonheart. This is the link to that dragon and see, it has saved his life already!"

He pointed to the scar running across the metal.

Ulf asked, "Is this over now, Jarl?"

"No, Ulf. There is one brother left and others who live in Jorvik. The Danes are growing in power there. I think that the days of Northumbria are numbered. Soon we will need to make war on them. When we are finished here have your warriors train. I will send word when we go to teach the Danes that this is not their land."

We did not leave straight away. We were all exhausted. Haaken and Ulf's men had had to travel without rest and we had spent three days fleeing across the land and fighting a relentless enemy. We headed for the nearby Roman fort and camped there. Snorri and the others were closely questioned by the other warriors. Everyone knew that what we had done was remarkable, I sat with Olaf, Haaken and Aiden.

"The Weird Sisters have woven a complicated web this time, Jarl."

"You are right Aiden. It goes from the Danes to Egbert and here to a time before the memory of man. I hope my son and the others are not entangled in this web."

"They will be, Jarl. The Norns do not do things by half and I fear I cannot see across the sea. I did not even see my own trap."

Olaf Leather Neck stroked the edge of his axe, "We rely on our weapons and our brothers. That is all that a warrior can do."

If there was something good to take from this encounter with the Danes it was the weapons, mail and treasure we took back home with us. Ketil and his men had the first choice. Had they not arrived when they had then we would be dead. But all of us benefitted. We took the sword from Harald Halfdansson and buried it with Vermund and the others who had fallen. He had earned it. His golden wolf we took, along with his share of the spoils, for his wife. He had no children and his wife was young. Another warrior would take her to his hearth. That was the way of the warrior. When we had taken our leave of my Ulfheonar we began the long journey home. For Aiden and I, it was a silent journey for we had much to ponder.

There was relief when we marched through the gates of Cyninges-tūn. I had had enough of riding and I had walked the whole way with my men. I know that Aiden wrestled with the problem of his powers and the significance of the dragon. I was planning my attack on the Danes. I had learned that if you did not punish your enemies then they took it as a sign of weakness and came back. When the Irish had kidnapped my wife and children we had inflicted such punishment that they never attempted anything like it again. I would do the same to the family of Halfdan the Black.

Kara greeted Aiden but I did not see Brigid. "Where is my wife?"

"It is nothing to worry about father, but she has a fever."

Fear gripped my heart, "Erika?"

"Your child is healthy. We found a wet nurse for her."

I stared at Kara, "A fever? You and your women normally have cures for such things."

Kara came closer. "It may not be a simple fever but I think she will recover."

"You speak in riddles. She will be fine and then it may not be a simple fever. Which is it?"

"Since the spirit of Myrddyn returned I have not thought clearly. I suspect my husband has not either. Is not that right?"

He nodded, "I told you that I should not have been caught so easily. My mind is clouded. "We must go to the cave and dream."

Kara smiled, "It is what I thought too. We will wait until Brigid is healed for we will need to leave Ylva with her grandfather."

"I thought you said that Myrddyn's return was good."

"It is but it was you who went to the cave and it should have been us."

I hurried to my hall. Uhtric and my wife's women were tending her. They bowed when I entered. "How is she?"

"She has warmed to the touch since the morning and her eyes fluttered as though she might wake."

"Did the nuns of the White Christ help her?"

"They have rarely left her side. It is only since we had word of your return that they have left."

I stroked Brigid's head, "Kill a chicken, pluck it and cook it. Pour in half of a small jug of the red wine I was saving. I will feed her!"

They scurried off. This was not what I normally did but I remembered that my mother had used chicken broth when we were ill. The wine was just an afterthought. The taste warmed me through and I believed it could not hurt. "Fetch me my children!"

Gryffydd and Erika were brought and poor Gryffydd looked fearfully at his mother. "Fear not, my son, we shall heal her. Come and sit on my knee."

He began to stroke the dragon around my neck. "What is this?"

"It is the sign of the dragon." I took it off and placed it around his neck. "There, you shall wear it."

He looked pleased and then he frowned and took it off, "Mother needs it more than I do father. Let the dragon heal her." He placed it around her neck. After a few moments, her breathing seemed easier. It became regular and a little colour came back into her cheeks and as we watched, her eyes opened. Gruffydd grinned, "See, I told you!"

She looked up at me, "I dreamed you were attacked. Was it true?"

"It was but I came to no harm and I am home now."

She put her hands on mine. "How long have I been ill?"

"A few days." She nodded and looked at my face and then Gryffydd's.

"The dragon cured you!"

"The dragon?" Gryffydd held it up for her to see. My poor wife looked confused. "I do not understand."

"I found this near the Roman Wall and it saved my life. I put it around our son's neck and he placed it on yours. It seemed to work."

She took it off and looked at it. Her eyes widened. "Do you know what this symbol is?"

"It is a dragon such as came to me in my dream. The old wizard, Myrddyn, said it was connected to me and was important."

She shook her head, "No, husband. I have seen this many times before and it is important. This is the symbol of my people. It is the banner under which we fight. It is said that one day this will unite all the peoples of this land." She clutched at her cross and closed her eyes. "This is pagan and cannot be happening!"

"You cannot fight your destiny. When I first took you from your home I did not know where the road would lead. I still do not but we cannot get off the path that has been chosen for us. I now see that the dragon ties us together. It is *wyrd*." It took some time to calm her down but eventually, she did.

After she had eaten some of the broth I had made for her I sent for Kara so that she could examine my wife. She was pleased and, when we told her of the dragon, she became even happier. The only person who seemed sad about the whole thing was Brigid herself. After she had fallen asleep Kara took me to one side. "Do not worry, father. There are two demons fighting inside of her. Brigid must make her own choices. But this is good. Your son shows that he too has a gift. He placed the dragon around her neck. We did not tell him to do so. Who did?"

After a couple of days, when Brigid was able to move around the hall and showed signs of recovery, Kara and Aiden left to sleep in the cave. Macha and Deidra came to stay in my hall to help Brigid recover. It left my son and I some time alone. I was aware that I had neglected him. The dragon had changed the lives of all in my home. I did not fully understand it but I was aware that it had some power. I hoped that the visit to the cave would bring with it some knowledge. I took Gryffydd to Bjorn Bagsecgson.

"I think, Master Blacksmith, that it is time for my son's first weapon."

Bjorn was a grandfather and knew how to speak with the young. "Indeed, and all of Cyninges-tūn has heard how he saved his mother's life. What would you have for him, Jarl Dragonheart?"

I had already decided what he would have but I was acutely aware that this was an important moment in my young son's life. It was his first step to becoming a warrior. "He has far to go to grow into Ragnar's Spirit but I would have a sword made for him rather than a seax. When he is a warrior grown he can wield a dagger which will be the equal of any sword."

"Let us test his strength then." There were iron bars laid out neatly in the workshop. They varied in length. "Come here, Gryffydd. Pick up each bar in turn and then lay it down."

The first three were easy for my son for they were short. When he came to the one which was twice as long as my hand he had to use his other hand to help him. "Thor himself has decided for you. That is the one!"

"But it is too heavy for me to lift with one hand."

"And when I have added the pommel and the guard it will be heavier but it will take a month to make and you will have to become stronger." He flexed his arm. "Put your hands around this." He tried but they would not reach and Bjorn laughed. "When I was your age then my arms were not like this. You work each day and you use your arms. Little by little they will become stronger. Your father did not learn to use Ragnar's Spirit in a day. When he was growing up, he hewed trees for old Ragnar and he learned to use a bow. You must do the same."

"I will." His eyes showed the excitement. It made me wonder why I had not paid him more attention before. He was the future and I had been too busy with the present.

"And the design?"

I looked at Gryffydd and took the dragon from around my neck. "I think the gods have decided that for us. There should be a dragon on the blade; this dragon."

Even Bjorn became excited. "Aye Jarl. *Wyrd*!" He held his huge hand out, "If I could have this for the day then I can study it." I hesitated. I was loath to lose such a precious item. My sword was rarely more than a hand span from me. Bjorn smiled, "I must know the way the dragon moves and make it so that its movement is reflected in the blade. You can trust me with this Jarl. I have never failed you yet."

I gave it to him, "I know Bjorn. Come, son, let us find a bow for you and then we will cut firewood!"

The young are eager to learn and my son took in every word with rapt attention I had not seen before. We practised with the bow and loosed arrows at a large oak by the Water. When his forearm was red from releasing the bow then we went and found a hatchet. I hewed the logs and he split them. It took me back to Norway when Old Ragnar, one-handed and crippled, had split logs with me. Those had been happy times. I did not know, at the time, how happy for I had been a slave. It made me realise that happiness came not from your station but from your state of mind.

When the sun was at its height, I laid down the axe. "Come, my son, we have earned our food this day!"

He was animated as we walked back to my hall. Brigid must have had servants watching for us. There was food and ale on the table as we entered. Macha and Deidra shook their heads when Gryffydd entered. "He is as filthy as a heathen! Come Gryffydd. It is time for a wash!"

"But father."

I shook my head, "Never argue with a woman, Gryffydd; you will lose!"

His head dropped and he allowed himself to be led. "What have you been doing husband?"

"Hewing logs and teaching my son to use a bow."

She studied me and my face and then said, "And where is the dragon?"

"Bjorn is studying it. He makes the first sword for our son and the dragon will be incorporated into it."

She made the sign of the cross. "Is this well done?"

"There is a connection between the dragon and my son. You can see that even though you may not like it. If this symbol of your past can protect not only our son but our people is that not a good thing?"

When she said, "Eat your bread and cheese. They are both freshly made." I knew that she agreed. She had a stiff neck and would never acknowledge that I was right.

Even my wife smiled when she heard the way Gryffydd spoke of his new sword, the dragon and the archery. She reached over and put her hand on mine. She said nothing but the touch was enough for me. By the end of the afternoon, my son could draw his small bow and release with far greater accuracy. He even hit the target four times out of five. We did not bother with the logs for I could see that he was tired.

"You must practice each day with your bow. Even if I am not here then I want you to spend as much time with the bow as you can. If enemies come then you will be on the walls defending our home. These are your first steps to becoming a warrior."

"I will."

"Now unstring your bow. When this becomes easy to draw we will get you a bigger one. I will have Snorri show you how to make a bow."

"Like that which he uses?"

Snorri had an expensive bow from the Saami people. It could send an arrow further than any other bow I had ever seen. "No, but when you are strong enough to use the longest bow that we can make I will send Siggi to the Saami and buy you one."

He became even more excited then and his words came out in a torrent as we headed for Bjorn's workshop. He took off his leather apron and came towards us. He gave me the dragon, "This is a wondrous symbol, Jarl. I have studied it closely. See how the muscles on the dragon's body make it seem real. It feels alive. That is not easy to do in metal. It is a shame about the mark on the body."

I laughed, "You mean the Dane's blade should have struck me and not the dragon?"

He grabbed his hammer of Thor, "Sorry, Jarl! I did not think. The dragon has a thick skin. See how it has scales along its body, Gryffydd. Your sword shall have such scales and, perhaps, your first byrnie. If you are to be the dragon warrior then you should look like one."

I had not thought of that but it seemed appropriate. I was the wolf warrior with the heart of a dragon. Perhaps my son would be the dragon warrior with the heart of a wolf.

Aiden and Kara did not return until noon the next day and, as they entered my hall, I saw how drawn they were. Macha and Deidra fussed over them. Gryffydd and I had spent the morning practising and hewing logs and we ate greedily as the two of them told their story. The three Christians clutched their crosses and silently intoned prayers as they heard what, to them, was blasphemy.

It was Aiden who spoke and Kara cuddled Ylva. "The old wizard came to us. You are right Brigid there is a connection to the old people of this land. The dragon was their symbol but it is more than that. The old man told us that the dragon came from a land far to the east; a land without mountains and without trees. It is from the land of the horse." He looked at me. "You were meant to find it. The grave had laid there since the time of the old wizard and the rain was sent to show you what lay within. It was *wyrd*."

"But what does it portend?"

"You are to be as the dragon. You must move quickly and when you strike do so with all the power at your command. A dragon is hard to kill for it wears armour over its body but every dragon has a weak spot. There is always one spot where a dragon can be hurt."

Kara looked up, "Your family. Each time you defend this land and fight our enemies then all of us in this hall and Wolf Killer and his family will be in the greatest danger. That is your challenge, father. You must be as the dragon and range far and wide to defeat our enemies and yet you must protect that which makes you strong; your family."

All those in the room looked at me. I had been set an impossible task. I had to be in two places at once. How would I do what had been foretold?

Part 3 The Dragon's Roar

Chapter 9

Wolf Killer and the warriors from Cyninges-tūn did not return until the summer was almost over. The air was still warm and the days long but the crops were ripening and the young animals no longer needed their parents. Our markets were filled with the bartering of lambs, calves and kids. A long line of horses and men trekked up to the gates of my hall. Even though Wolf Killer could have gone directly home more quickly he came to speak with me. The raid appeared to have been a great success. I could see that by the quantity of goods they brought but, as my jarls and my son sat and drank ale with me, they told me of the cost.

"The men of Neustria are fierce warriors and they have well-made burghs. We lost warriors; good warriors."

"Did they die well?"

"All died well."

"Then it is *wyrd*."

They told me of the rivers up which they sailed and the churches they had robbed. "We did not get as much coin from the holy books we took. They are not as good as the ones we take in this land."

"We met up with Gunnar Thorfinnson and young Hrolf. We both chose the same river in which to hide. They came on one raid with us. Your young apprentice is doing well, Jarl. He is like a son to Gunnar. They plan on spending the winter there. There is a river they make their own. It will be a hard battle for them but he has a determined crew."

"I am pleased for them both. I liked young Hrolf. He had spirit and it is good that he goes back to the land which enslaved him."

Wolf Killer had sharp eyes and he spotted the dragon about my neck, "That is new, Father. Is there a tale there too?"

We told him of the raid by the Danes and our escape. Aiden finished off the tale with their dream. "You are right, Father nothing we do is in isolation. Our raids in Neustria will have an effect. I know not what that will be but it will change our future. I would say that you were lucky to escape with your life but I know that it is not luck but the Weird Sisters." He stood, "And now I must return to my home. Your words have made me anxious about my family. My home is the closest to the Danes." He pointed to the chest his men had brought in. "I have left a share for you, father. I will not raid again this year."

"Thank you, my son. And I may have to take the rest of my men to Jorvik over the winter so it is good that you stay close by. The prophecy says that my land will be in danger when I am away and yet I must venture into the heart of our enemy's land. You will protect my family."

Gryffydd said, "I will have the dragon blade by then! I will protect the land!"

All smiled. Wolf Killer said, "I will tell you what, little brother, we will both protect this land. What say you?"

His eyes widened as he said, "Aye, Wolf Killer!"

After he had gone I sought out Siggi and Raibeart Ap Pasgen. Before he had captained my drekar Raibeart had acted as a spy for me. He had sailed a knarr and found information which we needed. "I have a task for you both but you can refuse if you wish."

Raibeart shook his head, "I will never refuse you, Jarl Dragonheart, for you have made me what I am today."

Siggi's face displayed his determination, "And I can never repay you for helping me to avenge Trygg. Ask."

"I would have you, Raibeart, sail '*Weregeld*' into Jorvik. I would know where the Halfdan clan live. If Siggi goes with you then it will appear less suspicious and you can protect each other" They both nodded. "With the goods, you have brought back from Neustria there will be goods we can trade with the merchants of Jorvik. There are still many Saxons who live there and they are Christian. There may well be a market for the holy books and goods you brought."

Siggi nodded, "Bjorn told me there is some low-grade iron ore at the mines. That is good ballast and they need that for the Saxon armouries."

"Good. See if you can trade for young animals. The vales around Jorvik have many fine flocks. But the most important part of your voyage will be to find where the Halfdans live."

"We will do so."

"I will ask for volunteers to sail with you. You will need warriors but the ones you take should look like sailors."

"Do not worry about that, Jarl. There are many young warriors who are keen for adventure. This will appeal to many."

It took us three days to gather the crews and the goods which they would take. I went with them, accompanied by my son, to Úlfarrston. I needed to speak with my drekar captains. Erik and Olaf were the only ones who were there. Bolli, my shipwright was working on *'Odin's Breath'* which needed repairs following the last raid.

"We will be taking our ships to Jorvik and we will do so in winter."

Olaf was new to winter raiding, "What if the river is frozen?"

"We will travel before Yule. If the river is frozen then it means we are not meant to raid and we will return home."

Erik was more philosophical about it all. So long as his drekar was on the water, then he was happy. "Will you be attacking Jorvik? It is a powerful fortress."

"I hope not." I pointed to '***Weregeld***' which was being loaded. "Raibeart and Siggi will find out where we need to attack."

"Then we have time."

I nodded. "I cannot see them being back here before the end of a month."

"Good, then I will replace some of the sheets and shrouds. Sailing in winter is demanding! How many drekar will we take?"

"That depends upon the information which our scouts bring back. It may be just your two but if needs be we will take them all. The Danes have troubled us three times this year. We rid ourselves of this particular boil with one sharp strike." I told them how the brothers we had sought had been involved in the attempt to attack the heart of my land.

Erik Short Toe frowned, "They died too well. You should have half-killed them and left them to be eaten by carrion. That is the punishment for traitors." He looked at Gryffydd. "Would you like to see your father's ship?"

I could see, by his reaction, that Gryffydd was fascinated by the drekar. Erik now had children of his own and they were swarming over the drekar. "You can play with them if you like. I have much to discuss with my captains."

He raced off, eager to play with some new companions. We spent some time discussing routes and charts. Olaf would have to copy the ones which Erik had. They were jealously guarded by my captains. Most Vikings did not have the luxury of charts and that was the reason many failed to return from voyages. Aiden ensured that my captains knew what the land and the sea would be like. Olaf was lucky that he had such a fine mentor as Erik. "The seas to the south of Jorvik are treacherous, Olaf. There are swamps and reeds which spill over into the river. It is easy to miss the channel. When we go you will follow Erik. His boat draws more water; if he can sail then so can you. "

Erik pointed to the side of Olaf's drekar, "We will be travelling light and will not draw as much water as we normally do but we ride lower in freshwater."

"There is much to learn and to remember."

"And you are learning, Olaf. I remember when Erik had to learn. Old Josephus passed all of his knowledge to Erik and he will do the same for you. It is our way."

There was a sudden shout and clamour from onboard '***Hear***t' we ran to see what it was. Gryffydd lay on his back and his nose was bloody.

Sven Eriksson who was a little older than him stood over him. Erik Short Toe shouted at his son, "What have you done? This is the son of the Jarl!"

Sven pointed a finger at Gryffydd, "He said this was his ship and he would be captain. I said it was mine and he hit me. I hit him harder."

I saw Erik ready his hand. "Stay your hand Erik Short Toe. My son is at fault." I helped him to his feet. "If you strike someone you should either be confident that you will win or suffer the consequences." I took a leather water container and poured it on Gryffydd's face. "There the blood has gone. Now can you play or would you stand with me and wait?"

"I will play."

"Good. This is how you learn to become a man."

Erik said when we were back studying the charts, "I am sorry, Jarl."

"Do not be. My son has to learn to take blows. This is my fault. I have not toughened him up yet. He has spent too much time with his mother. She is teaching him to read and he should be learning to fight. This lesson will be valuable and I am pleased that he went back to playing. I would have been disappointed had he walked away."

We headed back in the afternoon. The bleeding had long stopped but the congealed blood was still in his nostrils. We rode in silence until he said, "Is that your drekar, father?"

"It is but Erik is my captain and he spends longer on the drekar than any. It is his too. If you are going to pick fights then there are two things to remember: be in the right and make sure that you can win."

"But he was bigger and older than me!"

"I have fought much bigger men. Use your mind to defeat bigger enemies and if you are going to hit then do not hold back. A man, no matter how big, cannot fight if he has no wind. You hit the gut. If you hit the face then you hurt your hands. Look." I pointed to his grazed knuckles. He must have hit Sven Eriksson in the teeth. "It is the same with a sword. Unless you have a good blade then you will gain little from striking at mail. Better to strike flesh. That is some time off but you must use your mind. If you do not then you will not survive as a warrior."

I saw him looking at the knuckles on his hand as we rode back to Cyninges-tūn. It pleased me that he was thinking. I knew now that I had to let my son experience more of the rough and tumble of life in a Viking Stad. He could no longer be cosseted in my hall. I sighed, I would have a battle with his mother.

Brigid did not spy the damage until the next morning. I suspect one of her servants told her. "What happened to our son?"

"He got into a fight and did not win. He will do better next time."

"He is the son of a jarl. He should not be fighting with other boys."

"He will not become jarl if he does not know how to defend the land and before he can do that he has to learn to defend himself. He must become tougher."

"But he is a child."

"Ulf Olafsson had boys little older than Gryffydd and they stood a watch on the walls. They hurled their stones at the pirates. You know as well as any that an enemy will not spare Gryffydd because of his age or his size. Better to die fighting than accept death."

Both of us knew that I was talking about Christianity. The priests told them to turn the other cheek and not take a life. They promised them eternal life if they behaved. We wanted life on earth and, if we died well, then we would have just as good a life in the Otherworld.

She nodded, sadly, "I knew you for a pagan when I married you. I suppose I cannot complain that you wish to bring our son up as one too."

When I gathered the Ulfheonar to tell them of the raid I had my son seated at the table next to me. I told him to listen, not fidget and not fall asleep. The last would be the hardest for him. "Tell your families that we sail before Yule and we will be away for a month. I intend to end this feud with the Halfdan clan."

Vermund's death was on their minds and they all nodded their agreement. Erik Ulfsson asked, "Do we risk incurring the wrath of the other Danes?"

Olaf Leather Neck laughed, "I do not care if every Dane in the land wishes to fight me. Let them come."

"Erik is right, Olaf. The Danes are becoming like fleas. If we can end this with one battle, Erik, then so be it but if more wish to come then we will have to make them think twice about doing so. We have had a good year thus far and we are all richer. We fight to hang on to what we have."

Snorri asked the question which was on everyone's lips. "Do we replace Vermund?"

"We do but if we take someone with us to fill Vermund's oar then it will be a trial. The warrior will need to hunt the wolf after Yule."

"Then let us find four or five who wish to join our ranks. There are many who wish to do so."

"Then Haaken One Eye, I leave that task to you."

After they had gone Gryffydd asked, "Will I be an Ulfheonar? Wolf Killer is one is he not? He hunted the wolf when he was young."

"You will have the chance but it is more than just killing a wolf. Snorri will test the men's skills in scouting and hiding. Olaf Leather Neck will see if they have the skills with a sword or axe and then all of the Ulfheonar will decide if they wish to fight alongside them. We are all oathsworn. We never leave a man behind."

He thought about it and then nodded, "I will learn those skills. Perhaps, when Gói is gone I can spend time with my brother and he can teach me."

"I am sure that Wolf Killer will enjoy that and you can get to know your cousin, Ragnar." Ragnar was a little older. Soon he would accompany Wolf Killer on a raid. He might even do as I had done and be a ship's boy. Being the son of a jarl allowed few privileges.

Bjorn finished the dragon sword and the repairs on my dented helmet at about the same time. I saw, when he handed me the helmet, that he had added two large eyebrows. They made the helmet look more like a dragon's head but, more importantly, they added more protection above my eyes. "Thank you, Bjorn. It is an improvement."

"Each time it returns to me I see something else which needs doing. I have ideas for your mail too but let us not tempt the Norns. I will say no more." Gryffydd looked barely able to contain himself. Bjorn was a grandfather and he knew how to tease. "Now young warrior, what do I have here for you?"

I thought my son would burst. He was so excited he could barely speak. He just shook his head. Bjorn flourished the short sword like a conjurer. Gruffydd's eyes widened and I confess that I was envious. The engraved and etched dragon was a direct copy of the one I wore around my neck. It was so highly polished that I could have shaved using it. The detail was impressive. He had used oak for the grip and finished it off with a blue stone; a smaller version of mine. That would have taken as long to make as the rest of the sword for it would have been drilled by hand.

"There, your first sword. I have not bathed it in blood for it is your first and you will not use this once you are a man but I have put the fire of the dragon into its heart and it is tempered so that it is as hard as any sword I have ever made, saved that touched by the gods. Your father will help you to make the scabbard. That is a task for a warrior."

My son was silent. "What say you to Bjorn, Gryffydd?"

He could not speak and he threw his arms around the mighty leg of the smith and hugged. Bjorn was touched, "That is enough. He needs to say no more."

I reached into my purse for payment. Bjorn shook his head, "Jarl let me do this for you and my oldest friend. There are just three of us left from those days in Hrams-a. It is a gift."

I clasped his arm, "And a better gift I have yet to see."

"There is one more thing, Jarl, I would like to name it."

"You are the maker, it is yours to name."

"Then I would name it Dragon's Tongue. It came to me as I was making it. The sword is sharp as a tongue and fast enough to flick out. More importantly, when it speaks then others will listen. When your son is older and I make him his man sword then it will be called Dragon's Breath but this will do until then."

Gryffydd grinned, "I like the name, Dragon's Tongue!"

We returned to my hall and he clutched his sword as though it was made of gold. "What did Bjorn mean about the scabbard, father?"

"We must make a scabbard. It protects the blade and the wearer. You will have to help me make it for a scabbard made by another may take away from the power of the sword." I held up my scabbard, "I made this one when Bjorn first made my sword and Ragnar's Spirit has never let me down."

It took two days to make it. I did those things which he could not. I cut the wood and I gathered the materials but he, under my supervision, made it. He lined it with sheep's wool and he joined it together with horse glue. He looked at it proudly and went to get his sword.

I shook my head. "It is not yet finished. You need to cover it with leather or the wood will rot and you should have a design upon it."

A further two days of work saw it finished the satisfaction of us both. He was pleased with his efforts but his mother looked disappointed. She liked the effort it had taken and the detail but it was the function of which she did not approve. I shook my head, "Our son will be a warrior. It is in his blood."

" I know but I have seen too many widows and grieving mothers."

"That is why I will train him. You have to trust me. Our son will grow to be a man and will defend this land." Even as I said it I wondered if the Norns were listening. The Weird Sisters could be spiteful.

It was coming towards harvest time when the Danes returned. It was not a warband but it was a war party. Wolf Killer sent word that his hunters had found signs of men in his woods. When Wolf Killer examined the camps that they had used he determined that they were Danes. While he and his men continued to search for them he sent word of their numbers. There were ten of them. As soon as we discovered the news I sent riders to each Jarl and then sent out Ulfheonar with two or three warriors. It meant we had fifteen parties out seeking these intruders. Karl One Leg ordered our gates closed and we doubled the watch. I went with Rollo Thin Skin and Harald Einarsson. Against Brigid's wishes, I took Gruffydd. It was a risk but you learned by taking risks.

We wore no mail for we were hunting. When we found them then we would return to don mail and we would kill them. It would be a good lesson for Gryffydd. It would show him how men scouted. We took a quadrant of land from the road to Úlfarrston and the road to Windar's Mere. If we did not find them there then we would widen the search.

We used a raft towed by two fishing boats to sail down to the bottom end of the Water. It would save a long journey over land and, with the wind from the north was quicker. Olaf and his two men headed due south. Snorri and his two due east and I went between the two. Haaken had ridden down the water and he would complete the search to the south. Both Haaken and I believed that would be where the danger would be.

Rollo had good eyes and he had grown in stature, as a scout, in the last two years. We headed into the midge-infested wasteland where no one farmed. It was the time of the biting insect and there were many of them. We had found spies using this land some years earlier. As it had no people our enemies could freely move around. We searched for some time and saw no signs of humans. The animal tracks told us that this would be a good place to hunt if a man could fight the insects. Rollo and Harald asked if they could come back to hunt. There were many signs of game. "Aye that might be good but let us wait until the winter has come. The insects are less numerous then.

We reached the southern limit of our search and I said, "Let us head to Satter's Waite." This was the only farm for miles around. Old Satter might be able to tell us if he had seen anything untoward. We turned our horses and rode northeast.

Satter was an old recluse. He and his wife farmed the most inhospitable part of my land. I had no idea how he made it productive but he did. They had lost both sons when the Danes had come over to raid many years earlier. We had defeated them but they had left a trail of dead behind. Satter's two sons had been amongst them. Satter and his wife had been at Cyninges-tūn buying that which they could not grow. They never left their remote home again. He knew that part of the forest better than any. They were almost part of the forest. Both were like old gnarled trees. I would ask what he had seen. If he had not seen any then we would have to search to the north of my land.

The sudden cacophony of squabbling magpies and chuffs alerted us to danger. "Gryffydd, take out your sword and stay close by me."

I tightened my grip on my spear as did the other two. I waved to the left and right. The two warriors separated. We moved slowly towards the clearing. As we emerged the birds took flight, noisily. I saw that they had been picking over the corpses of Satter and his wife. They had been slain. I saw that they had been eviscerated and the birds had widened the wounds to feast on their flesh. The relatively untouched faces told me that it was recent. They had yet to begin on the eyes. We moved cautiously through the farm.

Rollo dismounted while Harald and I kept watch. I held my hand up to stop Gryffydd. Having examined the ground Rollo went into the hut Satter and his wife had lived in. While he searched within I looked for any sign of the Danes. It was obvious to me that it was they who had done this. If the bodies were fresh then that meant they might be close. I began to regret bringing my son. He sat, white-faced, on his pony.

Rollo came out and mounted his horse. He shook his head. They were not within. He pointed his spear north-west. I followed him as he led us towards the Danes. They had left the clearing and headed into the midge-filled forest. We saw their tracks on the trail. They had not bothered to hide them. Once we found them then I would send Harald back to Cyninges-tūn with Gryffydd and summon the rest of my men. I would not risk my son further. He had learned enough on this scout. I think they were the first bodies he had seen. His mother would not be happy but it would stand him in good stead. For warriors, this was a common sight.

When Rollo dismounted and waved his hand then I knew he had spotted something. I dismounted and went to Gryffydd. I whispered in his ear. "Hold my reins and stay here." He nodded. My son was learning quickly.

Harald and I knelt by Rollo. He pointed to the footprints in the mud. We had seen similar for some time. They were fresh. Then Rollo pointed to a bush. The urine was still dripping from it. I could smell it. They had passed this way not long before. I was slightly behind the other two and I heard a noise from my right. It was faint. It was a foot stepping onto a twig and trying not to make a noise. I spun around with my spear at the ready and saw Sven Green Eye. It was Snorri's patrol. He looked as surprised as I was. He held up two hands and then one hand. He made the sign for Danes and then pointed ahead. I pointed to the farm and made the sign for fetch help. He nodded and left. I hoped he had the good sense to take my son with him.

He had been gone but a moment when Snorri and Erik Alfsson appeared. I headed after my two warriors. There were now five of us. Better odds but with no mail and spears and swords only we could not risk taking on fifteen warriors. We caught up with Rollo and Harald half a mile further on. They had moved quickly. The ground dropped away and Rollo urgently waved us to the ground. We said nothing and I listened. I could hear the Danes. They had obviously taken food from the farm for they were eating and discussing which direction they should take. I could not see them. They had chosen somewhere hidden by low scrubby bushes and straggly trees. These were scouts who knew their business.

I lost track of what they were saying as a number of them all spoke at once. Then a voice barked out, "Jarl Ragnar Halfdansson has put me in charge of this raid. We do not discuss. I decide!" There was silence. "We were told to find the weakness of the Norse who live here. You, Karl Fine Hair, did not need to kill the old man and woman. When their bodies are found then they will know we are here."

"Did you see any path leading to the house, Gurt the Silent? I did not. They were alone and we needed the food they had. If we had not killed them then they might have told others that we were abroad. No one will find their bodies ten years from now!"

"No one kills without my permission. We are not here for treasure. We will get enough of that when the Jarl has gathered his forces. We have a month to discover all that we can and a month to get back. We have been promised our own drekar! That is a reward worth a little hardship. Do not throw that away for a full belly!"

"We have only seen one place they were defending. That looks easy to avoid."

"That was the stad they call Elfridaby. The son of the Dragonheart lives there. Jarl Ragnar will not avoid it. But make no mistake that is a hard place to take. It has high walls and deep ditches He has plans for the one they call Wolf Killer and King Egbert has promised much gold for the return of his wife.."

There was laughter. "I hear he plans to have her boiled alive for the disgrace of leaving him for another man."

"I care not what is promised so long as we get our drekar. We will head to Cyninges-tūn. There is a headland across the Water. I have been there before. We can make camp and study the walls. They are well made but we can find a way in I am certain. That is why we come for so long. We will examine the walls and the defences at night when the people sleep. We go back to Jorvik through the big water. That is the last place we were ordered to scout."

"What about food!"

"We have seen plenty of game."

"But not ale!"

"Two months without ale is not much to ask for Einar Einarsson. When we have a drekar we can sail the length of this land. There are many rivers and we will become rich. Now leave no sign. If they do find the dead farmer, I do not want them to find us."

Viking Dragon

I heard a noise as they moved around the clearing and then the leader, Gurt the Silent, said, "Follow me. We are not far from where we can camp. I have been here before."

We allowed them to move off and then I nodded to Snorri. He slipped through the undergrowth. A moment or two later he reappeared. "They have gone. I heard a little of what they said and, from their tracks, I think they head for the head of the Water. It will be the place close to where we had our hall."

"I agree. Where are your horses?"

"Just a mile back. We left them there when we followed the Danes."

"Meet us at the farm of Satter. He and his wife are dead. We can take the road by the Water and make faster time. We might pick up the men I sent for."

When we reached the farm I was relieved to see that Harald had taken Gryffydd with him. My son would be safe. While we waited we put the dead farmer and his wife inside their hut. When time allowed we would bury them. We had just mounted when Snorri and his two warriors appeared. We rode down the slope and through the woods to the road by the Water. We were halfway there when we ran into Olaf Leather Neck and his two men.

"We met Harald. He has ridden for Haaken."

"We have found them. They are heading for the hillside above my old hall. There are fifteen of them."

Snorri said, "The leader and two others wear mail. I found their tracks and glimpsed them when we followed."

"We can still take them, Jarl!"

"There is no need to take risks. They do not know they are being followed. Let us do this right, Olaf Leather Neck. Your axe will taste blood. It can wait."

The road to the Water passed beneath the high crag and then it dropped sharply through a twisting forest trail. This was slightly better used than the other paths for hunters who came here. We reached the road and I saw the sun beginning to slip behind Old Olaf. Snorri led us north. I heard hooves and we reined in with weapons ready. There were eight riders behind us. It was Haaken and Finni. Harald had used his head and found the nearest Ulfheonar. I saw Gryffydd flanked by two warriors. Haaken was taking no chances.

I quickly told them what we intended.

Olaf said, "Now we have enough Jarl. Even if they were all wearing mail then we could defeat them."

He was right. We had sixteen warriors. "We ride until we see Cyninges-tūn and then we walk the horses. Gryffydd and Karl Olafsson will watch the horses and we will approach them on foot. None must escape."

Haaken asked, "Do we not wish to know what they intend?"

Snorri said, "We heard what their plans are. If one escapes then they will know we are on to them and be on their guard. Is that not right, Jarl?"

I nodded, "It will be two months until they are missed. The gods have given us that time. We will use it wisely."

By the time we saw the glow from the fires of Cyninges-tūn, it was dark. We dismounted and prepared for war. Although we wore neither helmets nor armour we had the night to help us and we knew this part of my land. My first hall had been less than a thousand paces from where we were and my first wife's grave was almost within sight.

I turned to Gryffydd. "You have done well this day. I am proud of you. You and Karl must guard our horses and watch. Keep your blade ready. There is danger all around. Karl will watch over you for me."

Gryffydd had a serious look on his face as he put his hand on Dragon's Tongue. I glanced up at Karl. He was one of my youngest warriors. He had only seen thirteen summers. He nodded. I followed the others.

Snorri led and my men moved in a long line. We were a net and we would trap the Danes. I was under no illusions these men we hunted would know how to hide and how to use woods. They were scouts. We moved up the slope. Snorri was using his nose and his head. He knew where they would choose to watch. It was above the road and my old hall. We had cleared the trees from around the old palisade. The witch Angharad had burned my hall to the ground and now it afforded a fine view of my new hall. Our work had made it easier for our foes.

We moved slowly for we wanted no noise. The ground was still a little soft from the recent rains and the cushion of pine was spongy. The men I had chosen knew their business and they stepped carefully, measuring each step. There were clouds. The night was black and it was hard to see further than six paces. We were like a huge arrow with Snorri at the point. With Olaf, Haaken and me behind him, the others fanned out on either side. Snorri held up his hand as we reached a high point. He used his spear to indicate that the Danes were slightly below us. He touched his nose with his finger. He had smelled them. I was jarl but we were in Snorri's hands now. He knew what to do. He pointed to Olaf and waved his hand to the north. Olaf nodded and, tapping his men as he passed them, set off. He did the same to Haaken and Finni, this time indicating the path we had just taken. That left just our men. He took out his seax and set off. All of us copied him. We would need two weapons.

Many warriors fear the night. It is unknown and there are hidden dangers. My warriors relished it. We used it as an ally and so it was this night. I smelled their smoke. The Danes were confident enough to light one. I had no doubt that its flame was hidden from view but the smell of the smoke could not be hidden and it drew us like moths to a candle.

We moved together and when Snorri stopped, we all stopped. I saw him lay down his spear and move towards something I could not see. Then I heard the hissing sound of a Dane making water. Snorri moved so quickly that it was a blur. His left hand went up and he pulled the Dane back as he ripped his seax across his throat. It happened so quickly that the Dane was dead before he had finished making water.

Snorri picked up his spear and we continued down the slope. It was not easy. You had to pick your way around trees, rocks and loose pine needles. Although they had hidden the glow of the fire from Cyninges-tūn it was not hidden from above and we emerged just thirty paces from the dell in which they sheltered. Their leader had indeed been here before. It was the place I would have chosen. When daylight came they would be able to look down on my walls and my ditches. I did not think we had any weak spots but Gurt the Silent and his Danes would be able to discover those that they saw.

We halted, hidden by both the trees and the darkness. The fire cooked the Danes' food but it also spoiled their night vision. I counted the men around the fire. There were twelve. We had killed one and that left two sentries. Haaken, Finni and Olaf were there to mop up any sentries on their sides.

I watched as a warrior stood and said, "Olvir is taking his time!"

Another chuckled, "Perhaps he has found a sheep. Olvir has no taste!"

They laughed and the mailed warrior, I took him to be Gurt the Silent snapped, "Silence! Your voices will carry!"

"Not across the Water. I will go and find him. He might need help." The warrior came towards us. There was no way we could stay hidden. We had to time out attack well. The camp was thirty paces from us. When the Dane who was seeking Olvir was ten paces from us I waved my men forward. Snorri hurled his spear into the warrior and I ran past him.

Gurt the Silent did not panic. "Shield wall!"

His men had shields and they turned to face our attack. All that they saw were seven men. There were eleven of them. Even as they hurried to lock shields I threw my spear. I was but ten paces away from the Danes and I had practised throwing a spear since I was the same age as Karl Olafsson. It struck a Dane in the side and penetrated deeply. He pulled out the spear and I saw blood pouring from the wound. I sheathed my seax and drew Ragnar's Spirit.

The shield wall would not be solid for there were too few of them. My other men appeared and Olaf brought his men from behind the Danes. It was then that the locked shields to their front became a liability. Olaf's axe swung around in a wide arc. He knocked two men to the ground both had their backs ripped open to their spines. Just at that moment Haaken and Finni approached from the Water. I used my sword to counter the Dane who faced me. I grabbed the edge of his shield and pulled it towards me and then pushed. The sudden movement overbalanced him and he toppled backwards. He fell and I put my foot on his shield, pinning him to the ground before plunging Ragnar's Spirit into his chest.

Our sudden attack from three sides had taken them by surprise and they all lay dead. All that is save Gurt the Silent who faced Olaf Leather Neck. None would interfere. This was warrior combat and interference would risk the wrath of the gods. I looked to Haaken with a question on my face. I held up two fingers. He pulled a finger across his own throat. The two sentries were dead and we were safe.

Olaf did not have a shield and the Dane did. The Dane wore mail and Olaf did not. It should have been an unequal contest but when Olaf's mighty blow struck the Dane's shield and cracked it then we all knew it was a case of how long the Dane would survive. For a big man, Olaf was remarkably light on his feet and he danced away from the sword thrust of the Danish hersir. He then spun around and brought the axe in a wide arc. The Dane knew it was coming. He braced himself and his shield. This time the blow not only cracked the shield but I think the blow broke the Dane's arm.

The Dane thought he had the advantage as Olaf stood below him. With no helmet and no shield, Olaf looked to be vulnerable. As the Dane raised his sword for a mortal blow to Olaf's head, my Ulfheonar swung his axe at knee height, below the mail. The axe sliced through both legs as though they were pine logs. The surprised look on the Dane's face lasted but a moment before he went to Valhalla. He had been brave but he had faced an Ulfheonar. There was no contest.

Chapter 10

Harald Einarsson had died and two other young warriors had both wounds and scars which would mark them as warriors but we had done better than we might have hoped. By the time we had stripped the bodies and made a pyre on which to burn them, it was almost dawn. We headed home and wearily trudged through the gates of Cyninges-tūn. The fire of the dead would tell the other search parties that the threat was over. Even before I had greeted my wife I had sent a rider to tell Wolf Killer the outcome. When time allowed I would need to visit with him. He was in danger.

Brigid grabbed Gryffydd and hugged him. The look she threw at me would have turned a mortal to stone! I smiled. It was the best defence. "Our son did well. He saw the dead and did not shirk. He will be a warrior!"

Gryffydd's grin was worth the harsh words I would have to suffer later on. "Uhtric, take him indoors and bathe him. It is bed for you! Out all day and all night!"

Gryffydd ran to me and reached up for a hug, "Thank you, Jarl Dragonheart. I will work even harder to be a warrior. I liked Harald."

He had learned a valuable lesson. Death was indiscriminate. Gryffydd had liked young Harald Einarsson but he had been taken. Brigid grabbed our son's hand and dragged him indoors. Aiden and Kara had joined me along with my Ulfheonar.

"We have two months before the scouts are missed. We must strike before then or they will be forewarned."

"Raibeart and Siggi are not back yet."

"It matters not if they are back. We now know the plans of Ragnar Halfdansson. The gods have given us a gift. We will not spurn it. We make preparations and we move in the next ten days. Haaken, send riders to Sigtrygg, Ketil and Ulf. We hold a council of war here in three days."

"Aye."

"For the rest, you know what to do."

I was left with Scanlan, Kara and Aiden. "You have a plan already, father."

It was not a question. She had seen my thoughts. "I do. I cannot do as I had planned. I was going to take five drekar and attack with all of my warriors. There is a risk now that Ragnar Halfdansson may attack while we are at sea. I will take **'Heart of the Dragon'** and **'King's Gift'** with me. I will double-crew them. The rest can keep watch on this land. I will take only volunteers." I pointed to the old hall, now visible in the early morning light. "We need settlers yonder. Old Satter and his wife are now dead but they had the only farm we passed. Any enemy can pass through that land unseen."

"It is poor farmland. There are just trees, Jarl Dragonheart."

"Then let us use that, Scanlan. Bjorn needs charcoal and there are trees there. Encourage charcoal burners. Pay them a good price for their wares. We need their eyes and we need their charcoal. It is a wise investment. We can always get coin." I pointed to Harald Einarsson's dead body. "We can always get more gold but brave warriors are harder to find and more valuable than jewels."

When Scanlan had gone Aiden pointed across the Water. "Even though she is gone your wife watches over us still. To kill fifteen Danes and lose but one warrior is good."

"Perhaps but Harald showed me that he would have become a warrior for a shield wall. He would have been as a rock and now he is gone."

Kara shook her head, "He is not. His spirit is around the Water. The more that die the stronger the land becomes." She smiled, "My little brother showed his mettle today."

"He did but Brigid is not happy."

"No mother is happy about her son going to war. She will learn to accept it."

All of my jarls came. Wolf Killer brought Elfrida and his family. The encounter with the Danes had been a warning and it did not do to ignore such an omen. We gathered in my hall. I allowed young Ragnar and Gryffydd to attend but the women all gathered with the babies in Kara's hall. Kara would deflect my wife's fears.

I told them what we had overheard. "We have bought almost two moons, perhaps a little more. I had intended to journey before Yule but we may have to go just after the harvest is in. We are in the hands of Siggi and Raibeart now. We will sail as soon as all of our preparations are made and the men are gathered. We sail even if our knarr have not returned."

Wolf Killer said, "And what of the Danes? From what you have learned they covet our treasure and our land."

"I would not ask you to come Wolf Killer. You are a target as is Windar's Mere and Cyninges-tūn. We leave those guarded. I will take but two drekar; mine and Olaf Grimmson's. I will take Ulfheonar and volunteers. We have done this before and it works." I smiled, "It goes without saying that the jarls who are gathered around me would be a most welcome addition but, Ulf, Sigtrygg and Ketil, I need you to guard my borders with Wolf Killer. It is the land between Windar's Mere and Elfridaby which is the problem. We leave all of our horses and I wish you each to take sufficient so that that part of the land can be watched for signs of the enemy."

"We have many men who will wish to come, Jarl Dragonheart. Whom do you wish us to select?"

"I leave that to you Ulf Olafsson. I would say that it matters not how they are armed so long as they are handy with a sword and, perhaps a bow. I do not think we will be fighting the way the Danes wish to. There will be allies and confederates who will be eager to slay the Ulfheonar." I nodded to Aiden. "And we will be taking my galdramenn. We will need his powers."

Aiden smiled, "And a word of advice from the wizard. Prepare for winter. Lay in supplies."

Sigtrygg knew Aiden well, "You have dreamed of a bad winter?"

"Partly and it is partly the animals and birds. There was much blossom on the autumn berries and the birds have fledged early. They are signs that this will be a harsh winter. This could be a wolf winter."

Haaken looked at me and shook his head, "And we need warriors who seek to be Ulfheonar. They will hunt the wolf after Yule. *Wyrd*."

Ketil Windarsson said, "Some of the warriors I will suggest would be Ulfheonar."

"Then this raid will be a good test for them." Ketil had never been Ulfheonar but he knew the skills which were needed.

Aiden had brought a chest with him. "And we have this from the old ones to take with us." He opened the chest and took out the dragon banner. It had been repaired by Kara and her women. It looked new. They had sewn the dragon's outline in gold and filled it with red thread. The eyes were golden. It looked most lifelike and so much like the dragon around my neck that I knew they had been made by the same person.

Most of them had not seen it before and they did not know how it worked. I smiled, "Aiden."

He had brought a piece of willow in to the hall and he attached two lengths of cord to the end of it. The dragon drooped as though tired. "Come, let us go outside." Aiden took Gryffydd's hand. Once outside he handed him the willow branch and said, "Run around as fast you can in a circle and hold this high." He leant down, "Do not be afraid!"

Gryffydd was just intrigued but he obliged. The moment the wind entered the hold it began to make the wailing sound we had last heard on the northern wall. Women and children fled at the sound. Warriors ran for weapons. Far from being afraid Gryffydd was laughing. Ragnar ran up to him, "Let me try, cousin!" Gryffydd looked at me and I nodded.

Ragnar was that bit older and he could run even faster. The wailing became louder

Aiden shouted, "Behold the dragon roars!"

When the two boys tired of their game we returned inside. "This will be a secret weapon. We may not need to use it but the first time that we do will cause chaos." Aiden pointed outside. "You saw the effect here. Imagine this at night if we are attacking. And I will take with us some dragon fire."

Ketil Asked, "Dragon fire? How will you make that?"

"I have studied the writings of the Romans and I have found writings which give the ingredients to make a fire which burns on water. I have the materials and I will try it out before we go."

Ketil shook his head in wonder, "I am tempted to go with you just to see these two wonders in action."

"Do not worry Ketil, I intend to use both of them when we return. I will make people fear this land. If not because we are wolves then because we are protected by the dragon and by his mighty fire!"

When they had all gone I could see that my son was keen to speak with me. "Can I not come and carry the dragon?"

"You can." He became excited, "When you are one year older than Ragnar is now." His face fell and I felt remorse for my words. I put my hand on his shoulder. "You are not skilled yet. I would need a warrior to watch over you. This is not a game. It is war and that is serious. Come with me."

I took him to Uhtric who was sharpening the knives. "Uhtric when I am away I want you to take my son and have him hew logs and branches for one hour each day. Use a candle to time him. Even if his arm aches do not let him stop. He would be a warrior and he needs strong arms."

"I will do so, lord." His eyes twinkled. He was fond of Gryffydd.

Then I led him to my walls where Karl One Leg was working with the young boys of the stad. I waved him over. "This is Karl One Leg. He commands my garrison."

"You boys keep practising!" He came over to speak with us, "Aye, Jarl?"

"Gryffydd would be a warrior. Uhtric will have him chopping logs each day. He has a bow and he knows how to use it. I would have him get even better. Train him with the others. Make him into an archer and when I return I will make him into a warrior."

"I will and gladly."

Gryffydd gave him a queer look, "Why do they call you One Leg? You have two!"

Karl laughed and struck his leg with his sword. It rang. "You are sharp young Gryffydd. I have two but if Bjorn Bagsecgson had not put metal rods at each side then I would not be able to walk. I was one of your father's Ulfheonar but I was wounded. I can fight now but I do not move well. I will die protecting this stad and I will make you a warrior who is the equal of your father, the great Dragonheart."

As we went back to the hall he asked, "Are you a great warrior? Everyone says that you are the greatest Viking who has ever lived."

"Men say many things. You have to judge for yourself as you will with all men. Never take anyone's word for another's skill. Judge with your own eyes!"

"I will, father, and I will be stronger when you return. I will heed Karl One Leg's words."

"Remember too that you will be the youngest of those he trains. Do not expect any favours because you are my son. Being the son of Dragonheart is a burden you must bear. Ask Wolf Killer."

As we entered my hall he said, "Why am I just Gryffydd? You and my brother have names of honour. Why not me?"

"Because you have to earn it. Karl earned his by fighting bravely as did Haaken. Their names tell a story of their lives. When I was your age I was Garth. I didn't become Dragonheart until others gave me the name. Wolf Killer was named by my Ulfheonar for his courage when he killed his first wolf. Be patient. You have many years yet."

My knarr had still to return when we headed down to Ulfarrston. We could not wait. We had our volunteers and more. We carried fifty warriors on the *'Heart of the Dragon'* Asbjorn and Eystein had thirty on board *'The King's Gift'*. We would be too large a mouthful for our enemies and we had enough men to row most of the way if the winds were against us. It did not take long to load the two drekar and we pushed off without too much fuss. We had said goodbye to our families in Cyninges-tūn. We were keen to be away. The autumn was upon us and we could expect storms and wild weather. Often, at this time of year, sailing a drekar was like trying to ride a wild bull, bareback.

We rode and Aiden led a pony with two chests strapped to it. I looked at the chests curiously. "What have you there?"

"While you have been training your son I was reading. I think I have discovered Dragon Fire and how it works." He smiled, "That is wrong. I have rediscovered how the Romans made a fire for war. I have had to adapt it because I could not use all the things they did but it works; after a fashion. I have tried it. In these chests are small packages of wax, seal oil and ground-up powders. It took me some time to get the right combination of powders. I have collected them over many years. Some

Kara and I use for potions but others we collected and had no use for them. Now we do."

"How does this Dragon Fire work?"

"There is a piece of linen which we light and then we throw it. The linen lights the seal oil which burns and when the wax cylinder breaks then the burning seal oil ignites the powders and whatever it hits, burns. It even burns on water. It has a strange magic. It only goes out when the powders and seal oil are gone."

"It sounds like a frightening weapon."

"It is but it has its limitations. It is too heavy to fit on a war arrow and a javelin becomes unstable. You have to throw it."

I smiled. Aiden was no warrior and it was many years since he had had to fight. "But we have slings. They can hurl this Dragon Fire further. Every warrior on my drekar used a sling as a child. I think we can overcome your limitations." Once again my galdramenn had given us an advantage over our enemies. I knew now that our first meeting, when he had been a child, had been no accident. It had been *wyrd*.

It was evening when we sailed. Our double crews meant that we did not need to put in to shore at night. That would delay us and risk discovery. We sailed with a candle in a glass vessel. It was Aiden's idea and it worked. We had a ship's boy with a ready supply of candles replacing them as each one burned out. We had taken them from the churches we had robbed. It also helped us gauge the time and we used one candle as the measure for one shift of rowing. It was not precise but it worked. It also acted as a marker for Olaf. He knew where we were.

Thorir Svensson had been a ship's boy for some time and he was now almost a man. Erik had brought him on to be as a second captain and it enabled Erik to sleep. He was confident in Thorir's skill. Of course, when we reached the difficult waters around Corn Walum or the straits of Menai then Erik would take over. He was watching his apprentice as we sailed around the western coast of Ynys Môn. Aiden and Haaken were with us. The four of us were old shipmates who were easy in each other's company.

"You are making the challenge more difficult, Jarl. It would have been more than useful to know where we would find our enemies. They could be anywhere."

"I know Haaken but I dared not wait any longer. Ragnar Halfdansson will be expecting his scouts to be on their way back soon. When they do not return it will alarm him. We will have to sail the Humber and the Ouse and rely on Snorri and Beorn to sniff out our foes."

"They are both difficult rivers Jarl."

"I know. It is one reason I have brought Aiden."

Viking Dragon

"Captain," Thorir pointed to the island of Ynys Môn. There were Saxon ships there. We saw their masts. Saxons made good swords but poor ships. Ours could carry more men and sail in shallower water.

Erik nodded, "Just watch them, Thorir. We can outsail them at any time we like. So long as they are there then they are no danger."

I agreed with my captain. A Saxon would have to be moon-mad to take on a drekar. Haaken asked, "I wonder what happened to Siggi and Raibeart?"

"I am not surprised they have not returned. You are too used to a drekar, Haaken One Eye. If the wind changes then the crew rows. On a knarr, you go where the wind tells you and they are so tubby that any wind from the beam makes life uncomfortable. When we sail up the river we will be against the current and we will row. The knarrs have to tack from side to side. They may have completed the task the Dragonheart set them but they did not know that we needed the information sooner."

I smiled, Erik was defending his fellow captains. It was the brotherhood of the sea.

Once we had passed the island the Saxons now called Anglesey Erik lay down for some sleep. I saw how nervous Thorir was and so I stayed with him. Aiden and Haaken also slept. "Would you be a captain like Erik?"

"Aye Jarl Dragonheart. I envy Olaf. He has had more luck than any man deserves."

"Do not be jealous, Thorir. Your time will come. Learn all you can from Erik."

"I am not complaining Jarl and I am aware that I have much to learn but I can dream."

"Aye, you can." As I looked down I saw that Aiden was dreaming. His body and face twitched as they always did when he was in the land of the spirits. I looked to the east and saw Wyddfa and the cave we had found with the dead wizard, Myrddyn, lying within. No matter how far we travelled we never got far beyond this land. The old sword which hung from the wall of my hall was connected to my dragon and the standard and this mountain. It was just impossible to piece them together and to make sense of them. Perhaps when I was dead and in Valhalla, looking down it would make sense. I would say, *'Of course, that was why that was. Why did I not see it?'*

We had just passed Ynys Enlli when the ship's boy at the masthead shouted, "Ships to steer board! Two of them!"

Erik was awake in an instant as was Aiden. I went to the steerboard side of the ship. All that I could see were the dark sails of two vessels. Aiden said, "Erik, steer toward them."

Erik did not even question the order. He trusted Aiden but he gave him a quizzical look. Aiden shrugged, "I dreamed and I saw Siggi and Raibeart. If we are not afraid of Saxon ships then these two should not worry us."

The lookout shouted, "It is '***Weregeld***'!"

I clapped Aiden on the back. "You were right. You were both right. We need to stop, Captain."

"Haul down the sail!"

We must have been recognised too for the two knarr sailed directly for us and I saw their sails being hauled in too. My captains had great skill and soon we were touching '***Weregeld***'.

"We were worried, Raibeart, and we had to sail early."

I saw him nod. "We heard that Ragnar Halfdansson was preparing warriors to raid you. He is offering money to mercenaries to join him. He plans to come in the winter."

"He told you this?"

"It is common knowledge. All in Jorvik wish to have a piece of the treasure they believe we have."

"More importantly where does he live? In Jorvik?"

"No, Jarl Dragonheart, he has a hall on the river two miles south of the walls. He has a jetty and two drekar there. It is a place called Fulford. I think he makes his own kingdom."

"And how many men?"

"They are both large drekar with twenty oars on each side and he has mercenaries. In his hall, I would say between eighty and ninety but there are many more in Jorvik waiting for... well I am not sure what but the Danes are not yet ready to leave." I saw Raibeart laugh. "I said we were from Ynys Môn and he gave me a gold piece to spread the word that he wished more warriors to join him. You have a month at least."

"Then we will sail. Thank you, Raibeart, you and Siggi have both served me well. Steer towards Hibernia. There are Saxons ahead on Ynys Môn."

"Thank you for the warning. We shall steer well clear of them. May the Allfather be with you."

As soon as Erik lowered the sail we began to pull away. The darkness took the knarr. With just Olaf Grimmson behind us, the only ones ahead would now be enemies. Erik went back to his bed once we were underway but I sat with Aiden.

"Do you know this place, Aiden?"

"I have heard of it. When the Danes first came it was the place they used as a base. They used it to trade and the King of Northumbria allowed it. I think they kept it undefended to lull the King into believing that they were peaceful."

"In my experience, the Danes do not build great fortresses."

Aiden chuckled, "Neither do the Norse but then Jarl Dragonheart is not Norse. The gods made him."

"What do you mean?"

"We are the only people who build strong walls."

"No, I meant about being created by the gods. Do you mean as all men are made by them?"

"No Jarl. There is a purpose to your life and a long thread which the Weird Sisters wove. The thread begins over there." He pointed east. "It starts in the past with the old people of the land. When your mother, a volva was taken by the Saxons do you think that was not planned? Your mother was a volva. She could have escaped but she did not. All the time you were growing up she could have left. You told me that your father was often absent. Then you are taken to the Dunum. That was so that the young clay of Garth the Saxon could be reformed into Jarl Dragonheart of the Norse. You are like the caterpillar which turns into something wonderful, a butterfly. The gods formed you. Our dreams have told us that. Few men control their own destinies. You are completely controlled by the gods and the Norns. One day your work will be done and then... who knows? But this voyage is meant to be and the time is right. We would not have met Raibeart otherwise."

Even though I knew that dawn was not far away I lay down and tried to sleep. I wanted to dream while I was close to this land of the dragon. I touched the dragon around my neck and slept. The dream came but it was a strange one.

It was dark. There was no light. It was like the cave on Lough Rigg and it was silent. I wondered if I had died and then I heard a voice. It was my mother's. "No, my son, you are not dead. That day is not today. You will know the day of your death as I did. All of our family know when they are to die. It is a gift and a curse. You will dream your death. You were made by your past but you were also formed by the land. Every generation has a hero born who protects the land. It was my father and it will be you. When you die another will take your place. Trust to your heart for you are well named. The dragons that were are all gone. You will be the dragon. Be swift, be powerful but remember, my son, you must protect the land and the people."

There was no fall from the sky, no sudden jolt. I just opened my eyes and saw gulls flocking above me in the blue sky. I could hear the chant of my men as they rowed to one of Haaken's chants.

'Ulfheonar, warriors strong

> *Ulfheonar, warriors brave*
> *Ulfheonar, fierce as the wolf*
> *Ulfheonar, hides in plain sight*
> *Ulfheonar, Dragon Heart's wolves*
> *Ulfheonar, serving the sword*
> *Ulfheonar, Dragon Heart's wolves*
> *Ulfheonar, serving the sword'*

Aiden was asleep and his twitching told me that he was dreaming. Cnut Cnutson was speaking with Erik at the steering board and, when he saw me awake, he approached me with a skin of ale. "You have slept well, Jarl. We have changed oars twice and we have passed Corn Walum."

I drank the ale and wiped my beard with the back of my hand. "Any trouble?"

"No Jarl. We row for the wind is from the southwest but once we round the Dragon's Point we will have the wind and we can rest."

The Dragon's Point was the last corner of Britannia. It stuck out like a dragon's tongue. It seemed appropriate that, once we turned, the wind would speed us on our way. I looked astern and saw that **'The King's Gift'** was on station just a couple of boat lengths away. If the rest of our voyage was as smooth and as simple as this had been then we would, indeed, be favoured by the gods.

Chapter 11

Of course, neither the Norns nor the gods would make life simple for us. We were constantly tested to see if we were worthy enough for the rewards we earned. Five Saxon ships waited for us close to the island the Saxons called the Island of the Wights. The ship's boy on the cross tree spied them. "Five Saxon ships to landward!"

Erik was on the steering board. "Do we fight or run, Jarl?"

"We run. We cannot afford to lose any men before we reach Jorvik. If this was on the return journey then we would fight them for I have no doubt that our dragon ship could dance around them!"

Erik laughed, "Aye, Jarl. They are tubby and slow. Haaken, double-crew the oars. Let us show these Saxons how a dragon can fly!"

I turned and, cupping my hands, shouted to *'The King's Gift'*, "Double oars! We run!"

I saw the ship's boy at the prow of *'The King's Gift'* raise his hand in acknowledgement and then race to tell Olaf. It took time for Haaken and the men to get to their benches and the Saxons closed. They were just five lengths away when Haaken began to sing and the crew's chants transmitted to their hands and hearts. We began to surge through the water. It was as if the dragon ship was flying. The dragon prow seemed to lift us over the waves.

The storm was wild and the gods did roam
The enemy closed on the Prince's home
Two warriors stood on a lonely tower
Watching, waiting for hour on hour.
The storm came hard and Odin spoke
With a lightning bolt the sword he smote
Ragnar's Spirit burned hot that night
It glowed, a beacon shiny and bright
The two they stood against the foe
They were alone, nowhere to go
They fought in blood on a darkened hill
Dragon Heart and Cnut will save us still
Dragon Heart, Cnut and the Ulfheonar
Dragon Heart, Cnut and the Ulfheonar
The storm was wild and the Gods did roam
The enemy closed on the Prince's home
Two warriors stood on a lonely tower

Watching, waiting for hour on hour.
The storm came hard and Odin spoke
With a lightning bolt the sword he smote
Ragnar's Spirit burned hot that night
It glowed, a beacon shiny and bright
The two they stood against the foe
They were alone, nowhere to go
They fought in blood on a darkened hill
Dragon Heart and Cnut will save us still
Dragon Heart, Cnut and the Ulfheonar
Dragon Heart, Cnut and the Ulfheonar

Cnut Cnutson always swelled with pride when this chant was used for it was about his father and me. I looked astern and saw that even **'The King's Gift'** could not keep up with us and began to drop astern. She was, however, in no danger for the Saxons dropped back even further. They were not natural seamen. Had they been then they would have had half of their boats ahead of us to ambush us. We would still have beaten them but there would have been a sea-fight first.

Erik glanced astern and shouted, "You can slow down, Haaken. We have lost them."

As soon as the chant stopped then we slowed. The men rowed hard and it hurt but the song stopped men from feeling burning muscles and it fed their hearts. They were able to do more than they thought they could. If the Saxons ever discovered that then they might be better sailors.

Soon we were able to stop rowing and Olaf 's ship was back on station. Aiden looked at his charts. He kept a record when we sailed. "That little burst of speed has helped us, Jarl. Soon we turn north and this wind will still aid us."

I looked up at the mast, "Thank you Allfather."

I had told Aiden of my dream as soon as he had woken. He had not spoken of it since. As we sailed between the land of Kent and Frankia he did. "I have thought of your dream and it begins to make some kind of sense. If your family had not been kidnapped then I would not have been your hostage, would I? I would not have learned to read the words of the Romans. I might still be a galdramenn but I am not even sure about that. My powers came to me as we travelled through the land of the Cymri."

"You were born with those powers. Even as a child you were cleverer than most."

"I know not but I do know that each day with you and now your daughter increases my power. What I am saying, Jarl, is that the gods give you the means to do what you do. Looks at Haaken One Eye, he and

Olaf are the rocks upon which enemies break. Cnut died to save your family so that Kara and Wolf Killer would be reconciled. Prince Butar died so that you would leave Mann and go to Cyninges-tūn. I thought that all of this was just the webs of the Norns but I see a higher power now. The Norns serve the gods. What we do, we are meant to do."

He said no more but he had no need to. His words filled my head. Unconsciously one hand went to the hilt of Ragnar's Spirit while the other went to the dragon about my neck. My mother's words came back to me, '*All of our family know when they are to die. It is a gift and a curse. You will dream your death*' I knew then that each time I went to sleep I would wonder if that would be the night I would dream my death.

The voyage north to Jorvik was stormier than the one to reach the Saxon Sea. The wind was still with us but it blew in gusts, in fits and starts. It varied in strength and the crew were tested all the way north. There was one thing in its favour. Only fools were out in that storm and we had the whole sea to ourselves. It was just after dawn when Erik made ready to turn west to the mouth of the river. Haaken had the men ready to row as soon as we entered the huge estuary that was the Humber. It was deceptively wide. Erik knew it well. Many knarr had come to grief because they believe it was deep all the way across. It was not. There were shallows and there were mudflats. It shifted constantly as silt was deposited in one place and eroded in another. He chose the deepest channel. We could sail closer to the shallows but there was no need for such risks.

Haaken and the rowers were not needed, at first, for the wind, from the south-west still, helped us. Erik was busy and so I sought out Aiden. He knew the sea and river well. "How long to reach the hall?"

"The river runs due west for a while and then it begins its turns. When they are to the north and east we will be swift but when they turn we will be slow. Soon Erik will have to take in sail and then we will move at the pace of the rowers. In a straight line, we could be there in a couple of hours but with the twists and turns of this meandering river, it will take us all day. We will be close by dark."

Aiden would know exactly where Fulford lay. We would lie up below the hall. My warriors would land. Our drekar's skeleton crew could follow us up the river. The warriors would travel, unseen, across the land. I had spent some time during the voyage discussing our attack with the Ulfheonar. Although not as well made as a Saxon Burgh or even Elfridaby, the hall would have a ditch and a fence. If we could get over those without being discovered then we could burn the warrior hall. That way we could guarantee that the blood feud would be over. All of our enemies lay in Fulford. This raid might just bring us respite, for a while at least. I intended the attack to be swift, sudden and decisive.

We would use my men to secure the gate and then we could surround the halls. There would be at least two. One would be for the warriors and the other would be Ragnar's. There they would have his oathsworn and his family. That would be the one which the Ulfheonar would attack while Asbjorn and Eystein would lead the bulk of the warriors to attack and burn the warrior hall.

Those who were not rowing donned their mail and prepared for war. My sword and seax had been sharpened before we left Cyninges-tūn. I put on the cochineal and held my helmet. Since I had had the extra aventail and embellishments on the front it was slightly heavier. I would don it at the last moment. Besides I needed my eyes and ears to be unimpaired until we went into battle. We were now in the land of our enemies. There was not a single friend east of the great divide. The Saxons hated us but I hoped that they would take us for a Danish drekar sailing home. The two peoples, Saxon and Dane, had an uneasy alliance.

Erik was taking no chances and Thorir Svensson was at the dragon prow staring intently at the water to shout should we find a new shoal or mud bank. The boy on the crosstrees watched far ahead and the third kept an eye on Olaf in the drekar behind. I knew that Olaf and Asbjorn would be equally vigilant. Aiden was struggling into the short mail shirt I had insisted he wear. He was no warrior and we would be going against Danes in their home. If he was coming ashore then he needed to be prepared for war. He had no shield but a short sword and seax would have to suffice for protection.

Both Erik and Aiden were correct about the journey. It was torturous. Soon we needed every oar manned as we wound our way along the Ouse. We spied many Saxon settlements. The one at Gulle looked to be a strongly defended burgh in a loop of the river. Soon after Gulle, the river turned north towards our destination. It was early afternoon when we passed it. By the time we reached Riccall, it was almost dark and I wondered if we had misjudged the time.

Erik shook his head when I expressed my doubts. "We have six or seven miles to go. We will be there at midnight. By the time you have reached the hall then we will have turned the drekar around and have captured their jetty."

We were leaving fifteen warriors aboard to enable us to keep our drekar safe. They were the youngest and least experienced of our men but Erik and Thorir knew their business. They would not let me down. Disaster almost struck when we were but a mile from our destination. The hull ground on to a sandbank. Perhaps Thorir had been complacent I know not but we struck the river bed and we stopped. Erik quickly hissed, "Everyone, to the stern!"

All obeyed and, as the bow rose we began to move. Even as we shifted he said, "Now to the bow." Everyone ran to the bow.

There was a grating noise as we shifted over the sand and shingle mud bank but then we floated again. *'The King's Gift'* was smaller and had a shallower draught and they managed to sail over it without grounding.

Aiden scribbled a mark on the chart and murmured, "We will watch for that upon our return."

Thorir would be chastised by Erik but that would be much later.

All of the warriors were now armed and ready. The sail was down and we rowed the last mile up the twisting river. Our nose, Snorri, was in the bows and he whistled when he smelled the Danish hall. The smell of wood smoke carried, especially across water. Erik nudged us towards the shore. Snorri and Beorn leapt ashore first and disappeared into the night. The ship's boys were next and they wrapped ropes, fore and aft, around two trees. My men disembarked leaving a skeleton crew to row upstream.

I was the last one off, along with Aiden and as soon as we were on the river bank the boys leapt back aboard with their ropes. We followed our men inland. We did not run but watched where we walked. We had time enough. The Danes would be sleeping. If we had judged it right then we were less than a mile from the hall. Asbjorn and his men soon caught up with us. We did not move in a straight line but, rather, we swarmed. Every warrior was ready for action. I hoped we would reach the hall before we were seen.

The men before me stopped and made way for Haaken, Aiden and me. Snorri and Beorn stood there, panting. They had run hard. "The hall is a thousand paces to the northeast, Jarl. There is a low palisade but it is only the height of a warrior. The warrior hall is closest to the river and the Jarls' hall is raised and has two sentries at the door."

"Take archers and dispose of the guards." They tapped the archers on the shoulders as they led them back. I turned to Asbjorn. "You know what to do. Aiden has Dragon Fire. He will fire the hall. You will slay the warriors. The Ulfheonar will deal with the oathsworn. We will meet you at the jetty."

I took out Ragnar's Spirit and held it aloft so that my Ulfheonar could see me. I ran towards the hall. Our eyes were accustomed to the dark and I saw its dark shape above the palisade within a few steps. As we moved closer to the walls and the hall I could pick out more detail. We were in the hands of Snorri and his handful of archers now. If they did not kill silently then the alarm would be given and our task would be almost impossible. We walked slowly the last hundred or so paces. If the sentries were not dead then sudden movements would give us away. Snorri and Beorn rose like wraiths; they were almost next to us. Snorri pulled his finger across his throat. The sentries were silenced.

The archers led the way as we went towards the palisade. There was a ditch but it was for drainage. It would not deter us. Most of us jumped it although Olaf Leather Neck contemptuously waded it. When we reached the palisade, pairs of Ulfheonar stood with their shields at the ready. I put my foot on the shield and was pushed up to the level of the wooden wall. I could see the Jarl's hall. It was on the far side and the sentries did not appear to be looking in our direction. As I slipped over I saw Asbjorn and his men as they, too, scaled the walls.

Between the walls and the halls lay thrall's huts and animal pens. We would have to move quietly and not disturb the animals. Snorri and Beorn led the way across the open area. Suddenly a huge dog began to growl as Snorri passed. He put his hand out and murmured something. The growling stopped and I saw the dog's tail wagging. If there was such a thing as a perfect scout then it was Snorri. He was prepared, even for savage guard dogs. He and Beorn went around the rear of the warrior hall to head to the Jarl's hall.

We moved along the side of the warrior hall. I could hear the noises of men snoring, talking in their sleep and, inevitably, farting. Aiden stayed there and waited for Asbjorn and his men. They carried faggots with which to fire the hall. I halted in the shadow of the warrior hall to watch the sentries. There was but one door into the hall and they guarded it. There were steps up to it. A Danish hall was often built below the ground to create a high roof. This looked to be one such. It explained why it was on slightly higher ground.

Haaken and Erik Eriksson stood behind me. I saw Beorn creeping along the side of the hall. I guessed that Snorri was on the other side. We had fifty paces to cover as soon as the two sentries were dead. Beorn was about to strike when Loki played a trick. One of the sentries decided to make water and he turned to go down the hall. He saw Beorn. Beorn's blade was fast but the sentry shouted, "Vikings!" before he fell.

There was no time to waste and we sprinted across the open ground. Behind me, I smelled burning as Aiden lit the first fire. With men guarding the one door in the hall I hoped that they would be able to kill the warriors with few losses to themselves. Even though we ran as fast as we could we could not reach the door before the oathsworn reacted to the alarm. I saw Snorri and Beorn fighting five men. They stood back to back. A mighty giant raised his axe to decapitate Snorri but an arrow flew from nowhere and struck him in the side of the head. One of

Snorri's archers was alert. The Dane fell as though poleaxed. Even so, the odds were too great and I saw Beorn fall to a blow from behind.

As the warrior raised his sword to finish him off I saw that Rolf had sprinted ahead of us and he brought his axe around to scythe through the Dane's leg. Rollo was close behind and before the second Dane who had been fighting Beorn could change his attack Rollo had run him through. There were more Danes rushing from the hall but we were all at the gate and we met them sword to sword. I saw that Snorri, too, was wounded. As I blocked a sword from a Dane I shouted, "Get Beorn to the drekar!"

I punched the warrior in the face with my shield and, as he reeled brought my knee up hard between his legs. He was not wearing mail and he fell backwards. I stabbed him in the throat. Behind me the warrior hall was on fire; the flames raced up the sides of the bone dry building and I heard the screams of those within. My target was Ragnar Halfdansson. Olaf Leather Neck and Rolf Horse Killer cleared the door to the hall with two mighty swings from their axes. The Danes wore no mail. The three who had stood there fell backwards writhing as they tried to hold in the nest of intestines which were spilling out.

Haaken made the door before I did and he roared his challenge, "I am Haaken One Eye! If you face me then you die! I am Ulfheonar!"

He was almost berserker as he ran to the nearest Danes. The fact that there were three of them did not discomfit him in the least. I followed him for Haaken was not as young as he had once been. He slew one and blocked the sword from the second but the third had stepped to the side and was about to run Haaken through under his outstretched right arm when I brought down my sword and took the Dane's arm. Even as he stood bleeding I brought the blade backhanded into his chest.

"Find Ragnar Halfdansson!"

Haaken might have only had one eye but it missed nothing. He pointed to the far end of the hall where I saw Ragnar and four of his oathsworn. They had been donning mail. Now that they saw us they ran towards us.

I raised my sword and shouted, "Ulfheonar! To me!"

Leif the Banner and Finni the Dreamer appeared as though by magic and I heard a roar which told me that Olaf Leather Neck was on his way. He would not let his jarl fight alone!

Ragnar spat out his words as he raced to me, "When I had no word from my men I should have known you had used magic to defeat them!"

"I used the same weapon on Gurt the Silent that I will use on you, Ragnar Halfdansson, Ragnar's Spirit!"

None would interfere in our combat. It would be jarl to jarl. He was a much younger man than me. I was at least fifteen years older. He was in the prime of life. He was a big man. I remembered that from the Wall but we were fighting in a hall. It would be speed and skill which determined the outcome of this contest. The hall had a high roof and Ragnar Halfdansson brought his sword in a huge swing. It was aimed at my head. I did the unexpected; I stepped into him below his swing. I pulled my shield up as I did so and his right arm struck my shoulder and then the edge of my shield smashed up into his jaw. I had not even bothered swinging Ragnar's Spirit which hung from my hand.

Ragnar Halfdansson stumbled backwards with his shield up to block the blow which never came. His mouth was pouring with blood. "Trickster! I knew you could never defeat Halfdan the Black without such tricks. Tricks and magic! You are no warrior!"

"Then this will decide that!" I feinted with my shield and he moved his own shield to block the strike. The tip of my sword darted out and plunged into the flesh above his knee. I twisted the blade as I did so.

This time he screamed with pain and I was showered with gobs of blood from his mouth. I wanted him annoyed and reckless. I wanted him to try to kill me with brute force. He lurched towards me with a flurry of sword blows from his sword and his shield. I had to dance out of the way blocking as best as I could. Each blow weakened him for he was bleeding now from the mouth and from the knee. He had struck me with such fury that he had bent his sword.

It was time for me to go on the offensive. I did not strike at his shield; instead, I made a sweep at his head. He brought up his own shield and swung at my shield. My strike was the first I had made with any force and I saw that it had hurt his arm. Because his sword was no longer straight it had little force behind it. It bent a little more when it struck my shield. He looked at the blade as though it had betrayed him and he threw it at me before reaching down and picking up an axe. The way he hefted it told me that he was a skilled axeman. He grinned and it almost made me laugh for blood oozed from the sides of his mouth.

"Dance away from this, Dragonheart!"

He brought the axe over his head with as much force as he could muster. I knew it would hit my shield and I angled it at the last minute as I stepped to the side. It slid down the face of my shield and caught on the boss. It stuck between the wood and the metal. As he tried to jerk away I lunged in with my sword. I put my whole force behind it and it tore through his mail. In his hurry to fight us he had not put on his leather byrnie and my sword found flesh. I twisted as I withdrew the sword touched by the gods.

Ragnar Halfdansson was hurt. He was dying but he could still hurt me. He swung again at my head and I was barely able to sway away from the strike. His weak knee and the power of the swing carried his body forward. As he tumbled towards me I brought my sword over and took his head in one swift move. I spun around and saw that the hall was like a charnel house. The dead lay everywhere. Through the door, I saw dawn breaking. In another part of the hall, I heard screaming from the families of the Jarl.

"Take what you can and then back to the drekar." Fetch our wounded." I took Ragnar Halfdansson's axe and helmet. They would remind me of the Halfdan clan.

When I emerged the warrior hall was still blazing. My Ulfheonar formed a wedge around me for there had been other Danes living nearby and they were already gathering. They were wary of attacking us and they stood blocking our way to the gate and the river. Haaken said, "It looks like we will have to fight our way out."

Olaf Leather Neck had not had enough of death and destruction. He roared, "Come on you Danes! Taste my axe!" He swung it in a figure of eight and Rolf joined him. We made our way to the river. There were one or two heroes but they were swiftly slain by my Ulfheonar. We burst through and marched towards the river. Some carried treasure and trophies but of more value was the fight that we had had. We had defeated Jarl Ragnar Halfdansson and his oathsworn in their own hall. It would be a tale told by fires long after we were all dead and in Valhalla.

Aiden and the rest of my men had made a shield wall by the jetty. Erik and Olaf had tied up next to the Danish drekar. They had placed gangplanks across them and I shouted, "Back to our drekar. We have done enough!"

Aiden waited for me. "We have soaked the Danish ships in seal oil and we have the fire ready. They will not raid again."

I stood on the jetty until there were only Danes before me. I took a step forward and raised Ragnar's Spirit, "This is a warning to all Danes. Stay away from my land. I will punish all who dare to threaten me, my family or my land!" I pointed my sword at the glow from the burning hall. "This is the punishment for such transgressions."

I turned and walked slowly to my drekar. *'The King's Gift'* was already pulling away. I turned as I stepped onto my ship and nodded. "Cast off!"

Using their oars my crew pushed us into the middle of the river. Aiden, Olaf, Haaken and Erik all hurled their burning brands into the drekar. With a whoosh, the bone-dry drekar burst into flames. The heat was so great that I felt it from ten paces away. As the sail was lowered we moved away from the doomed dragon ship. Ragnar Halfdansson had thought he could take on the Viking dragon. The flames of his burning hall and ships proved him wrong.

We needed no oars for we had the wind and we were moving downstream. Warriors were being tended to by comrades but I saw Aiden and Snorri. They were kneeling close to Beorn. It seemed like an age since he had been wounded. I hurried to his side.

"How is he?"

Aiden did not look up. I saw that Snorri had his hand held to Beorn's thigh. "He has taken a bad blow to his leg. I fear the blade has cut the bone. We must stitch it. We have no fire to cauterize it. We must stop the bleeding."

Snorri said, "He took a blow to the head too. He breathes but he is not in this place."

I could see that Snorri was concerned for his friend. The two of them were inseparable. "Aiden is a good healer. If he can be saved then Aiden is the man to do it and if not...it is *wyrd*."

"You are right, Jarl. None of us are getting any younger. We are now like Old Olaf and those older warriors with whom we first fought. We thought them old because we were young and full of life. Time has caught up with us and we did not see it."

"We are not yet ready to go to the Otherworld, Snorri. Beorn is a fighter. He will fight this."

We were aided by the fact that we sailed down a slow river. Erik had to navigate carefully and it meant the deck did not move over much. Haaken was watching the land as we passed through the land of Northumbria. "They are watching us, Jarl. Word must have spread for the signal towers flame. They are warning their men."

"Have the men ready to fight if we have to. Issue the bows."

My worry was not men on the shore with weapons; those we could deal with. It was the river. If they blocked the river with a chain or a rope then we might be stranded. Until we reached the confluence with the Humber then we were in danger.

"Jarl, fetch some water. Pour it over my hands and Snorri's. There is so much blood it is hard to see the wound."

I was grateful for something to do. There were buckets of seawater kept in case of fire. I knew that the salt in the water would keep the wound cleaner. I picked one up, "How is Beorn?"

"He is fighting Erik, as we all do."

"Aye we come into the world kicking and screaming and, if you are a warrior, then you leave the same way."

I stood over Aiden, "Just pour it, Jarl."

I did so and as the blood was washed away I saw that the wound was as long as my hand and I could see the white of bone. It was a bad wound. There was some water left and I poured it on his head. I saw that his skull was not as depressed as Haaken's had been but it was another bad cut. This bled but not as fast as the one in his leg. "What about his head, Aiden?"

"It needs sewing but I have but one pair of hands."

He sounded irritated. "If you have a spare needle and gut we will see what I can do then eh, galdramenn?"

"Small stitches! No one will see his leg but his young wife will not want a monster to return to her!"

I had seen Aiden stitch enough men to know what to do. It took me some time to thread the bone needle but I managed. I washed away some of the blood and joined the two flaps of skin. I began to sew. It was fortunate that Beorn was between worlds for I am certain that my clumsy hands would have made him cry out and move had he been awake. I finished before Aiden did. I had tried to make the stitches as small as possible but I had closed the wound. He now just bled from his leg.

Eventually, Aiden sat back. "I have done all that I can. It is now in the hands of the gods. We must watch him and keep him warm. Snorri, try to get some ale into his mouth."

"I will, Aiden, and I thank you. You have done all that you can to save my friend. He is in the hands of the gods now."

Aiden stood and looked to the land. "How far have we come?"

Erik shouted, "We are halfway to the Humber. We are not out of danger yet."

The bends in the meandering river meant that we travelled further than a man on a horse. We had to travel sixty miles on the river to reach Gulle but a horseman only had to ride twenty miles. A rider could have left Fulford and ridden to Gulle. The huge loop in the river formed a natural barrier around Gulle. It was a strong burgh. The lookouts reported that the walls were manned. They had been warned. We avoided scrutiny before by travelling in the dark but now we had a bright day with which to contend.

"Put shields over the wounded. Get your bows and prepare to be attacked."

Erik said, "If we man the oars we can pass quicker."

"Is the river wide enough?"

"It will have to be." He pointed to the walls of the burgh. They were lined with archers and we saw the telltale trail of smoke. They had fire arrows.

Haaken began to organise the rowers. He used the men who had no bows. He took a bench along with Olaf, Rollo and Rolf. Every oar was manned although it was just by one man.

I took the empty bucket and ran to the side. I trailed it over and hauled up river water. We might need it soon. I donned my helmet. "Leif, get the dragon banner and go to the prow. Stand close to the dragon and hold up the banner. Let it roar!"

"Aye Jarl!"

It would have been better at night but I hoped that the effect would stun the defenders. I donned my helmet and picked up my shield. I took out Ragnar's Spirit. I would not be using it as a weapon but it gave my men confidence. The oars took us down the river much quicker and I saw more men man the burgh's walls. They had not released any arrows when Leif unfurled the banner. The speed of the drekar through the water created a natural wind and the dragon began to wail. I smiled as I saw the men on the walls look around for the source of the noise. It delayed the arrow storm which I knew would be coming.

"Snorri, we need your bow!"

"Aye Jarl."

Snorri and Beorn both had bows made by the Saami people. Snorri could send an arrow far further than the Saxons on the walls of the burgh. Within the walls, someone must have taken charge for the hiatus of the dragon's wail was ended with a few ranging arrows. Most fell short and the ones that reached us were taken on our shields.

"Take in a couple of reefs on the sail, Thorir. If they have fire arrows then I want a smaller target for them to aim at."

"Aye, captain." He and the ship's boys swarmed up the ropes to the cross trees.

I saw Snorri pull back on his powerful bow and release. The archer on the tower who thought he was safe from the drekar was plucked from the ramparts and fell from the walls. The rest took cover until the mailed warrior shouted his orders again.

We were as close to the walls now as we would ever be. The wailing dragon and Snorri's bow had bought us time but now they used fire arrows. A fire arrow is harder to use accurately than a normal arrow. The shaft has to be balanced just right. Twenty arrows soared but almost all fell woefully short. Some did not even make the river. Two struck the hull but the river's spray doused them. To do damage they needed to hit the sails or the dry deck.

The next twenty were more accurate but Erik's foresight meant that the ones that hit the drekar hit the deck. They were doused by Aiden and his pail of river water. I raised my sword, "The sword that was touched by the gods defies you Saxons!"

It had an immediate effect on my men. The rowers pulled harder and the rest cheered. By a quirk of the wind and the river, the dragon's wail became louder and, once again, the archers on the walls hesitated. Their leader shouted and pointed at me. The next ten arrows were aimed at me. I held up my shield and felt the impact as four of them thudded into it. A fifth clanged off my helmet and four struck the deck around my feet. I felt the heat as the fire caught on the dry deck. There was a whoosh and a hiss as the flames were doused by three buckets. I took Ragnar's Spirit and chopped off the hafts of the arrows in my shield. The heads continued to burn.

Aiden said, "Jarl, your shield!"

"Let it burn a little longer. I want them to see that I do not fear them."

It had an effect for the arrows became fewer as we passed beyond their effective range. Olaf's drekar did not suffer as much for we had been the prime target. As we passed around the bend I allowed Aiden to put out the flames. When I looked at my shield I saw that fire had burned close to the mouth of the wolf which was painted upon it. It looked like the wolf was grinning.

As soon as **'The King's Gift'** passed out of sight of the burgh my men all began cheering and banging weapons on the deck, "Dragonheart! Dragonheart! Dragonheart! Dragonheart!" It echoed down the river as we headed for the safety of the sea.

Chapter 12

Once we reached the sea the danger from the land was over but we now had to face the dangers from the sea. The waves were huge as we left the protection of the land. Erik had to sail on reduced canvas and we needed men constantly on the oars to maintain our position. If a wave had struck us beam on there was a danger that we might have broached. Aiden had all the wounded brought to the centre of the drekar and he had a piece of old torn sail used as a shelter. The motion there was less severe and they were protected by the rowers. Beorn had still not awakened but Aiden was happy that he was breathing easier and a little colour had returned to his cheeks. I looked down at him and Aiden said, "The gods send us sleep to heal us, Jarl. You have been in the land of dreams; you know that."

I did but that did not stop me from worrying.

The stormy weather continued all the way down the east coast. It was night as we did so and I wondered how Erik could steer and navigate when the coast was hidden from us. We passed the Saxon Kingdoms but we were safe for none but a fool would have ventured out in such weather. At dawn, the unpredictable wind took us too close to the Tamese for my liking. I knew that we were seen from the burghs one on the bank and, sometime later, the one on the southern bank. Egbert and his warriors would know that we were abroad. Erik managed to drag us away from the shore so that we rounded the dangerous coast of Kent from a safe distance. I kept peering behind at Olaf Grimsson in *'The King's Gift'*. It was a smaller drekar and suffered more in such weather. My young captain appeared to be coping well. While we had lost warriors in the battle of Fulford, his boat had been lucky and he was still with a full crew. It helped.

When we began to head west the weather eased. The wind came from the south-east and Erik took the decision to stop rowing and rely purely on the wind. "We still have Corn Walum and Syllingar to contend with. There we will need rowers. They can rest along this stretch." Erik smiled at me, "And I think that you should rest too, Jarl."

Aiden had just finished examining Beorn. "Erik is right Jarl, you should rest. Beorn is sleeping and there is no change."

I nodded. They were both right and I did need the rest but I feared sleep for I feared my dreams. My mother's words still haunted me. '***All of our family know when they are to die. It is a gift and a curse. You will dream your death***' I wondered if I would ever enjoy a pleasant sleep again. Her words appeared to have murdered sleep. However, I lay down and covered myself in my wolf skin. I held my dragon as a protection against the dreams which I feared.

I awoke and could not remember a dream. I had not dreamed of my death nor any death and I found myself smiling with relief. Behind us, I saw the first hint of dawn. Thorir was on the steering board. "That is the Isle of the Wights ahead. Captain Erik told me to steer well to the south."

"A wise move." I picked up the ale skin and drank deeply. Most of my men, including Aiden and Snorri, were asleep. I went to the stern to look for Olaf. There he was, two lengths behind us. He knew how to obey orders. Like us, he was just under sail and I guessed that most of those on board his drekar were sleeping too. I went to the rail on the steerboard side and leaned over. That was Wessex. We had cowed the Danes, at least for a while but I wondered if King Egbert had forgotten our raid on his prized Lundenwic. I was about to turn away when a movement caught my eye. It was a sail. It was ahead of us. Just then the ship's boy on the crosstrees shouted, "Saxon ships to the north!"

Erik was waking up as I shouted, "To arms!" I ran to the stern and cupping my hands shouted, "To arms!" Even as I looked astern I saw another two Saxons heading for Olaf. They had learned from their mistake. There were five Saxons and they had us between them. It was an ambush. The three ahead could cut us off for the wind was still from the northeast and favoured them. We might escape but I knew that there would be no chance for Olaf. I would not desert my men.

"Erik, steer towards them!"

Thorir said, "Towards them? That is suicide."

Erik snapped, "You still have much to learn. By sailing towards them we take the initiative. There are two more coming astern of Olaf. With Olaf, it will be two against three and that is better odds than five against two."

Haaken and the men were already armed. I looked to Aiden. "You had better prepare Dragon Fire. Choose four men. That is all that I can spare. Snorri, organise archers and wait until I decide which shall be your target."

The three Saxons ships were all smaller than my drekar but they were bigger than Olaf's threttanessa. They were tubbier than a drekar and rode higher in the water. Most importantly we had many oars and, when we needed to then we could escape quickly.

I went to the stern. "I want your drekar next to mine! Fighting platform!"

I saw the warrior at the prow, It was Eystein; he waved and he hurried aft. If *'The King's Gift'* was next to us then neither of us could be taken by two Saxons. As I looked astern I saw that the two Saxons were already losing ground as the swifter drekar flew through the water. They sailed reasonably well with the wind astern but this was from their quarter and they were as slow as a knarr. I donned my helmet and picked up my shield. The blackened wolf still grinned at me. "Leif, let us try the dragon again. If it worries them for but a moment we can take advantage."

I wandered over to Erik. "Take us between the two which are closest to us. With Olaf, we stand a chance of destroying one of them. If it is two against two we might win."

"We will need an overhaul when we return home. We have taken damage already and three against two means we will suffer more."

"Then you believe that we will return home?"

"When I sail with Dragonheart I am always confident. It is when I sail with others that I clutch the wolf about my neck!"

Olaf was bringing his drekar up to the seaward side of us. It was a fast drekar. I went to the rail closest to him. "We will engage the two end Saxons. Tie your drekar to ours and we will destroy the one to seaward first."

Asbjorn waved, "Aye Jarl."

Aiden said, "This Dragon Fire is as dangerous to us as the enemy. I have a plan."

"Go on."

"When we fight the Saxon to landward you will attack with your warriors?" I nodded. "Then I will follow with my four warriors and we will attack the other Saxon. He will do one of three things: support the ship you assault, attack your stern or attack your bow. Whichever he does we will attack with Dragon Fire. If it works that will be one ship out of the way."

"But?"

"But there is a danger that it may set light to the ship you attack and you will need to flee quickly."

"So be it." I turned to Rolf. "When Aiden goes aboard the Saxon ship your task is to guard him."

"I will, Jarl Dragonheart."

The Saxons were turning towards us now. They kept in a line to prevent us from sailing past them. They could not know what we planned. "Now Erik put the steering board over!" I turned and shouted the same to Olaf. Both ships turned, almost as one. We took them by surprise and the three of them tried to turn to stop us. They merely succeeded in stopping themselves. "Ready with grappling hooks!"

Erik shouted, "Take in the sail!"

As our bows touched the bow of the middle Saxon we started to slide down the side, "Throw!"

The four men who held the grappling hooks sent them across to hold the Saxon tight. On the other side of our drekar men tied us to Olaf's ship. I took out my sword and using the grappling ropes climbed up the side of the Saxon. Snorri and his archers sent their arrows into any who tried to cut the ropes. It was only a climb of an arm's length and as Snorri felled the Saxon who leapt at me I clambered on the deck. We had to clear enough space for Aiden and his throwers to reach the far side of the ship. Already the third Saxon ship was coming to the aid of the ship we were attacking.

The decks were filled with Saxons but most had no mail. I hacked at the middle of a Saxon who was too slow to bring his shield across. I gutted him and as I withdrew my sword I ripped it across the side of a second Saxon. Haaken and Olaf joined me and the three of us carved a path through the middle of the milling warriors. Had we not had the finest of armour, the strongest of shields and not the best-trained warriors to walk the earth we might have died for we were assaulted on all sides. We took most of the blows on our shields and armour. They swarmed over us. A few spears were jabbed at our faces but by turning my head I avoided them. Those who struck us died. Olaf took two men with one blow.

We reached the steerboard side of the ship as the other Saxon nudged alongside. As the ships were the same height the Saxon warriors just had to clamber over the side. They had not seen Olaf and his axe. He hewed limbs as though they were trees. As warriors climbed over the sides their heads were smashed to a pulp. Their legs were hacked in two. Haaken and I used our swords to take those who tried to avoid Olaf's berserk attack. The Saxons moved to the bow of their ship to cross there.

Rolf appeared next to me. His blood-spattered armour was testimony to his passage. Behind him came Aiden and his throwers. Olaf and Haaken stood on one side and I stood with Rolf. We held off any who were foolish enough to challenge us. Aiden had all the time in the world to light his Dragon Fires and hand them to his throwers. They threw them to the bow and the stern of the packed Saxon ship. The men who stood there merely lifted their shields. When the missiles struck there was a flare of flame which shot into the air. The shields which were ignited became infernos. The deck caught fire. One missile hit the sail and the flames raced up. Aiden had another eight deadly packages and his throwers plenty of time to spread their fire around the Saxon ship.

Aiden turned to me and his face bore a worried expression, "I would order the retreat, Jarl. This ship will be engulfed in flames by the time we return to ours."

I yelled, "Fall back!"

We charged the angry Saxons and as they fell back to the other side of the ship we moved backwards and dropped down onto our own drekar.

"Cut the lines!"

There was panic on the Saxon ship as they realised that there was a fire ship next to it. A gap appeared as the fireship drifted away.

"On to *'The King's Gift'*!"

I led my men across Olaf's drekar. He had fewer men and I knew that he would be struggling. The Saxons had filled their ships with warriors.

As we tumbled over the side I saw that Eystein had led half of the warriors to take the bows while Asbjorn had taken the others to the stern. Eystein was having the worst of it. He was outnumbered and surrounded. I shouted, "Snorri, clear the bows. Rollo, Erik, Finni, with me!"

I brought my sword diagonally across my head and it swept across the backs of three warriors trying to get to Eystein and his beleaguered warriors. I did not kill them all with the one blow but they were wounded and injured enough to be out of the battle. Rollo and Finni hacked and slashed at my side. Two warriors guarding Eystein fell and a mailed Saxon with three oathsworn fell upon my Ulfheonar. He slew one with a blow which took his head but then the other three attacked from three sides. Eystein fought courageously. I saw a wounded warrior reach up with his seax and hamstring Eystein the Rock. One leg crumpled and, as it did so the mailed warrior hacked at Eystein's shield arm. He managed to swing and hack into the mailed warrior's leg even as half his arm drooped. The other two fell upon Eystein and hacked him to death.

It was too much for me. I roared like a dragon and brought my sword down with such force on the warrior who had taken Eystein's head that I cut him in two, slicing through to the spine. He shivered as he fell. Rollo and Finni slew the mailed warrior and the last Saxon. The wounded warrior held up his hand and said, "Mercy. Spare me, lord."

His treacherous blow had slain a great warrior. I brought my sword up and laid him open from the crotch to the chest. He was not dead yet but some time later he would die and in pain.

"Get Eystein aboard his ship. Fall back! Aiden, destroy this ship!" I waited until Eystein was carried to safety and then I backed away, daring any Saxon to face me. They did not. They were terrified. When I reached the side of the Saxon I turned and jumped down into Olaf's ship.

"Cut the ropes!"

As the ropes were severed Aiden had his men throw the last of the Dragon Fire high into the air. They landed together and the flames leapt high to set the mast and the sail on fire. We hurried back to our drekar and let loose the ropes which bound us together. As Olaf and Erik lowered our sails and pulled away I saw three Saxon ships burning. The two which raced towards us would pick up the survivors, that was all.

We watched, as we headed west, the efforts of the Saxons to save their comrades. The sea was on fire. There would be few survivors. "Well Aiden, the Dragon Fire worked."

Erik shook his head, "And I pray that our enemies do not get the secret for there is no answer Jarl, to this Dragon Fire. It spells the doom to every ship afloat."

We had left Eystein's body on his ship. Asbjorn had fought alongside him his whole life. He would find it hard to fight in the future. We, too, had lost warriors. There were homes in Cyninges-tūn which would wait in vain for their sons to return. It was not even as though we would be bringing home treasure. Any treasure was now at the bottom of the sea. All that we returned with was security and honour. Yet I knew that none of my warriors who had died would regret their deaths. They had died for their families. That was all a warrior could do.

The day promised to be a stormy one. The skies were filled with thick black clouds. I went to check on the wounded. "How is Beorn?"

Aiden had just examined him. "He is asleep but he is not improving and the wound feels hot to the touch. I fear it may be infected."

"Can you do nothing for him?"

"Not at sea. If we were on land I could use fire or perhaps maggots but here..." His voice tailed away.

Snorri said, "Beorn would not wish us to take a risk landing. He would take his chances."

I shook my head, "But I will not. Tell me, Aiden, is there somewhere we could land?"

"This is Wessex, Jarl and it is filled with enemies."

"They should fear us! Find somewhere quiet. We have enough warriors to defend ourselves. I have spoken."

Aiden took out his precious charts and went to speak with Erik. Erik and he spoke for a while and then Erik said, "Tell Olaf that we will head inshore."

Haaken and Olaf joined us. "This is *wyrd*. We can honour Eystein with a Viking funeral!"

Haaken was correct. It was the right thing to do.

Olaf said, "And if any warrior of Wessex interferes then they will risk the wrath of Olaf!"

We headed towards the coast and Aiden and Erik spoke the whole time. Eventually, both seemed satisfied and we headed towards a strange white rock with an arch which stood in the middle of the sea. I wondered had they gone mad until we passed it and I spied a beach with a steep path up a cliff. Once again they had saved us for we could guard the clifftop and heal our men while burying our dead. It was not an easy landing for the waves and the currents were quite strong but when the ship's boys had secured us to the land we disembarked. The two ship's crews would affect repairs while most of my warriors would climb the path to burn the body of Eystein. Aiden would move the wounded to the beach and then begin to heal them. As I climbed the path I knew that I had done the right thing.

"Jarl Dragonheart, I will take some men and search for maggots. It may be the only thing to save Beorn."

"Rollo and Rolf go with Aiden and find maggots."

We laid our dead at the top of the cliff. We would gather wood to burn them later but first, we owed it to the living to help them. Aiden had had Beorn brought ashore and he lay on the beach of the small cove. A warrior and four ship's boys watched him. Snorri was already building a fire. I had the men search nearby for maggots but there were no dead animals there; at least not recently dead. It would be up to Aiden to find the creatures.

"Gather wood and we will build a fire. We shall be ready to light it when Aiden and the others return."

There was a great deal of dead wood. There must have been a recent storm and broken branches were strewn everywhere. We placed the bodies of our dead on the top with Eystein, as a Hersir, in the centre. He had no sons or daughters but a young wife. I took the golden wolf from around his neck. She would have that as payment for his death and I would give her some of my animals. Eystein deserved no less. With his sword between his hands, he was ready to meet Odin. Satisfied that we had done all correctly we waited for the return of Aiden.

We heard them as they hurried through the undergrowth from the north. "Have you found maggots?"

Aiden grinned. He looked, once more, like the young boy who had once followed me. "Aye Jarl and we found more besides. There is a settlement in the next valley and a monastery. The Norns directed us here. It is *wyrd*."

"Then you see to Beorn. We will light this pyre when we have raided the Saxons. The families of the dead shall not go unrewarded."

We were not dressed for war but a Viking is always ready to fight. We each had a shield and a weapon. It was all that we needed. Rollo and

Rolf led closely followed by Asbjorn. There was anger within the heart of my jarl. It had been Saxons from Wessex who had hacked his friend to death and it would be Saxons from Wessex who paid the weregeld.

The monastery and settlement were not far away. We could smell the animals and the smoke from their fires. There would be no time to scout. We would just descend upon them. Rollo raised his sword and pointed. They had built the monastery on a hill and it was a hundred or so paces from the village which was lower down the slope. Since he had become a Christian King Egbert had built many such monasteries. I ran next to Asbjorn. "You take your men left."

"Aye Jarl."

I waved to Olaf, "You take half of the Ulfheonar and half of the other men and go right. I will lead the rest towards the centre."

He nodded and began tapping men on the shoulder and pointing. Soon I was left with just twelve warriors. Haaken was with me and I still had Rollo and Rolf. There was a sudden shout from the left. Asbjorn and his men had been spotted. It could not be helped. The palisade around the village loomed up and as we approached I shouted, "Break through!"

Rolf's axe soon hacked a gap wide enough for two men to get through and we burst into the village. I saw, in the distance, a hall which was raised up on a mound of earth. That would be the hall of the Gesith and his warriors. I ran towards it flanked by my Ulfheonar. The doors burst open when we were twenty paces from it and warriors appeared. From their mail, this was a rich Gesith for four of the men we spied wore mail.

The leader stood on the step and shouted, "North Men! Sound the horn!"

The man next to the Gesith blew hard on a horn. It was as loud as any I had heard before and it echoed across the countryside. It was summoning help. Before I could worry about that we had to deal with these warriors. We charged them and that took them by surprise for there were but four of us and I saw that there were ten warriors who were preparing to meet us.

Rolf's axe swung horizontally and it hacked through the legs of two men. I took the blow from the warrior with the horn on my shield and rammed my sword up under his byrnie. The stroke ripped him open from the crotch to the chest. The Gesith realised that being above us gave him no advantage and he shouted, "Kill these pirates!"

As he jumped down he swung his sword. I blocked it with my sword and they rang together. I was wide awake and I had fought more often than this Gesith who had just awoken and looked a little rusty. I brought my hand back and feinted towards his middle. He brought his shield around and I flicked the tip of the sword towards his face, It was not a full helmet and my sword tore across his nose and cheek up to his forehead. I saw bone. He reeled and as he did so I punched with my shield. I hit the back of his sword hand. He held on but I knew that his hand would be numb. I brought Ragnar's Spirit around in a wide sweep. The blood from his face running down across his eye made it hard to see. He made the mistake of trying to wipe it and raised his shield arm. My sword struck him in the ribs. His mail was good and I did not penetrate the links but the blow had been so hard that I had hurt him. I brought my hand back and this time lunged towards the bloody mess that was his face. It came out of the back of his skull.

The warriors were dead and, as I glanced around I saw that we had taken the village. I reached down and took the horn from the dead warrior. I placed it around my neck. "Hurry they summoned help. Let us take their mail and arms. I will go in the hall."

I ran up the steps and found six thralls cowering in the corner. "You six come with me." They hesitated, "Obey me and you shall live!"

They stood and followed me.

"Pick up the mail. Rollo, take this back to the ship and then let the thralls go."

"Aye Jarl Dragonheart."

"Come Haaken, let us see what else we can find. Rolf go and find Asbjorn and Olaf. Tell them that help comes and we need to return to the ship. Asbjorn can fire the pyre. There is no cause for secrecy anymore."

"Aye Jarl Dragonheart!"

There was a sconce inside the hall and I grabbed the brand from it. As we moved silently through the hall I heard sobbing from a room off to the side. We moved towards it. Haaken tore open the hanging which acted as a door and we saw a woman and three children. The woman guarded a box."Who are you?" I spoke in Saxon but she saw just a warrior dressed as a wolf. The children looked terrified. "Answer me and you may live. Remain silent and you will not." It was a bluff. I was not the kind of warrior who killed women just for the pleasure of it.

The woman was not afraid of me. I could see that and, when she spoke, I heard iron in her words. She spoke with authority as though she was used to giving orders and having them obeyed. "I am the Lady Maud, wife of Ethelfrith, Thegn of Radipole. I am precious to King Egbert. Harm me at your peril."

I laughed, "I do not worry about upsetting Egbert." I leaned down to take the box. " She gripped it and darted hatred from her eyes. "Whatever is in the chest is not worth your life is it? I give you my word that if you give me the box then you and your children shall live." She hesitated,

"You have the word of Jarl Dragonheart and even King Egbert knows that I honour my word."

She released the box and her mouth fell open, "You are the Wolf Warrior?"

I nodded as I took the box. "I am."

Haaken said, "Jarl, enough of the pleasantries. Time is pressing and they have summoned reinforcements."

"Farewell." I saw that she gripped her crucifix as I left and her lips moved. Was it a prayer or a curse?

Clutching the box, which seemed heavier than it should have, I followed Haaken. My men had fired the village and the monastery. It would draw those sent to find us and buy us time. We had less than a mile to run to reach the cove. As we passed we saw some of the younger warriors from Cyninges-tūn who were still seeking treasure. Haaken shouted, "Leave that and follow us. If you stay then you die!"

No one argued with Ulfheonar. As we neared the cliff top I saw the glow of a fire. Asbjorn had lit the funeral pyre. Haaken's hand held his sword and he pointed to the north. "Jarl look!"

I saw, illuminated by the fire from the burning village, riders. This would be close. The warriors with us wore no mail. "Run and tell Jarl Asbjorn and Olaf to form a shield wall!"

There was little point in turning around. We would hear the hooves of those following. The worst thing to do in such a situation was to panic. If they reached us quickly then it meant they were not wearing mail and they would struggle to defeat us. They might waste time in the village and the monastery. There were too many imponderables. I just worried about what I had to do.

The flames were licking around the top of the pyre when we reached them and Olaf was already organising the shield wall. Asbjorn stared at the bodies of his friend and his comrades. Olaf had ten warriors with mail and the rest had none. I gave the chest to Audun Larsson and said, "Take those without mail back to the ship. Aiden and Snorri should return to the drekar with the wounded." I took the horn from around my neck. "Have them sound this three times when it is done."

He took the chest and handed the horn to Leif the Slow. "Aye Jarl."

As he ran I shouted, "Asbjorn the Strong! Do you wish to join your friend on the pyre or are you a warrior still? There are enemies coming."

He unsheathed his sword, "I come, Jarl! I have not yet bathed in enough blood!"

He stood next to Olaf and Haaken. Leif the Banner and Rolf stood next to me. I saw the last of our men disappear over the cliff and head down the narrow path to the sea. We needed to make these Saxons fear us. There were twenty of them. The leader had a fine helmet and all wore leather armour which had metal scales upon it. Each had a spear and a shield. They looked to be identical. They charged straight at us. Many would have fled at such a charge. We had faced men like this before. Their horses would turn rather than run at a shield wall and the spears they held posed no threat to us. They were brave and I think that they were used to making enemies flee before them.

Rolf Horse Killer lived up to his name as he and Olaf swung the axes into the chests of two of the small horses. There was a sickening crunch and a wild scream as the first of the horses suffered the axe blow which ended its life. The two riders flew from the backs of the horses and, as they lay at our feet were butchered. A spear was thrust at my head and, rather than block it with my shield I hacked at the head with my sword. It sheared it in two. Haaken pulled at the spear which was thrust at him and pulled. The rider did not let go and he was pulled onto the sword of Rollo Thin Skin.

Asbjorn was fighting like a man possessed. He waited not for the horsemen to close with him, he charged at them. Olaf and Haaken hurried behind him to protect his flanks. The smoke from the pyre now drifted across the field making it hard to see. When I heard the horn sound three times I shouted, "Back to the ships!" I turned to those near me who just stood, "Back!"

A single rider rode at me and he tried to use his spear like a lance. I braced myself and as he thrust I put my weight behind my shield. He was pushed backwards from his horse. He fell and landed at my feet. I ran up to him and, before he could rise, took his head. I saw Olaf and Haaken dragging Asbjorn towards me. "He went berserk, Jarl!"

"Get him down the cliff. I will watch the rear." As I backed towards the cliff path I saw that the survivors had lost their appetite for a wild charge. Too many men and horses lay dead. They had thought to make us turn and run. We had not and they had lost.

I stood at the top of the cliff and, raising my sword, shouted, "I am Jarl Dragonheart! Beware my sword for it is Saxon Bane!"

I descended the cliff. I was the last one to leave the beach and I waded out to my drekar. We had come to bury our dead and to heal our wounded but we had taken treasure and gained a great victory. *Wyrd*.

Chapter 13

"How is Beorn?"

"The wound had begun to mortify, Jarl. I had to cut open the stitches I had used. It was filled with pus and mortification. I let the blood wash away most of the evil and then sealed it with fire. I have packed it now with maggots and seaweed. If he is still as ill by the time we reach the Sabrina then he will lose the leg." He saw the look of horror on Snorri's face. He shrugged. "Better that he lose a leg than lose his life." Aiden was not a warrior. He did not understand our minds. Beorn would choose death over the loss of a leg.

Snorri shook his head, "With but one leg then Beorn would be as well dead. I will stay with my friend."

Aiden nodded, "That is good for your spirit can help to heal him. I will stay here too. Erik knows the waters."

I went, with Haaken and Olaf, to the stern where the treasures had been gathered. Erik nodded to them. "If we have storms when we round the tip of this land we may lose them. Better they are stowed, Jarl."

It was as close to criticism as Erik would come. I nodded, "Have the mail and the swords put beneath the decks. I will examine this chest. The Saxon seemed reluctant to let it go. I wonder why."

As soon as I opened it I saw the reason. It was the royal jewels. I recognised the small coronet which was given to the queen of Wessex for Elfrida had worn it when we had first met her in Lundenwic. The crown of King Egbert was not there but there were other royal rings, crowns and jewels inside the chest. Haaken's eyes widened, "Who would have thought that such a small village would hold such a great treasure."

Olaf said, "The monastery was richly endowed. They had fine ornaments as well as good linen and some holy books. It has been a profitable raid. The treasure from there is on *'The King's Gift'*."

"And we know that Wintan-ceastre is not far away. Those riders came quickly. I wonder if the King was close by and the riders were with his army. I have rarely seen warriors thus armed. They were not fyrd. To me, they were more like mounted hearthweru. They all wore the same armour."

Haaken nodded, "I think you are right, Jarl. In which case we were more than lucky. Had King Egbert and his army reached us then who knows what the outcome might have been."

"We will need to speak with Elfrida when we reach home. She may know the thegn and his wife and shed some light on this treasure. For now, we will do as our captain suggests and store the chest somewhere safe."

As the chest was taken to safety I went to the stern. I had thought it was an accident that we had landed at that cove. Now I saw the Norns at work. They were weaving once more. The webs continued to confound us. And they had not yet finished with us. Storms erupted when we were close to Syllingar. I saw Aiden clutching his amulet. We had been driven into the clutches of the witch who lived there. We had been stopped too often to ignore the gods. Perhaps she did not want us that day for we passed the jagged teeth which were a threat to every sailor and turned to sail north towards home. The closer we came to the Sabrina the more concerned we all were with Beorn's health. None of us wanted him to have to lose a leg but part of me wondered if this might be the end of the days in the Ulfheonar of Beorn the Scout. Would he end up crippled like Karl One Leg? Although Snorri said nothing I knew that was his fear too. He had lost Bjorn, one close friend and I knew that he would find it hard to bear to lose another.

I had lost Cnut, another old friend when we had saved my daughter and Elfrida. Now I watched Haaken each time we fought together. If he went then I would be the last of the old ones. Haaken and I were like Olaf and Old Ragnar had been. When Ragnar had died in Norway Olaf the Toothless had begun to shrink both in size and to withdraw from the world. It had been as though he had been preparing for death. I felt like Aiden, a galdramenn, for I was reading Snorri's thoughts.

I went over to the three of them. I could detect no change in Beorn. It had been two days since the maggots had begun to do their work. I could tell that Snorri was keen to know if the treatment had worked.

"How is our comrade?"

Aiden said, "I am hopeful. He sleeps better and his breathing is regular."

"Is there heat still from the wound?"

"There is but that might not be a bad thing. Sometimes heat means it is healing."

"Can you not look, galdramenn?" Snorri could not keep the anxiety from his voice.

"We wait for three days."

"But you said by the Sabrina..."

"And that is because I thought it would take us three days to reach here. It is not yet three days. The gods have given us a good wind. Would you rather we were still at Syllingar?"

"No Aiden, I am sorry but...."

"But you are worried about your friend as are we all. You need to have faith in the Allfather and in your friend. He is a fighter."

Snorri had also been wounded in the fight at Fulford but his had just resulted in a long scar running down his face and the back of his hand. It would be a visual reminder of his brush with death and, if Beorn died, of the day his friend went to the Otherworld.

Haaken was busy composing another of his sagas to chant while we sailed. He was honouring Eystein the Rock. It was not yet complete but I sat and listened as he played with the words. Once he had the chorus he was happy for that gave him the beat he needed for the rest.

> **Through the stormy Saxon Seas**
> **The Ulfheonar they sailed**
> **Fresh from killing faithless Danes**
> **Their glory was assured**
> **Heart of Dragon**
> **Gift of a king**
> **Two fine drekar**
> **Flying o'er foreign seas**
> **Then Saxons came out of the night**
> **An ambush by their Isle of Wight**
> **Vikings fight they do not run**
> **The Jarl turned away from the rising sun**
> **Heart of Dragon**
> **Gift of a king**
> **Two fine drekar**
> **Flying o'er foreign seas**
> **The galdramenn burned Dragon Fire**
> **And the seas they burned bright red**
> **Aboard 'The Gift' Asbjorn the Strong**
> **And the rock Eystein**
> **Rallied their men to board their foes**
> **And face them beard to beard**
> **Heart of Dragon**
> **Gift of a king**
> **Two fine drekar**
> **Flying o'er foreign seas**
> **Against great odds and back to back**
> **The heroes fought as one**
> **Their swords were red with Saxon blood**

And the decks with bodies slain
Surrounded on all sides was he
But Eystein faltered not
He slew first one and then another
But the last one did for him
Even though he fought as a walking dead
He killed right to the end
Heart of Dragon
Gift of a king
Two fine drekar
Flying o'er foreign seas

He looked to me for approval. "Very dramatic, Haaken but Asbjorn was at one end of the Saxon ship and Eystein the other. They were not back to back."

He waved an airy hand. "Dramatic effect. You are no poet, Jarl Dragonheart! This honours Asbjorn!" He wagged a finger at me, "Are you annoyed that I did not mention your part in the battle!"

"You know me better than that. It is a fine saga. There are you satisfied?"

"It still needs work but I will make changes after we have reached home. I will sing it to Unn and the children. They appreciate my work and their voices help me to sharpen the rhythm."

We passed the Sabrina and continued north. When dawn broke we were just south of Ynys Enlli. Snorri had not slept. Aiden shook his head as he approached the Ulfheonar. "You need faith, Snorri. Let us see if the maggots have done their job."

I stood and watched as Aiden untied the bandages. There was a disgusting smell but Aiden seemed happy enough. I asked, "Should it smell that way?"

"That is the rotting seaweed." He picked the decaying weed and laid it on one side. He leaned over and began to pick out the maggots. When he had a handful he said, "It is going well. These are dead." He sniffed the wound. "He is healing. He will not lose his leg."

I felt a great sense of relief but Snorri asked, "Then why does he not wake?"

"The Allfather is wise. He makes the body sleep so that galdramenn such as me can heal the wounds. He will wake when he wakes." Haaken had wandered over. "Remember Haaken when I put the plate in his skull?"

Snorri asked, "Where were you when the Allfather made you sleep?"

"I was wandering the earth and seeing places I have never seen. Believe me, Beorn is not unhappy, Snorri. The only one who is worried is you."

Aiden added, "And that is because you feel guilty that it was he who was wounded and not you."

Snorri's hand went to his golden wolf, "You are reading my mind?"

"I know you, Snorri. And you have naught to feel guilty about. You were unlucky that is all. If the warrior had not gone to make water then Beorn would not have a wound. *Wyrd*. Perhaps this is good for you, Snorri. It will teach you about wounds, eh?"

"Perhaps but if you say that Beorn will live then I will sleep."

Aiden, Haaken and I watched the coast of Cymru as we sailed north. Always the mountains there seemed to draw me as though part of my life lay there. Aiden too was preoccupied. "That is where Myrddyn lived. His spirit is there still. I can feel it."

Haaken snorted, "It is typical that I miss one trip with you and you meet a ghost from the past. I would have made a great saga from that!"

"Some stories are best untold. What I heard heralds my doom."

"Your doom?"

"I know now that I will dream my own death. Each night sleep has become torture. When I close my eyes the blackness enfolds me." I held the dragon out. "This is a double-edged weapon. It brings great power but it also warns me of my end. I have no peace and no sanctuary to which I can retire." It was getting on to dark when we edged into the estuary we called home. Beorn awoke as the ropes were thrown to tie us to the jetty. "Where are we?"

"You are home, Beorn."

He tried to move and winced with the pain. Snorri laughed, "You almost lost that leg. We will have a litter made and you can be carried home. It will be some time until you walk again."

Aiden added, "Let us see if the wound heals before we speak of walking."

Beorn looked horrified, "I will walk, will I not?"

"It depends upon how much rest you get and if you listen to me! Snorri is right, we will make a litter for you."

Coen Ap Pasgen came to the jetty. He looked concerned, "You managed to defeat the Danes?"

"Aye, we did. I hope that we have deterred them for some time."

As the wounded were brought off he said, "You must stay with us this night."

"We will."

Coen Ap Pasgen was a good host and we discovered much while we ate with him. "The Irish have decided that Anglesey, as the Saxons call it, is ripe for raiding. They have sent their pirates there rather than here or Ljoðhús. The Northumbrians are not as strong as they once were. It pleases us for they do not raid here now." He smiled, "Your reach is long Jarl. They would rather sail further than risk your wrath."

I found myself touching, unconsciously, the dragon around my neck. When we had passed Wyddfa I had felt its pull and I felt it now. "Perhaps. And is my land safe?"

"Your son and Karl One Leg each send a messenger every three days. Your land is unharmed and your people prosper."

I felt relieved beyond words. I had worried that things had gone so well that it must have meant ill at home. I had been wrong.

We left at dawn for the ride north. The weather changed even as we headed through the forest. The wind was in our faces and it was a vicious north-easterly. It was what we called a lazy wind: it did not go around you, it went straight through you. I was happy that I was at home. I looked forward to nights in my hall with my wife, son and daughter. The wind and the wolves could howl but so long as I was in my hall then all would be well with the world.

The younger warriors hurried home. We had more tales than treasure but all had something to show for the month away. Their early arrival meant that we had a reception as every wife, mother and daughter came to greet us. Kara and Brigid did not. They would wait in our halls. That was as it should be. I was Jarl and Aiden was our wizard. It allowed our people to greet us. Inevitably there were those waiting to greet warriors who now lay as ashes in Wessex. We had treasure for them but that was as nothing compared with the treasure they had lost. I made sure that I spoke with each of those whose son or husband had been killed on the raid. It was little enough but a word from the Jarl made the loss somewhat easier.

Haaken handed me the chest of treasure. "Here Jarl. You had best determine what we keep and what we sell."

"I will speak with Elfrida. We will visit there before seven days have passed."

When I entered my hall I was bowled over by Gryffydd who tore into me like a tornado. "Let me greet your father, Gryffydd! Then you may have him." Brigid had a smile on her face as she admonished our son.

I nodded and he backed off. Brigid threw her arms around me, "I have missed you." She kissed me hard and then pulled away from me. "Have you any new wounds that I should know about?"

"No, but Eystein was killed and Beorn badly injured. My Ulfheonar suffered. It was a warning that I am mortal."

She linked my arm and led me to my table. "We have food ready. I dare say that ship's rations have made a wraith of you."

It felt good to have my family about me. Erika still did not recognise me, she was still a baby, but I could see that she had grown. I told them the tale of our journey. I spared both Brigid and my son the gory details. It was not seemly. I was forced to bring forth the treasure and Gryffydd was fascinated by the treasure within.

"I will see Elfrida first. It may be that we can have ransom from Egbert for some of these jewels and crowns."

"Beware my husband. Egbert has not forgotten Elfrida and your son. It would not do to anger him."

"I cannot worry about a Saxon king who lives many leagues hence. We destroyed three of his ships and many of his warriors. It is he who should fear us!"

Even as I said it I regretted it. The Norns heard everything. They heard my boast. The words went to the cave in the far north beyond the unending sea and they heard.

Gryffydd dragged over Uhtric, "Tell him Uhtric! Tell how I have hewn wood every day and practised with Karl One Leg! Tell him how I can pull a bow and release an arrow as well as those who are Ragnar's age!"

The old servant smiled, "It seems you have done this for me but he is right Jarl. He has been diligent and not slacked off once."

Brigid sniffed, "And he is outgrowing his clothes! The boy has the appetite of a wild boar! He takes more feeding now than he used to."

"Good. I am pleased, my son. You are on the road to becoming a warrior." It was the best thing I could have said and he visibly grew before my eyes.

Kara's touch was what Beorn needed and within three days of his return, he was walking once more. It was slow and it was measured but Snorri, especially, was delighted that he could actually walk. I waited until he had managed five steps and then I left with Gryffydd, Leif, Rolf and Rollo for Elfridaby. We took the chest with us. For my son, this was a treat. He rarely travelled east and the last time he had done so we had met the Danes. I reflected as I rode south and east. The land had been tamed since first we came here. We had put down roots. Our roads, while not the equal of the Romans, left a mark on the land.

I know not why but I headed up past Satter's farm. I had a mind to speak to the spirits of the old man and woman. As we neared it I heard noises and laughter. We reined in when we reached the farm. There were people living there. It was a community. I saw three families. Some had converted Satter's old farm while the other two were newly built. They gathered around us.

An older man approached me, "Welcome Jarl Dragonheart. We are honoured that you have come to Satter's Waite. I am Ragnar Gunnstein. Satter was my uncle."

"I am just pleased that the farm continues. I thought his sons died."

"They did and when we heard that he had died we decided to come here. Our father always said that our uncle had a fine eye for the land." He looked suddenly worried, "We have not done wrong, have we? Did you have it in mind for another?"

I shook my head, "Take it, Ragnar. I am more than pleased. I had thought it would be an empty shell. This is *wyrd*. Take it with my blessing, Be my hersir here. When I need men I will send to you."

"And we will serve, gladly."

I clasped his arm as warriors do and mounted. Gryffydd asked as we entered the forest again, "What is a hersir, father?"

"It is a headman. Most times they are appointed by those who live close by. It is a title only but it means they are not bondi."

"Bondi?"

"Free farmers. They are the backbone of my land. Each bondi has to provide himself with arms and protect their land from enemies."

He nodded as he took that in. Rolf said, "You should demand that each has a shield and a helmet Jarl. It is in their own interests to do so."

Leif laughed, "Have you not noticed, Horse Killer, that the Jarl has the helmets collected from the dead enemies we slay and they are given out to those without helmets? He does the same with the shields."

"I am sorry Jarl. I had not noticed but now I can see that you have always done so."

"And I would do more. It is a shame that we could not bring back more of the weapons and armour from Fulford."

"Perhaps we were not meant to. The gods work in strange ways. Those at Satter's Waite will be the first to be given the weapons we next take."

By the time we had emerged from the forest and taken the road to Elfridaby Gryffydd had taken all of our words in. He had learned to listen more than he used to. "Are you finished fighting for the year then, father?"

"I do not know. That is not in my hands but those of our enemies." I pointed to the leaves on the trees. "See how they are turning brown. Soon they will fall and it will be winter. Most of our enemies do not like to fight in winter. It is unlikely that they will do so but we have fought in the snow before now. Let us say that we are always prepared should an enemy come.."

Leif leaned over, "And after Yule, those who wish to become Ulfheonar will hunt the wolf."

He was right. Beorn's wound and Snorri's lucky escape had shown me that I could not afford to lose more Ulfheonar until more were trained. What had been a small group of elite warriors, in the beginning, had now grown to be vital to the security of Cyninges-tūn.

Wolf Killer and his men had not been idle. The stronghold which nestled in the bend of the river had walls as high as those at Ulf's Stad. They were only made of wood but an enemy would bleed to death upon them. Ragnar and his father rode to meet us. It was a month since I had seen my grandson but I could see that he had grown.

When they reined in next to us he said to Gryffydd, "Race you back to the hall!"

Even though he only had a small pony my son was up for the challenge and they hurtled off at full pelt for Wolf Killer's stronghold.

Wolf Killer was smiling as he shook his head, "If they fall and break anything then Elfrida will make the blood eagle of me!"

"They are young enough to shrug off such injuries. It is we who should fear to fall."

"Did you defeat the Danes?"

"Aye, we did," I told him all. Even after we had dismounted and entered his hall I was still telling him what had happened on that long and fateful voyage. By the time I was finished we were all seated around his long table. Elfrida had poured us ale and they all looked expectantly at the chest.

Elfrida had been quiet when we had told our tale and now we looked at her expectantly. She looked up at me, "Before I open the chest I know what will be within." Rollo and Rolf clasped their golden wolves. They thought she had become a witch. I knew better. Elfrida was a bright and clever young woman. She had worked it out when I had said whence the chest came.

"You know this Maud and Ethelfrith?"

She nodded, "They were at court and the Lady Maud did not like me. She comes from an ancient line. Her ancestors ruled the land around the old fort they called Maiden Hill. King Egbert and she were often close. Now that her husband is dead I think that she will occupy the King's bed more openly than she did. It was an open secret and her husband benefitted from lands and titles. She seeks power. You have inadvertently done exactly what she would have wished. The King will give her the lands of her husband." She put her hands on the chest.

"Within here is the crown of the Queen of Wessex and, I daresay, those of Kent and Essex too."

Wolf Killer frowned, "Why would he not keep them close by him?"

I answered for his wife, "He is often away on campaign. Whom best to guard them than his mistress and most powerful of thegns. This makes sense now."

Elfrida opened the chest and identified each crown as she laid them on the table. "This red jewel came from a sword which was taken from a Mercian King a long time ago. This, as you know, is the crown of Wessex and these two of Kent and Essex. The seals are those of the large estates which lie close to the King. The other jewels I do not recognise but this is a mighty hoard, Jarl. I fear that King Egbert will not rest until he has them again."

I finished my ale as I reflected on this. Ragnar and Gryffydd seemed fascinated by the crowns. To me they were unnecessary. My sword was worth more for the gods had touched it. My helmet was more valuable because it protected me and the dragon I wore about my neck... well that had a power I had only just begun to harness. The richly decorated crowns were just that, adornments for women who had not fought for them. However, Elfrida was quite correct. King Egbert would not rest knowing that I had taken them. I had seen steel in the eyes of Lady Maud. She would want them back and, if she was Egbert's mistress, then she had power over him.

"What of these mounted hearthweru? We have not seen them before."

Elfrida had been staring at the crown which she had once worn and now she dragged her eyes away. "In the west of the land, there were horsemen. It is said that they were from the old people. They fought on horses."

Wolf Killer said, "Did we not meet such warriors on Ynys Môn? They wore mail."

I nodded, "But the ones we saw were not like that. They all had leather mail with metal plates sewn on. They looked like fish scales and their helmets had a guard protecting the back of their necks."

"We have seen those before, father, they are like the ones worn by the Romans."

Leif looked up from the jewels, "And Jarl, remember what Aiden said. The dragon banner we found was from the time of the Romans. They must be connected."

It was then that I realised that Aiden had not seen the horsemen and he had been too preoccupied with Beorn to take much notice. I needed to speak with him. "When I return home then I will speak with Aiden.

Thank you, Elfrida, you have told us that which we needed. Had I not discovered the true worth of these crowns I might have just sold them."

"And now?"

"And now we hang on to them because King Egbert will want them back. Kara and Aiden will need to dream."

Chapter 14

We stayed for two days. It was mainly so that I could see my grandchildren and to allow Ragnar and Gryffydd to play together. The more they played then the closer would be the bond when they grew older. There would come a time when the two of them would stand shoulder to shoulder and fight for my land. Once we set off home I hurried and headed for the southern end of the Water. We summoned a boat so that Gryffydd and I could get home quicker than by horse. My men would ride our horses to Cyninges-tūn.

When Aiden saw me he knew that there was something on my mind. "You have troubled thoughts, Jarl Dragonheart."

"I have," I told him what I had discovered from Elfrida and we went into his hall to speak with Kara. They both listened.

Kara said, "We do not need to dream. There is a woman involved. They have always been our most dangerous enemy. Remember Angharad? I have no reason to doubt Elfrida and her recollection of this woman. If she was able to have a husband and to service the King then she is a formidable foe. She will make sure that King Egbert punishes you."

"I can see that. Perhaps I should have left the chest there."

Kara laughed, "And do you think the Weird Sisters would have approved of the spoiling of their web? No, father, you could no more leave them there than you could stop the sun rising each morning. It was meant to be."

"Then we need to work out what Egbert will do."

Aiden had been quiet. "King Egbert has a problem. There are many leagues between Wessex and Cyninges-tūn. How does he get here?" He went to the chest and took out one of his maps. He laid it out. Gryffydd climbed on to a chair so that he could see. I doubted that he would understand the squiggles and lines but it was good that he was interested. Aiden pointed to the land of the Cymri. "He cannot come this way for we both know that the land is hard enough to cross in peacetime but with an army is impossible. He could come by sea but we have destroyed three of his ships and it would be a perilous voyage. The Saxons are no sailors. That leaves him with one route; he will come through the land of his vassal King, the East Angles. Northumbria is a spent force and he can pick up more men at Jorvik."

I shook my head, "I would hope he would try that for it would mean he could not come before next spring. You cannot cross the high passes in winter."

Suddenly Gryffydd leaned over and drew a line from Wessex to Cyninges-tūn with his finger. "I would come that way! It is the straight road!"

I ruffled my son's head, "And that way is barred, my son for he and the Mercians are implacable enemies."

Aiden slapped his head, "I am a fool and your son is right, Jarl." He opened the chest and took out the red stone. "This is what will join the two Saxon kings together. He will offer him this stone back. King Egbert now controls Corn Walum. Coenwulf is old. He will not relish another war with Egbert. If he could reclaim the stone without losing warriors and face then he will do so." He banged his hand on the map. "This way King Egbert takes all the risks and King Coenwulf reaps the reward. He will come through Mercia."

I smiled at Gryffydd, "Well done, my son. You have seen what these old eyes and mind could not."

Kara kissed her half brother on the head, "You know what they say father that the eyes of the innocent see things clearer than others. We make things too complicated."

"And now you need to tell me when they will come."

Aiden swept his hand at the land of Mercia. "The borders to the north of Mercia are not hard like those of Northumbria. They are soft. There is a flat plain north of Wrecsam. Once past the Maeresea, the land is gentle until it reaches the land of Sigtrygg. The men of Northumbria will not stop the passage of a Saxon army come to punish Norsemen. I believe that King Egbert will be raising an army now. You need to warn Sigtrygg for his stad lies directly in the path of our enemies."

"Then we prepare for war. And this time we will be fighting an enemy who knows how to win. These will not be Northumbrians whom we have trounced each time we meet them nor will they be faithless Danes. The army of Egbert knows how to fight. We shall need your magic, Aiden."

As we walked back to my hall Gryffydd asked, "Will I be fighting, father?"

"Answer that yourself, my son. Which of my warriors shall I take from the shield wall to make sure that you are protected?"

He nodded. We climbed the steps to my hall and he looked at the walls which ran around the stad. "And if you lose the battle?"

I smiled, children were ever honest. "Then you will get to fight for you will stand on the walls with your bow and loose arrows until you are struck down and then you will fight with your sword, Dragon's Tongue, until you, too, are slain and then I will see you in Valhalla."

He smiled, "Then I am satisfied and I will practise until these Saxons come."

Brigid had heard the last part and her face showed her fear, "The Saxons come?"

"Probably. You will have to help Scanlan organise the people. We need food laying in and all will have to defend the stad for I will take all the men except for Karl One Leg."

"And me!"

"And you, Gryffydd the Fearless!"

I summoned my Ulfheonar and my Jarls. The exception was Sigtrygg. I sent a message to him warning him that there may be Saxon attacks from the south. It took two days for them all to reach me. We sat in the hall. I had already spoken with the Ulfheonar and Asbjorn. They did not attend the council of war. They had warriors to train and to arm. Bjorn was busy making more weapons while my Ulfheonar brought out the helmets, shields and spears which we had captured and were deemed to be of inferior quality. Every man who went to war needed arming.

"You need to leave men to guard your stad but I want the best of your men ready to march as soon as I summon them."

Ulf looked troubled. "It is a day's march to here Jarl Dragonheart and then another to Sigtrygg's stad."

"So long as you reach us that will be sufficient."

Wolf Killer added, "For us, it is but half a day, if we march hard." He looked at me. "Will you wait for the summons from Sigtrygg, father?"

"No, I intend to march in the next three days."

"But Aiden may be wrong."

I smiled and spread my hands, "And when has he been wrong before? If he is wrong then my men will have a long march and some hunting in Sigtrygg's land and Aiden will have to suffer the sharp edge of my Ulfheonar's tongues. I will take Aiden with me for we may need his Dragon Fire."

None of the three jarls who sat around my table had seen Dragon Fire used. Ketil said, "Did it work?"

"The Saxon ships burned and the fire continued to burn even when it was laying on the sea. It is truly a terrible weapon. I know not how the sorcery works but I am grateful that we have the wizard with us."

"But in the end, it will come down to sword against sword."

"It will, Wolf Killer, but we also have another weapon the Saxons do not have. Our archers. I intend to use Snorri to command the archers. We will not need him to scout. Our enemy will come to us. I think that there will be such numbers that they not try to hide."

Ketil nodded, "I can see the way Aiden's mind works. King Egbert regains his jewels and vengeance for the loss of Elfrida while King Coenwulf gets back his jewel but his ally conquers the land which Northumbria and we stole from him. Until we spoke I was not certain that Aiden was right but I now believe it in my heart."

"It matters not if we are wrong. I will still take my warband south. The rest will wait until I send a rider and then you will move instantly. Use horses and ponies. I will only have half of our forces. You three will have the rest and we will need all of our men to defeat Mercia and Wessex."

Aiden had not attended the meeting as he was busy making maps for the three of them. It was important that we all met at the right place. He came in towards the end of the counsel and handed the maps out. Ketil said, "I believe your predictions, galdramenn."

Aiden looked puzzled, "And why should you not?"

Wolf Killer laughed, "Because we live in the real world and you live in the spirit world. But I, too, believe you are right." He tapped his head. "Since I have been here I feel my mother's spirit and she tells me it is so." He turned to me. "I will send my wife and family here and march directly to Sigtrygg, father. We will only have to await Ketil and Ulf. Our banners will stand together!"

Elfrida and her children arrived the day we left. Wolf Killer had sent an escort of his oathsworn. They would accompany us south. Gryffydd was disappointed that Ragnar was not there. "It is not fair, father! Ragnar goes to war and I do not! And I am his uncle!"

There was much laughter at that. Elfrida ruffled his hair, "Your time will come soon enough, Gryffydd, besides we need you to protect your baby sister and the women."

"Remember Beorn is not coming with us and he is as disappointed as you. I leave the three of your to guard my stad."

He was still not happy but he nodded, "And I will fight in the next war!"

We used all the horses and ponies that we had. Many men still had to march but we had mobility and we could take more arms. Aiden had two pack horses with his Dragon Fire. He had refined it since the fight off the isle of the Wights and was more confident about its use. I left Olaf to lead the warband and rode ahead with Haaken and Leif to speak with Sigtrygg. His stad was on a war footing. I saw many animals gathered in pens and the pens had high walls with wooden towers.

"I made these preparations when I received your warnings but I am still uncertain if they are true."

"They are," I told him the reasoning. "Even if Egbert comes by sea it is well that we gather here for we could attack him from two directions but I do not believe he will use the sea. I have Siggi and Olaf watching the waters off Ulfarrston. The two knarr are crewed by my drekar captains. We will have adequate warning."

Sigtrygg said, "Then I am satisfied. We need to choose our ground well."

"You have the high ground to the east watched?"

"Two of my best hersir are there and they are well mounted."

"Then we guard the ford of the Ēa Lōn. That is our best opportunity to hold them. Our archers can use the bluffs above the river. Send your scouts south to watch for them but they should not allow themselves to be seen." I pointed to the area behind the new animal pens. "We will camp there. I intend to send for Ketil and Ulf when we know more. There is little point in hunting your animals to death. My men will need feeding."

Sigtrygg knew the land well and he said, "If we have the men hunt south of the Ēa Lōn then it will not harm my people and it will give us warning of the Saxons."

"Good."

My war band arrived just after dark. Sigtrygg's people had prepared both food and the camp. The weather was damp and it would not be pleasant for our warriors but we had the satisfaction of knowing that our enemies would have to march in the wet and would be far more uncomfortable than we were. Wolf Killer arrived the next day and I was happier. We could now contest the ford. Our two warbands were the best trained and the best armed as well as being the two largest.

We went to the ford the next day while my Ulfheonar went hunting. The rest of our warbands made the camp more habitable, digging drainage ditches and erecting better shelters. Aiden was the one who had the ideas for making the ford more difficult for our enemies.

"They will be forced to the middle part of the ford. If we build a small dam upstream then we can burst it and make the ford deeper."

"Will they not cross where the dam is?"

"We build it well upstream and have a few men to guard it. Remember, Jarl Dragonheart, that this is the main road north to your land. Egbert does not come here to attack Sigtrygg. He comes for his jewels and for you." He turned to the bank. "We can make this bank slippery. I will have water laid in at the top. As soon as we see them we make it slick with water. They will get up the slope but they will have to fight the earth as well as our arrows. Then, at the top, we will make a barrier of bramble and willow. Once again, they will get through but it will take them some time. We need to make them bleed when they advance."

"And have you given thought to those horsemen we encountered?"

"Aye, I have. Bjorn's grandsons have been making these for three days." He took out the wicked three-pointed spikes with which we could sow our flanks.

"And Dragon Fire?"

"We save that for the shield wall. If we use it before then it will be wasted. They will use a shield wall." He turned and pointed behind him. "The land between here and the stronghold is where they will form up. I assume you will fall back to the stad?" I nodded. "Then the boys with the slings can hurl it over your heads to the shield wall."

"Well done, galdramenn. You have done your part. Now it is up to warriors to face them beard to beard."

Aiden took a party of villagers and young warriors east to make the dam. The warriors were delighted to be working with such a famous wizard. I knew that they would make a good job of it. As we headed back to his hall Sigtrygg said, "I have quarters for you, Jarl Dragonheart."

Shaking my head I said, "No Sigtrygg. I will sleep amongst my warriors and endure the same hardships that they do. This is not high summer and it will be cold. When they know their jarl suffers the same privations as they do then they will fight that bit harder."

Leif had already put up my shelter for the night. He was unpacking my mail as I reached him. He looked up at the skies and shook his head, "This damp will do nothing for the mail, Jarl."

"Coat it in seal oil and that will give it protection." Ragnar's Spirit hung from my waist. That was protected by a sheepskin scabbard which was coated in oil.

Haaken approached me. He looked bedraggled and his hair hung lankly down his head. I saw that he was losing hair now. It was a sign of our age. He shook his head, "My only consolation is that King Egbert is suffering as much as we are."

Olaf shook his head, "He may be safe in Wintan-ceastre. Perhaps it is we who are the fools."

"And a few nights in the open is a small price to pay, Olaf Leather Neck. The alternative is for us to wait until they have devastated the lands to the south of us and we are penned in Cyninges-tūn."

"You are right, Jarl. Anyone would think I was a warrior on his first raid complaining because his mother had not cooked his meal!"

Wolf Killer arrived the next day at noon. Our hunters brought in game but no news of the Saxons and we continued our preparations for war. It was Sigtrygg's people for whom I felt sympathy. They were forced to stay within his walls and to have two large warbands nearby.

A rider galloped in from the north just after the sun had set. He threw himself from his horse, "Jarl Dragonheart, I come from Siggi. He has been to the Dee and spied upon Caestir. There is a great host assembling: Mercians, the men of Wessex and some Danes."

"Did he estimate numbers?"

"No Jarl for Saxon ships chased him to sea."

"And when was this?"

"Three days since."

"Tell Siggi he has done well. Ask him to wait at the mouth of the Ēa Lōn. Watch for our signals."

I sat with Sigtrygg, Wolf Killer and Haaken. "We know he comes. The question is when?"

Sigtrygg said, "Although it is but a two day march from the Dee if he has baggage and horses to carry it then it will take up to four days. There are few roads from the south and the poor weather means he will not travel swiftly."

"Then tomorrow I send for Ketil and Ulf. We will need their men. They have Danes." The Danes were nothing more than mercenaries. They would fight for any master but they were devious. When they had served they stayed and took the land anyway. It was a worry.

Raibeart Ap Pasgen and his men arrived the next day. They were a mixture of Norse and the warriors of Úlfarrston. Although there were just thirty of them they had fought alongside us on many occasions and all were well-armed. Six had full mail byrnies and he had six archers. In times such as these every stone, we had made a larger wall. Our warriors were the wall against which the Saxons would break.

Two days later first Ketil Windarsson and then Ulf Olafsson arrived. There was still no sign of the Saxons but we knew that they were somewhere to the south of us. Aiden had built the dam and the water level at the ford was much lower. The enemy would be tempted to cross in greater numbers. Aiden would be responsible for ordering its destruction. He had young boys placed at intervals between the ford and the dam. When the Saxons were in the vicinity he would be at the dam. We gave him and his messengers good horses for we would need every man that we could muster to fight such a mighty host.

Snorri was not happy that he could not be out with the hunters and the scouts but I insisted that he organize the archers. We had over fifty of them and they were almost a third of our entire force of warriors. We had another forty farmers but I was loath to risk them in the shield wall. They would defend the walls.

It was the Ulfheonar who brought us news of the enemy. Erik and Rollo were the first ones to return, "Jarl, we have seen Saxon scouts. They are ten miles south of us."

Aiden mounted his horse, "I will go to the dam."

Over the next few hours, the rest of our hunters returned and each brought the same story. A large army was heading north. Then we had disastrous news. The warriors assigned to signal Siggi came back to tell us that four Saxon ships were in the estuary and were landing men on the northern shore.

"Jarl, there are fifty warriors. They will be landing even now."

"Do they have mail?"

"No Jarl."

"Haaken stay here with the Ulfheonar. Wolf Killer bring your warband. We will meet these before they can organize themselves."

We had rested for some days and we ran the two miles to the mouth of the estuary. I knew that landing from any ship was difficult but a Saxon ship had to land further out in the water. They would be like drowned rats when they got ashore. We had to hit them and hit them hard. Wolf Killer had forty men and half were mailed. More importantly, all were oathsworn. They were called the Wild Boars and they were ferocious fighters.

As we ran towards the coast I said, "We just hit them as hard as we can. It will take the rest of the day for Egbert and his men to get to the ford. I am guessing this landing is to catch us by surprise. They will not have anticipated that we would be waiting for them."

We saw their masts before we reached the coast. I was aware that the younger warriors were leaving me behind. I forced myself to catch them up. As we reached the headland which overlooked the sandbanks of the treacherous estuary I saw that only two ships had managed to land their men. The other two lay grounded on the mudflats some way from the shore. The tide went out very rapidly in this bay. When we were seen an alarm was raised and those that had reached the beach tried to form a shield wall. It was hard for they were covered in mud and their clothes were soaked.

"For the Dragonheart!"

Wolf Killer's cry heralded our attack and we tore into the shambolic shield wall. We had no order but we needed none for we had all fought together before. They were slow to move and we were fresher. They hurried to the firmer sand of the shore. As the spear came towards my head I easily fended it off with my shield and, pressing close, stabbed the warrior through the chest. The warrior behind did not even have time to thrust at me and I brought Ragnar's Spirit over my shoulder to hack him across the neck. We were through the flimsy shield wall and the rest ran from our ferocious attack. They ran back to their ships.

"Hold, Wolf Killer! If we go out on to the mud we, too, might get stuck."

"But we cannot leave them! They are a threat!" My son pointed his sword at the two ships which were less than forty paces from us.

"Not for long." I pointed at Siggi's knarr. Siggi knew the waters as well as his own hand and he had sailed in these channels many times. The Saxons could do nothing about him and I saw Erik and his crew with fire arrows. They might not have been the greatest of archers but they could not miss at twenty paces. They set the sails and masts alight and soon it spread to the hulls. Both of the ships which were stuck began to burn. Their crews threw themselves overboard and the thick, cloying mud dragged them down.

Siggi turned and headed out to sea again. Wolf Killer said, "Why does he leave?"

"Watch, he will block the mouth of the estuary. These ships are going nowhere." The two ships to which the survivors of our attack had fled were both stuck on the mudflats. When the tide came in Siggi and his two knarr would do the same to them.

Even as we watched we saw Saxons sinking beneath the mud and the waves. As the tide came in they began to drown. A few managed to make it to the remaining two Saxon ships but they would not trouble us. Egbert's plan had hit a problem; the river. We took Saxon weapons, shields and helmets and headed back to our camp. We reached there at dark. When we peered across the valley we saw the first Saxon fires being lit on the southern bluff above the river. Egbert and his allies had come. We had had the skirmish, next would come the battle and I was under no illusions. The next one would not be as easy.

Chapter 15

Wolf Killer shook his head, "We were lucky that they landed the way that they did, father. Had the mud not held them they were a formidable force which might have caused us trouble."

"No, Egbert planned badly. He did not scout this river. We all know that it has mud flats and shoals. Our luck was in having Siggi and an experienced crew patrolling. I know that Erik Short Toe had much to do with that victory. He knows how to win. And it is now that we have the advantage for Egbert will not know the fate of his ships. He will camp and expect his men to be creeping up for an attack on our western flank. Come the morrow he will be disappointed."

Sigtrygg joined us, "I am glad that you were here Jarl. What now?"

"We light no fires to tell the Saxons we are here. We make them wonder. They will see your stad but the land between will be bathed in darkness. One in four men will be on guard and we rotate every two hours. I want all of our men to be rested for the battle."

I went to see my Ulfheonar. "Tonight I want you to be ready to battle."

"You want us to attack the Saxons?"

"No, I want you to go half way between where we killed the Saxons and our camp. When I come we will make a noise as though we are being attacked. I want Egbert to think that his men have succeeded and attacked our right flank. In the morning he will attack this flank and we will be waiting. After we have feigned an attack we camp on this flank. We stand no guard this night but I suspect we will hear them if they try anything. We are, after all, Ulfheonar."

Wrapping ourselves in our wolf skins we lay down on the slopes of the northern bluff. We were not a large number but, if the Saxons tried a night attack, then we would be the first to know.

I said, "Ready?"

The Ulfheonar were keen to play this trick and they said, "Aye!"

I counted to three and then we began banging shields with the shafts of our spears and shouting. Haaken made some wonderful noises as he died at least ten times. I said, "Gradually quieten down as though we have all been slain!"

Inevitably it was Haaken who was the last to die and then there was silence. The grins on their faces told me that my warriors had enjoyed the trick. We lay down. As with the others, one in four would watch. I wondered what the rest of our army had made of it. We were well to the west and isolated. All that they would have heard would have been a cacophony of battle noises.

When I awoke Haaken was sitting up and looking south. "Do you hear something?"

"No Jarl, at least not here." He pointed to the east where there was a faint lightness in the sky. "But they are stirring."

"Then when I have made water we will rejoin our brothers. If they try to come now we will see them. There is no dark of night in which they can hide." As I walked down the slope I felt the breeze from the west and the smell of the smoke from the burned-out Saxon ships. I knew that when dawn broke I would see their skeletons on the mudflats. Over years they would be broken up by the sea and disappear but, for now, they were a reminder of the failure of the Saxons. It gave me hope.

I finished and returned to my men. They had awoken, disturbed, no doubt, by our earlier words. "Come let us join the rest of the army."

We headed east into the rising sun. It would be a grey day. I could see that from the thin sun which peered over the hills to the east. If the wind was from the west then that would bring rain. It always did in this part of the world. It might aid us for it would make the bank up which they had to climb even more slippery. When we reached Wolf Killer and my other jarls I saw that the water barrels had been emptied down the slope during the night.

He laughed, "That sounded a fierce battle last night but I am guessing that they did not come then, father?"

"No. Perhaps they knew their attack had failed or were waiting for a signal which never came. It does not matter we know where they will attack today. Are Aiden's messengers in place?"

"They are."

I nodded, "There will be a delay between the signal to break the dam and the water arriving. I want some of the men of Wessex on this slope before the water strikes them."

I went to find Snorri. He and his archers were close by the walls of the stad. There was a dell just below the ridge and the rest of the army was on the other side of the ridge. Snorri could not see the Saxons but, more importantly, they could not see him either. He was awake already although some of his men slept. "You are ready Snorri?"

"I am but you know I would rather stand in the shield wall with you. This feels wrong. There is no Beorn and I lead strangers."

"But we both know that you and the archers you lead can swing this battle in our favour. Egbert will be looking for archers before he launches his attack. You and your men must remain hidden until he has committed to the attack. When the attack is broken then you can join us."

"Erik Ulfsson says that he counted their fires and they have almost double our number of warriors."

"Perhaps but we have played that trick before have we not? We have lit fires and had them tended by one warrior. Besides these men have marched many leagues and are far from home. I will take these odds."

"And yet we now have less than fifteen Ulfheonar."

"True but we have Wolf Killer's Wild Boars and the oathsworn of Sigtrygg, Ketil and Ulf are doughty warriors. Asbjorn was Ulfheonar and the men he leads are well-armed. Trust in our people." He nodded. "It is Beorn who is on your mind is it not?"

"He came so close to death that I began to dream of my own. I have neither wife nor son. All that will remain of me when I am killed is a line in one of Haaken's sagas. That will soon be forgotten. I see Cnut Cnutson and see his father. Young Ragnar is evidence that Wolf Killer has lived and yet what do I have?"

"You have the chance to make that right when we return from this battle. We defeat the Saxons and you take a woman. Spend the winter making babies!"

He stared at me and I could almost see the thoughts in his eyes. Was I becoming a galdramenn? Then suddenly he smiled as a brief shaft of light from the east lit up the dragon which hung around my neck. "We will prevail, I have seen the dragon smile. When the dragon roars then we shall win!"

It was as though the scales had been removed from my own eyes. I had a sudden idea. "Thank you, Snorri!"

I raced to find my son and grandson. "Ragnar, find yourself a horse. A good horse; for today you ride!"

"I am not leaving you am I grandfather?"

"No, my young warrior. Today you carry the dragon banner. I want you to wait with it by Aiden and when he releases the river then you will ride down the valley holding the dragon banner and making it wail."

He looked puzzled but Wolf Killer knew what I intended. "And the Saxons will see the water but to them it will be a dragon, hurtling towards them."

I nodded, "And if you are on the sky line then they will see the dragon too. You must wear a helmet. Now go and I will get Leif to bring you the banner."

Leif carried both banners, my dragon and my wolf. Today we would fight under the wolf banner but it would be the dragon who would bring victory. Ragnar returned as the sky was becoming light enough to see the Saxons stirring. "Now do not open the banner until you reach Aiden. Tell him what we plan and he will tell you when to ride."

Viking Dragon

Wolf Killer reached up and clasped his son's hand. "Today you fight in your first battle, my son and it will be under the eyes of Jarl Dragonheart and his Ulfheonar. There is no greater honour!"

I saw Ragnar's eyes light up at the thought and he galloped off. If any sharp-eyed Saxon saw the young rider heading east they would think he went for reinforcements.

More confident about our plans we now rejoined our warbands. We would not be one continuous line. I was trying to deceive Egbert. I wanted him to think that there were divisions amongst my men. I knew that his Saxons would not trust each other. I wanted him to believe that we were the same. In addition, I wanted him to think we had fewer numbers than we really had. Each warband would be separate from all of the others. The largest warband was that of Wolf Killer and he had but thirty men. Mine had sixteen. We would look pathetically thin in numbers. Our success relied on a number of factors but the control my jarls had over their men would be the most crucial.

Egbert was being careful. He had fought me before. When I saw his men dismantling trips and traps by the river I could not help but smile. He had expected a night attack with my Ulfheonar. They had feared us so much that they had put cord and dug pits to catch us as we came. He would have had many sentries out at night and they would now be tired. Egbert would watch for more tricks from me. The ones we would use were Aiden's magic and he would not have seen them before. I saw him and King Coenwulf as they gathered with their eorledmen and priests on the bluffs opposite. Their priests carried their cross and the boxes containing the relics of their saints. The two kings were looking at our battle lines and seeking our strategy. I saw his horsemen. They were to the east of his main battle line. They would, no doubt, ride upstream and try to cross there. Between the main army and Aiden were a line of boys. They would signal and they would seed the banks with horse killers. The three-pointed spikes would come as a nasty surprise.

After a long discussion, five warriors descended to the ford and, with shields held before them, began to cross. They used their spears to poke the bottom of the ford for spikes and holes. They found none but they were wary. We allowed them to cross. They were less than fifty paces from Sigtrygg and his men. Suddenly the ten boy slingers who were behind the warband raced to the side and whirled their slingshots. The river stones flew at the five Saxons. One was too slow to raise his shield and he fell in the river. As he was dragged to safety by the others Sigtrygg's band cheered.

The leader of the scouts reported back to Egbert. He seemed satisfied that he had seen what he thought was our trick, slingers behind a shield wall. He turned and spoke. A horn sounded. I saw the horsemen head up the valley and a column of men began to march down towards the river. It was not a wedge. It was a block of men ten wide and fifteen ranks deep. The front and the sides were mailed men. It was more than two-thirds of his army. I waited until they had reached the river before I had Leif signal the first of the boy messengers. We had practised this. The message to release the dam would not reach Aiden until the column was just emerging from the river. I guessed that at least four of the ranks would have crossed before the water struck.

"Ketil, Ulf, forward!" Almost anticipating my order the other two warbands marched down to join Sigtrygg. They now formed one line. The thirty boy slingers who were attached to them hurled their stones. The Saxons raised their shields to protect themselves from the stone storm. None were hurt but they had to slow and they bunched up. As they stepped ashore they found that their feet had no purchase on the slippery bank. The water Aiden had poured down the hill had made it slippery. The more that men used it then the muddier and more slippery it would become. Three warriors fell when their feet slipped and stones struck those within the column. They halted while they reorganised. This caused bunching so that the river was completely filled by the column. The three ranks in the northern bank had to move before the column could continue its progress.

In the distance, we heard the wailing begin. My men had all heard it but not the Saxons and the Danes. I looked across the river and saw the consternation amongst the Saxons. What did this portend? There was a ripple in the column as the Saxons looked upstream to discern the cause of the strange and eerie noise. The clatter of stones on the shields suddenly sounded like an ominous drumbeat and still, the wail came closer as Ragnar galloped down the valley. I trusted my grandson. He would be keeping pace with the wall of water which was hurtling down the river. Sigtrygg would not need any more orders. As soon as the water struck he knew what he had to do.

I looked to the left and saw Ragnar approaching, the banner held high. As I glanced to the river I saw the wall of water. It was almost as high as a man. Turning back I saw Ragnar pull back in the reins and rear his horse. He spun the horse around in a circle to maintain the wail and then Sigtrygg launched his attack at the three ranks who had made the northern bank of the river. The eyes of the column were upstream and not on the spears of Sigtrygg, Ketil and Ulf. The water and the spears struck together. The power of the water took me by surprise. It swept those in the river from their feet. I saw some struggling a hundred and fifty paces downstream, towards the sea. Many disappeared beneath the wave never to reappear. Their armour and shields dragged them to the bottom. The slingers moved closer to hurl stones at the now bare heads of warriors who tried to swim to safety. The front three ranks were slain to a man as three warbands stabbed, hacked and hewed at warriors who had no idea just what was going on. This was not war this was magic. The Saxon horn sounded and those that could made their way back.

Just then I heard a shout from Wolf Killer and saw his warband swing to face north. It was the horsemen. They had crossed the river. The horse killers had thinned their number but twenty of them rode at the Wild Boars. I had placed our strongest warband there for just such a purpose. My Ulfheonar also turned but there was no urgency. I trusted my son and he would hold these horsemen. If they thought to intimidate us they were wrong. The wall of shields never wavered. The horsemen flowed around the shield wall and their horses had to suffer spears and axes as well as the stones from ten slingers.

Their leader survived. He and five others saw Ragnar, still whirling around on his horse and making the dragon wail. Although he was two hundred paces away they charged towards him. The Saxon leader was trying to leave with some glory. The dragon banner would make a fine trophy. Neither Wolf Killer nor my men could reach the horsemen. My grandson saw the danger and he galloped towards the stad. The Saxon riders tried to cut him off. It was a race. Ragnar had chosen a good horse but the Saxons were superb horsemen. I saw their leader as he raised his spear. He pulled his arm back when he was twenty paces from Ragnar. Suddenly a line of archers rose from the undergrowth and forty arrows knocked the six horses and riders to the ground. I saw Snorri raise his bow. My grandson was safe!

I turned my attention back to Egbert. The attack of the horsemen had been hidden from the Saxons by a fold in the ground. He would not know the fate of his horsemen nor the presence of my archers. He had lost a good thirty men in his attack. Many others, perhaps fifty or so, were so far downstream that, by the time they rejoined the army they would be exhausted. The river at the ford was gradually returning to its normal level. My men had stripped the bodies of those they had slain and left them as a barrier to the next attack.

"Leif, signal the warbands to fall back."

My three warbands made their way back slowly up the slope. It was slippery with water and they placed their feet carefully. They filled in the space between the Wild Boars and the Ulfheonar. We locked shields. I saw many of those in the front ranks make water. It made the ground even more slippery and it was always better to fight with an empty bladder.

It took some time for Saxons to decide on their next course of action. They were used to fighting Vikings who hurled themselves at their shield wall. We were not obliging them. The forty Danes they had formed the front four ranks of the next column. Behind them came the men of Mercia and finally the Wessex warriors who had reformed. There were about a hundred and twenty warriors. As they moved towards the slope I saw that they were gathering the ragged remains of their army to exploit the success of their attack. When the hundred and twenty punched a hole in our lines then the last forty of their reserve would join in.

As they moved ponderously towards the river Aiden and his boys rode up. "It worked then?"

"It did and Ragnar did well with the Dragon Banner. When you reach the stad then send him back to me."

"I will, Jarl Dragonheart."

Wolf Killer asked, "Are you not finished with him?"

"We know that the rush of water was made by the dam. The Saxons do not. If you were a Saxon and you heard the wail of the dragon coming down the valley again then what would you think?"

"That the river was flooding again. That might work but what if there are Saxons up the valley?"

I pointed to Aiden's messengers. "You boys, find a weapon. You will guard the bearer of the banner!"

When Ragnar returned he looked excited. His father said, "You did well Ragnar. Jarl Dragonheart has another task for you."

"Furl the banner. We will be attacked again soon. I want you to ride, when I tell you, to the dam and then unfurl the banner and ride down the valley once more. These boys will be your protectors."

"I need no protectors, Jarl!"

"Nonetheless you shall have them. The Dragon demands an escort at the very least." He nodded. "Now wait on the other side of the hill so that the Saxons cannot see you. Wait with Snorri. When you see the banner raised and lowered three times then ride to the dam."

Snorri and the archers could see my wolf banner which Leif held. We waited. "Slingers advance."

The boys with the slingshots moved from behind us. They knew how slippery the grass was and they moved cautiously. The Danes marched from the ford and started to ascend the slope. They knew now of the dangers and they were more cautious. The slingers hurled their stones and soon the shields came up to protect the warriors. It sounded like hailstones as they clattered off shields and helmets. Inevitably warriors slipped and, as they did so, the slingers found flesh. A well-thrown stone could kill or render unconscious a careless warrior. Four Danes fell. They were not dead but they were no longer in the column. Some of the Danes became angry at the incessant rain of stones and they made the mistake of running towards the boys to rid themselves of the irritation. They slipped and the steepness of the slope caused some to slide back down, disrupting their ranks. The boys took advantage of the chaos, hurled their stones even faster and more warriors fell.

    The Jarl who led them was a huge warrior with a winged helmet, axe and a skull on his helmet. He roared. "Shields! Form ranks! Wait until Erik Skull Splitter gives you the order to move!"

    The effect was instantaneous. The Danes halted. The boys managed to hit another eight warriors. Some would have broken limbs but the Danes formed up again. They now had three ranks of seven. As they moved forward I realised that the slingers were in danger. "Slingers! Retire behind the shield wall!"

    They moved around the side and formed up behind us. They all had plenty of stones. The river bed had been full of them and they had chosen wisely. They were only boys but they knew the shape of the stone they needed. Without the boys in front of them, the Danes moved steadily up the slope. We were standing on dry ground and we had taken a flat piece of the hill where we had solid footing. The Danes would be advancing up the slippery part of the slope.

    "You know what to do, Sigtrygg."

    "Aye Jarl!"

    Sigtrygg's men had a wall of double shields. I shouted, "Ketil, Ulf, now!"

    The two warbands moved quickly to form up behind Sigtrygg so that there were six ranks. They would match the advancing Danes. As the Danes neared the top of the hill Sigtrygg shouted, "Charge!"

    They took three paces on the dry ground and struck the Danes as they crested the rise. Their spears were at eye level. I saw Erik Skull Splitter as Sigtrygg's spear was rammed through his mouth. It was such a powerful blow that it knocked the helmet from the Dane in the second rank. The Danes lost their footing and fell to the floor as the weight of three warbands hit them. King Egbert had made a mistake. He played into our hands by using a narrow frontage. He should have employed a long line and outflanked us.

    I yelled, "Ulfheonar!" and attacked the left side of the Danish line as Wolf Killer led his Wild Boars against the right side. The Mercians who were following were bowled over by the falling bodies of the Danes. The men we slew lay on the ground wounded or were knocked from their feet. They were slain as they lay below us. I saw King Egbert as he ordered his reserves and I shouted, "Leif, signal Ragnar!"

The banner was raised and lowered three times. "Fall back!" I did not want to risk my men slipping on the slick slope. The water had been augmented by blood and guts. It would be treacherous underfoot.

As we retook our original positions I saw that we had lost warriors too but the Danes had been finished. There were not enough of them to mount a serious opposition. The Mercians too had been disrupted. However, someone had realised our weakness. They began to form a long line. When the reserves joined the line then they would be able to overlap our short frontage and the slaughter would begin. I watched as the priests and the Saxon kings joined their men. King Egbert had seen our weakness. He still outnumbered us and he thought he had seen through our strategy.

As his men reached the river and began to cross we all heard a wailing in the distance. "Slingers, advance!"

As the Mercians and men of Wessex looked east and those in the river began to look fearfully for the wall of water, the slingers threw more of their deadly missiles. The enemy lost another six warriors before they regained their composure. I saw that some of the reserve had fled up the hill on the other side of the valley. They had had enough. As the dragon banner drew close I could hear the priests as they chanted their prayers to the White Christ. It seemed to halt the flight of those who were afraid and the reserves crossed the river. My ploy had not worked as well as I had hoped but there were at least twelve warriors who would not fight for they had fled. The priests might have convinced their men that it was their prayers which had saved them but I knew differently.

"Slingers, withdraw!"

The boys ran quickly to shelter behind our shield wall. This time the Saxons were well aware of the slippery nature of the slope and they moved cautiously. They used their spears as walking sticks to offer themselves support. As they ascended the slope I shouted, "Listen for my orders! Every man obeys instantly!"

They all shouted, as one, "Aye Jarl Dragonheart!"

The shout was so loud that I saw the advancing Saxons slow as though they feared we would charge them. We each held a spear and we were in two ranks. The front rank of the Mercians had their mailed warriors spread out. I guessed that the ones in mail were the Gesith with their oathsworn. The line would overlap ours by twenty warriors on each side. The two flanks of our line were held by the two best warbands we had. I had to hope we would hold.

When they slowly reached the top and were just five paces from us I yelled, "Charge!"

We did not run but walked purposefully. It was but five strides. However, we hit them with two solid lines of warriors. I thrust my spear into the chest of a warrior who was standing next to the Gesith. Haaken stabbed at the mailed Gesith. My spear struck him in the chest and I felt the head of my spear sink into flesh. His arms splayed wide as he fell back. The Gesith was punched by Haaken's spear and he too took a step back. I withdrew my spear and punched at the next Mercian. He had not quite made the firmer, drier ground. My spear hit him in the cheek and tore out through the back of his skull. Two spears jabbed out from behind me and two more warriors were knocked to the ground.

I lifted my shield and yelled, "Push!" While punching with my spear I joined Olaf and Haaken to push hard with our shields and hit the struggling Mercians.

It would have been easy to get carried away and push them down the hill but that would have been a mistake. We would have slipped and we were in danger of being outflanked. Leif, in the second rank, shouted, "'Ware right!"

That was the signal to withdraw. He had seen enemies outflanking us. "Fall back! Fall back!"

We each punched at the enemy and then began to walk backwards. It was Haaken to my right and Rolf behind him who would have the most difficulty for they had Mercians attacking them. Rolf and Haaken threw their spears as they took long steps back. I threw my spear too and took a long step. We were echeloning back with Sigtrygg and his men as the point of our arrow. We had five hundred paces to march before we dropped below the dell. There Snorri held a surprise for the Saxons.

I drew Ragnar's Spirit. The spears had bought us time and three men lay writhing with the spears we had thrown. The slingers, behind us, continued to hurl stones at the Saxons. They could not run for fear of tripping over the wounded and dying front rank. We continued to move as quickly as was prudent. Some of the Mercians chose glory and they ran at us individually. It was brave but foolish. I blocked the axe of one Mercian on my shield and rammed my sword into the warrior's gut. Haaken and Olaf, protecting my sides, did the same. Leif used the wolf banner as a spear to gouge into the eyes of any warrior who came too close to me.

As soon as we started to drop down the slope to the dell before the stad I began to shout out orders. "Steady and lock shields!"

While still walking backwards we half turned so that every shield was locked with its neighbour. The front rank had no spears. We would have to rely on our comrades in the second rank. The Saxons stopped on the ridgeline. Once again there was someone giving orders. I saw the men of

Wessex form the front rank and they too tightened shields. The delay enabled us to walk back to the archers and the ditch which surrounded the stad. As the Saxons began to move forward I heard Snorri snap out the order, "Release!"

Fifty arrows soared high into the air followed a heartbeat later by another fifty and then another. A hundred and fifty arrows falling on unsuspecting warriors can be devastating. Those with quick reactions were able to protect themselves with their shields. Those with mail had some additional protection but thirty odd warriors fell. Some killed and some wounded. The gaps created meant that another ten fell with the next flight and then they locked shields to protect them from all sides. We were in the position I wished us to be. We were anchored to the two sides of the stad. The slingers were now in the two towers while Aidan and his specially selected slingers were on the gatehouse.

I saw that the field had some of our own warriors lying upon it. They had lost more men but then they could afford to. Any loss for us was most grievous. The Saxons gathered themselves for their next attack. I knew when King Egbert had arrived for there was the sound of a horn and the Saxons formed a boar's head. It was a double wedge and the points would strike at Ketil and Ulf's men. Egbert had realised that the flanks held our best warriors. We had to hold them until Aiden and his men could use Dragon Fire.

As the Saxon line began to advance I heard, in the distance, the wailing of the dragon. I did not expect it and neither did the Saxons. They hesitated and it cost three men their lives as Snorri and his best archers targeted them. My grandson had taken it upon himself to inspire fear in the enemy. Wolf Killer's son was a true warrior. Then the Saxons hit us. They had many more men than we did and we felt the weight. Before the shields collided their spears darted out. They did not hurt us for we had large shields and mail beneath. I suspected that Ketil and Ulf's men would suffer more. We were being pushed back by sheer weight of numbers.

The spears in our second rank duelled with the Saxon spears. I held my blade low and waited for my chance. I began to bring it up. As the shield of the warrior facing me began to rise I pushed my sword and shield up at the same time. The warrior could not stop his shield from rising. The tip of my sword touched something and I pushed hard. It was the warrior's flesh. I punched up and my sword's tip appeared from his shoulder. I tore it out and he fell. The pressure lessened and, as his face slid down my shield, I punched with the boss at the man behind. It caught him square on and he reeled. We were not having it all our own way and I felt a spearhead slide down the side of my helmet. The warrior who held it roared his delight until Rolf brought his axe over and took his head.

We now had a straight line. Sigtrygg was no longer the point and, in places, the line was one warrior deep. The archers were also scoring more hits than misses. It was at that moment that Aiden launched his Dragon Fire. It coincided, or perhaps he had planned it that way, with Ragnar and his Dragon Banner. They approached, this time from the west. I saw the flaming pots of death rise high above us. Aiden was taking no chances and he was aiming at the press of men at the rear of the huge wall of Saxons. The flames flashed and ripped through the rear ranks. We felt the wave of heat as it surged forward. I had never been as close and it was terrifying. It must have worried Aiden for there was no second shower.

"Fall back!"

We stepped back as one. The bodies of our slain lay before us but there were more bodies of the Saxons. I could see shields on fire and three unlucky warriors were like human candles.

"Lock shields!"

As we locked shields Aiden's slingers sent over their second wave of Dragon Fire. We saw it as it struck. Shields caught fire and were thrown away. Snorri and his archers used the opportunity to slay the ones who did so. I think Aiden and his throwers only hurled ten or twelve of the weapons but they broke the back of the Saxon attack. As the archers thinned out those who still stood we heard the horn sound and the Saxons fell back. Had we had more men we could have pursued them but we had lost warriors and I would not risk it.

"We hold what we have!"

As the Saxons fell back those in the stad and the army began chanting, "Dragonheart! Dragonheart! Dragonheart!"

We had not yet won but I could not see how Egbert could defeat us. Unless he had a vast army waiting to reinforce him he would struggle to take the stad. "Have the enemy bodies stripped of armour and weapons and then make a pyre of them on the banks of the river. Make sure the Saxons can see them."

"Aye Jarl."

"Snorri, take your archers and make sure that the Saxons cannot interfere."

"Aye Jarl."

"Aiden, see to our wounded."

I took off my helmet. I saw that all of my jarls were still alive. They were bloodied but alive. Ragnar rode up. His horse was lathered and close to exhaustion. "Well done, my grandson and bearer of the Dragon Banner. You had best dismount and let your mount rest."

He slid from its back and his father grabbed him and hugged him, "Well done, my son! You are a hero!"

"I felt scared when those horsemen chased me but I knew that Snorri and his archers would save me."

Wolf Killer smiled, "Then I owe Snorri an honour. I will order a fine quiver for him. It shall have a dragon on it."

I walked with Haaken and my jarls to view the Saxon position. "Things went better than we might have hoped, Jarl Dragonheart."

"They did, Ulf Olafsson, and we were fortunate that they tried to batter us with that huge column. Had they tried a long line first they would have found that it was only the centre which was slippery."

"What will he do now, father? You have fought him before."

I pointed to the bluff opposite. There was a heated debate going on. "I think that there is some disagreement over their plans. I am guessing that they are blaming each other. Coenwulf and Egbert were always going to be strange bedfellows. I think they will not attack again tonight and then we shall see what the morrow brings."

The Saxons did not bother to try to disrupt the funeral pyre. The bodies sizzled and hissed by the water. I had chosen that as the site for the fire deliberately. If they attacked the following day they would have to pass the ashes of their dead and it would be a clear reminder of how many men they had lost. Once the bodies were well alight we headed back to our camp. We had not eaten all day and we were hungry. Sigtrygg's alewives had brewed fresh beer. It was what our warriors needed.

I had not lost any Ulfheonar but all of my jarls had lost warriors who would be irreplaceable. I made sure that the armour and weapons we had captured was shared out evenly. It was small enough compensation but it was all that we could do.

I slept well that night. We had held the armies of Wessex and Mercia. That in itself was a cause for celebration but we had done so while keeping my land safe. They had taken none of our soil, not one grain! We made sure that we were up before dawn. I expected King Egbert to try a sneak attack. As the sun rose the Saxons remained in their camp. Our sentries reported much shouting from their camp and the clash of weapons. It seems that discord was still in the air.

We had our weapons sharpened and we even had enough time to have our armour oiled. We had more barrels of water prepared to make their ascent of the hill as difficult as the day before. By noon it was obvious that there would be no attack. We knew that when we saw a peace emissary make his way to us. They sent a priest across the river to conduct negotiations. I wondered if they thought that we would show respect to his robes. We allowed him to approach. As he passed the still smoking funeral pyre he made the sign of the cross. He struggled up the hill which was now black with dried blood. When he reached us I could see that he was out of breath.

He attempted to speak to us in our language but he was not fluent. I stopped him. "I speak Saxon as do most of my jarls. Speak your own language so that there is no mistake over the words used."

He nodded, "Thank you Jarl. I struggle with your language." He readied himself and then launched into his speech. "King Egbert and King Coenwulf have had enough of fighting and they wish to have a truce so that we can discuss peace."

I nodded, "As it is King Egbert and King Coenwulf who attacked us then why do they just not leave?"

He looked at me sharply, "They wish to speak with you about... perhaps if you would agree to meet at the river?"

"And what assurances do I have that there will be no treachery?"

"I will stay here as a hostage!"

I burst out laughing. "You think I value your life priest? I care not if you live or die. Tell your kings that I will meet with them. I would have a priest there too. No other warrior is to be closer than two hundred paces. I will bring my galdramenn and two jarls. Four on each side should be sufficient."

He nodded and scurried down the hill; grateful no doubt to be alive. "Do you trust them?"

"Not really, Haaken, but I will have Snorri two hundred paces from me. With his bow, he can hit a target three hundred paces away. I will be safe. Wolf Killer and Sigtrygg, you come with me." I turned to Ragnar. "You stay here with my Dragon Banner. Leif will be by your side. Make sure the Saxons see your banners eh?"

"Yes, grandfather."

"Good boy!" I waved Snorri over and told him what to do. He nodded. He would not miss.

We did not wear our helmets as we descended. We were going to talk. We reached the river before they did and we waited at the ford. The fourth member of their delegation was a Dane. He had his arm in a sling. He had been wounded in the attack and as he neared us I saw that his beard was singed. He had suffered Dragon's Fire.

I waited. King Egbert glared at Wolf Killer. There was little love lost there but Wolf Killer kept an impassive face. Anger was pointless at such times. King Coenwulf looked older. His helmet had hidden his features.

It was many years since I had fought against him for King Egbert and now he was an old man. He looked unwell. I did not think he was long for this world.

Eventually, King Egbert was forced to speak; if only to break the silence. "You raided my lands and stole a box of jewels from Radipole!"

I smiled, "We are Vikings it is what we do." I paused, "But I left the Lady Maud alive. Surely you, of all people, should be grateful for that."

He coloured, "If you had touched a hair of her head..."

"What? You would have brought an army here to my land to punish me?" I pointed to the pile of smouldering ash. "We see how that turned out. What is it that you want? Speak or let us get back to fighting. My men have not killed enough Saxons or Danes yet!"

The Dane pointed his good hand at me. "I am Thorir the Troll Burster. You killed Erik Skull Splitter. He was a formidable warrior. You seem to make a point of killing Danes. Halfdan the Black was a good friend of mine."

"And now he and his brothers are dead. Perhaps you Danes will think twice before you risk my wrath. Stick to fighting Saxons, Dane. You and your men will live longer." He thought to say something but realised that most of his men were dead. "And you, King Coenwulf, you have said little. What made you ally with a snake-like Egbert? He cannot even lie straight in bed!"

"You go too far, Dragonheart!" King Egbert was not used to such insolence.

"This is my land and I go as far as I like. I answer to no king! You do not like my words? Then go and let us fight some more."

King Coenwulf coughed and a little blood came from his mouth, "I will speak, Dragonheart. You are a fierce opponent but a man can talk to you. I will speak plain and simple words to you. You have, in your possession, a red jewel. The jewel was taken from me." He glared at Egbert. "I am close to death and I would have it returned before I die."

"And you can have it."

Only Aiden was not surprised by my statement. "Truly?"

"Yes, truly."

"And what is the price?"

I turned to the priest who was watching it all with interest. "You, go and fetch a holy book or one of your relics; the most important you have with you." I turned to Aiden, "Fetch the chest."

Sigtrygg and Wolf Killer knew me well enough to stay silent but King Egbert was suspicious. "And what of my crowns? Do they get returned as easily?"

"Firstly, you have not heard the prices yet and secondly only one is your property. The other two belong to Kent and Essex. I see neither of those kings before me."

Wolf Killer smiled. He began to see the direction in which I was going. Aiden reached us first. He was younger and we had placed the chest close by the Ulfheonar. The priest was older and slower. When he returned, he had a small box in one hand and a large book under the other. He was out of breath and could barely speak.

I held up my hand, "Take your time." Aiden opened the box and I took out the red stone. "Is this the stone?" He nodded, "Then swear on," I pointed to the box, "what is in there?"

"The finger bone of St. Oswald."

"As he was killed by your ancestor, I do not think that you will swear on that. " I pointed to the book, "Swear on your Holy Book that neither you nor your successor will ever make war on my people again."

"That is all that you want?"

"It is."

He put his hand on the book. "I swear that neither I nor my successor will make war on Jarl Dragonheart and the land of the wolf."

I handed the jewel over and said quietly, "Choose your allies more wisely next time, King Coenwulf."

King Egbert said, "And I suppose you want me to swear the same thing?"

"Not quite. You may have the crown in exchange for an oath not to make war on my land and you will grant us trading rights with Lundenwic. My knarr and those of my allies will be welcome in your burgh."

"That is preposterous!"

"Then these talks are over." I turned and Aiden closed the lid on the chest.

"Wait! What of the other crowns?"

"Those are for sale. Do you wish to buy them?"

I had him beaten, I could see that. He was desperately looking for a way out which would save him face. There was no way out and his shoulders sagged, "Very well; I agree."

"A hand on the chest and another on the holy book." He flashed a look of pure hatred but he did as I asked. "Now swear."

"I swear that I will not make war on Jarl Dragonheart and the land of the wolf. I also swear that he and his allies have trading rights in Lundenwic." I handed him the crown. "And the others?"

"Have you fifty golden pieces for each one with you?"

He shook his head, "We came to make war and not to barter!"

"Then I suggest you come to barter next time for you are no General. Send a ship to Ulfarrston with the ransom and the crowns will be there."

He said as he turned, "Then our business here is concluded."

The Dane asked, "I am curious. How did you make the river flood, the dragon roar and dragon fire?"

Aiden said, "Did you not know? Jarl Dragonheart is the Viking Dragon and we have the power of the dragon protecting our land. Remember that and fear its power."

Epilogue

Seven days later as we marched north to Úlfarrston and then Cyninges-tūn, my men were still full of the victory. Haaken, however, asked, "Why did you not ask for King Egbert's successors to agree not to attack?"

"King Coenwulf will not live another year. I could see it in his eyes. King Egbert will keep his word but it will only last a year or two. His hatred for me and for Wolf Killer will fester. He will remember the humiliation. King Coenwulf's successor will be told of the dangers of attacking us. Egbert is Mercia's enemy and not us. It was why I could afford to be generous."

"And have we made an enemy of the Danes again?"

I shook my head, "You saw the Dane's reaction to the Dragon Fire. He did not understand it or the flooding river. He will be our greatest ally for he will return to his land and tell all of the magic of the land of the Wolf. We will be safe. This winter we can hunt wolves and, perhaps, next year we can raid but someday the men of Wessex will remember us. When that day comes we will be ready."

The End

Glossary

Afon Hafron- River Severn in Welsh
Alpín mac Echdach – the father of Kenneth MacAlpin, reputedly the first king of the Scots
Alt Clut- Dumbarton Castle on the Clyde
Balley Chashtal -Castleton (Isle of Man)
Bardanes Tourkos- Rebel Byzantine General
Bebbanburgh- Bamburgh Castle, Northumbria Also known as Din Guardi in the ancient tongue
Beck- a stream
Belesduna - Basildon
Blót – a blood sacrifice made by a jarl
Blue Sea- The Mediterranean
Bondi- Viking farmers who fight
Bourde- Bordeaux
Bjarnarøy –Great Bernera (Bear Island)
Byrnie- a mail or leather shirt reaching down to the knees
Caerlleon- Welsh for Chester
Caestir - Chester (old English)
Casnewydd –Newport, Wales
Cephas- Greek for Simon Peter (St. Peter)
Chape- the tip of a scabbard
Charlemagne- Holy Roman Emperor at the end of the 8th and beginning of the 9th centuries
Celchyth - Chelsea
Cherestanc- Garstang (Lancashire)
Corn Walum or Om Walum- Cornwall
Cymri- Welsh
Cymru- Wales
Cyninges-tūn – Coniston. It means the estate of the king (Cumbria)
Dùn Èideann –Edinburgh (Gaelic)
Din Guardi- Bamburgh castle
Drekar- a Dragon ship (a Viking warship)
Duboglassio –Douglas, Isle of Man
Dun Holme- Durham
Dyrøy –Jura (Inner Hebrides)
Dyflin- Old Norse for Dublin
Ēa Lōn - River Lune
Ein-mánuðr - middle of March to the middle of April
Eoforwic- Saxon for York

Faro Bregancio- Corunna (Spain)
Ferneberga -Farnborough (Hampshire)
Fey- having second sight
Firkin- a barrel containing eight gallons (usually beer)
Fret-a sea mist
Frankia- France and part of Germany
Fyrd-the Saxon levy
Garth- Dragon Heart
Gaill- Irish for foreigners
Galdramenn- wizard
Gesith- A Saxon nobleman. After 850 AD they were known as thegns
Glaesum –amber
Gleawecastre- Gloucester
Gói- the end of February to the middle of March
Grendel- the monster slain by Beowulf
Grenewic- Greenwich
Gulle - Goole (Humberside)
Hamwic -Southampton
Haughs- small hills in Norse (As in Tarn Hows)
Heels- when a ship leans to one side under the pressure of the wind
Hel - Queen of Niflheim, the Norse underworld.
Here Wic- Harwich
Hersir- a Viking landowner and minor noble. Ranks below a jarl
Hetaereiarch – Byzantine general
Hí- Iona (Gaelic)
Hjáp - Shap- Cumbria (Norse for stone circle)
Hoggs or Hogging- when the pressure of the wind causes the stern or the bow to droop
Hrams-a – Ramsey, Isle of Man
Hywel ap Rhodri Molwynog- King of Gwynedd 814-825
Icaunis- a British river god
Itouna- River Eden Cumbria
Jarl- Norse earl or lord
Joro-goddess of the earth
kjerringa - Old Woman- the solid block in which the mast rested
Knarr- a merchant ship or a coastal vessel
Kyrtle-woven top
Lambehitha- Lambeth
Leathes Water- Thirlmere
Ljoðhús- Lewis
Legacaestir- Anglo-Saxon for Chester

Lochlannach – Irish for Northerners (Vikings)
Lothuwistoft- Lowestoft
Louis the Pious- King of the Franks and son of Charlemagne
Lundenburgh- the fort in the heart of London (the former Roman fort)
Lundenwic - London
Maeresea- River Mersey
Mammceaster- Manchester
Manau/Mann – The Isle of Man(n) (Saxon)
Marcia Hispanic- Spanish Marches (the land around Barcelona)
Mast fish- two large racks on a ship designed to store the mast when not required
Melita- Malta
Midden- a place where they dumped human waste
Miklagård - Constantinople
Nikephoros- Emperor of Byzantium 802-811
Njoror- God of the sea
Nithing- A man without honour (Saxon)
Odin - The "All Father" God of war, also associated with wisdom, poetry, and magic (The Ruler of the gods).
Olissipo- Lisbon
Orkneyjar-Orkney
Penrhudd – Penrith Cumbria
Portesmūða -Portsmouth
Pillars of Hercules- Straits of Gibraltar
Ran- Goddess of the sea
Roof rock- slate
Rinaz –The Rhine
Sabrina- Latin and Celtic for the River Severn. Also the name of a female Celtic deity
Saami- the people who live in what is now Northern Norway/Sweden
St. Cybi- Holyhead
Scree- loose rocks in a glacial valley
Seax – short sword
Sheerstrake- the uppermost strake in the hull
Sheet- a rope fastened to the lower corner of a sail
Shroud- a rope from the masthead to the hull amidships
Skeggox – an axe with a shorter beard on one side of the blade
South Folk- Suffolk
Stad- Norse settlement
Stays- ropes running from the mast-head to the bow

Strake- the wood on the side of a drekar
Suthriganaworc - Southwark (London)
Syllingar Insula, Syllingar- Scilly Isles
Tarn- small lake (Norse)
Temese- River Thames (also called the Tamese)
The Norns- The three sisters who weave webs of intrigue for men
Tilaburg - Tilbury
Thing-Norse for a parliament or a debate (Tynwald)
Thor's Day- Thursday
Threttanessa- a drekar with 13 oars on each side.
Thrall- slave
Tinea- Tyne
Trenail- a round wooden peg used to secure strakes
Tynwald- the Parliament on the Isle of Man
Úlfarrberg- Helvellyn
Úlfarrland- Cumbria
Úlfarr- Wolf Warrior
Úlfarrston- Ulverston
Ullr-Norse God of Hunting
Ulfheonar-an elite Norse warrior who wore a wolf skin over his armour
Vectis- The Isle of Wight
Volva- a witch or healing woman in Norse culture
Waeclinga Straet- Watling Street (A5) Windlesore-Windsor
Waite- a Viking word for farm
Werham -Wareham (Dorset)
Wintan-ceastre -Winchester
Withy- the mechanism connecting the steering board to the ship
Woden's day- Wednesday
Wulfhere-Old English for Wolf Army
Wyddfa-Snowdon
Wyrd- Fate
Yard- a timber from which the sail is suspended
Ynys Enlli- Bardsey Island
Ynys Môn-Anglesey

Maps

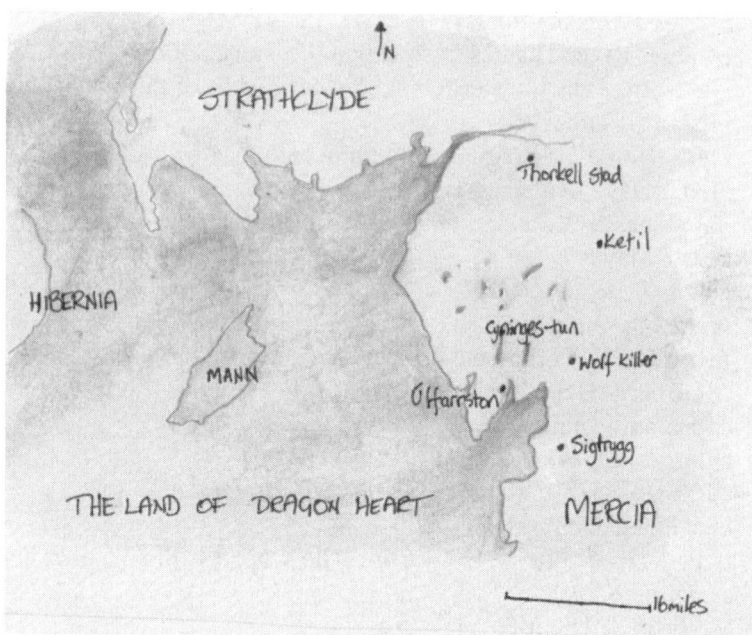

Historical note

The Viking raids began, according to records left by the monks, in the 790s when Lindisfarne was pillaged. However, there were many small settlements along the east coast and most were undefended. I have chosen a fictitious village on the Tees as the home of Garth who is enslaved and then, when he gains his freedom, becomes Dragon Heart. As buildings were all made of wood then any evidence of their existence would have rotted long ago, save for a few post holes. The Norse began to raid well before 790. There was a rise in the populations of Norway and Denmark and Britain was not well prepared for defence against such random attacks.

My raiders represent the Norse warriors who wanted the plunder of the soft Saxon kingdom. There is a myth that the Vikings raided in large numbers but this is not so. It was only in the tenth and eleventh centuries that the numbers grew. They also did not have allegiances to kings. The Norse settlements were often isolated family groups. The term Viking was not used in what we now term the Viking Age beyond the lands of Norway and Denmark. Warriors went a-Viking which meant that they sailed for adventure or pirating. Their lives were hard. Slavery was commonplace. The Norse for slave is thrall and I have used both terms.

There were many Viking raids on London in the ninth century. They increased dramatically after 825. Dragonheart's raid is the first. 842 and 851 saw the largest raids. One was reputed to have 350 drekar! It was in the ninth century when the Danes finally conquered what is now East Anglia, Essex and, of course, Northumbria. They were not uniquely Danes. Some were Norse from Norway while others were the Rus or Swedes. However, Denmark and the lands of the Low Countries were the closest and they had the majority of the raiders. Rising sea levels at this time meant that much of their own lands were becoming submerged. The warriors came first; made homes and then brought their families.

I used the following books for research

British Museum - 'Vikings- Life and Legends'
'Saxon, Norman and Viking' by Terence Wise (Osprey)
Ian Heath - 'The Vikings'. (Osprey)
Ian Heath- 'Byzantine Armies 668-1118 (Osprey)
David Nicholle- 'Romano-Byzantine Armies 4th-9th Century (Osprey)
Stephen Turnbull- 'The Walls of Constantinople AD 324-1453' (Osprey)

Keith Durham- 'Viking Longship' (Osprey)
Anglo-Danish Project- 'The Vikings in England'
Anglo Saxon Thegn AD 449-1066- Mark Harrison (Osprey)
Viking Hersir- 793-1066 AD - Mark Harrison (Osprey)
Hadrian's Wall- David Breeze (English Heritage)

Griff Hosker February 2016

Other books by Griff Hosker

If you enjoyed reading this book, then why not read another one by the author?

Ancient History

The Sword of Cartimandua Series
(Germania and Britannia 50 A.D. – 128 A.D.)
Ulpius Felix- Roman Warrior (prequel)
The Sword of Cartimandua
The Horse Warriors
Invasion Caledonia
Roman Retreat
Revolt of the Red Witch
Druid's Gold
Trajan's Hunters
The Last Frontier
Hero of Rome
Roman Hawk
Roman Treachery
Roman Wall
Roman Courage

The Wolf Warrior series
(Britain in the late 6th Century)
Saxon Dawn
Saxon Revenge
Saxon England
Saxon Blood
Saxon Slayer
Saxon Slaughter
Saxon Bane
Saxon Fall: Rise of the Warlord
Saxon Throne
Saxon Sword

Medieval History

The Dragon Heart Series
Viking Slave *
Viking Warrior *
Viking Jarl *
Viking Kingdom *
Viking Wolf *
Viking War
Viking Sword
Viking Wrath
Viking Raid
Viking Legend
Viking Vengeance
Viking Dragon
Viking Treasure
Viking Enemy
Viking Witch
Viking Blood
Viking Weregeld
Viking Storm
Viking Warband
Viking Shadow
Viking Legacy
Viking Clan
Viking Bravery

The Norman Genesis Series
Hrolf the Viking *
Horseman *
The Battle for a Home *
Revenge of the Franks *
The Land of the Northmen
Ragnvald Hrolfsson
Brothers in Blood
Lord of Rouen
Drekar in the Seine
Duke of Normandy

Viking Dragon

The Duke and the King

Danelaw
(England and Denmark in the 11th Century)
Dragon Sword *
Oathsword *
Bloodsword *
Danish Sword
The Sword of Cnut

New World Series
Blood on the Blade *
Across the Seas *
The Savage Wilderness *
The Bear and the Wolf *
Erik The Navigator *
Erik's Clan *
The Last Viking

The Vengeance Trail *

The Conquest Series
(Normandy and England 1050-1100)
Hastings
Conquest

The Aelfraed Series
(Britain and Byzantium 1050 A.D. - 1085 A.D.)
Housecarl *
Outlaw *
Varangian *

The Reconquista Chronicles
Castilian Knight *
El Campeador *
The Lord of Valencia *

The Anarchy Series England 1120-1180

Viking Dragon

English Knight *
Knight of the Empress *
Northern Knight *
Baron of the North *
Earl *
King Henry's Champion *
The King is Dead *
Warlord of the North
Enemy at the Gate
The Fallen Crown
Warlord's War
Kingmaker
Henry II
Crusader
The Welsh Marches
Irish War
Poisonous Plots
The Princes' Revolt
Earl Marshal
The Perfect Knight

**Border Knight
1182-1300**
Sword for Hire *
Return of the Knight *
Baron's War *
Magna Carta *
Welsh Wars *
Henry III *
The Bloody Border *
Baron's Crusade
Sentinel of the North
War in the West
Debt of Honour
The Blood of the Warlord
The Fettered King
de Montfort's Crown

Sir John Hawkwood Series

France and Italy 1339- 1387
Crécy: The Age of the Archer *
Man At Arms *
The White Company *
Leader of Men *
Tuscan Warlord *
Condottiere

Lord Edward's Archer
Lord Edward's Archer *
King in Waiting *
An Archer's Crusade *
Targets of Treachery *
The Great Cause *
Wallace's War *
The Hunt

Struggle for a Crown
1360- 1485
Blood on the Crown *
To Murder a King *
The Throne *
King Henry IV *
The Road to Agincourt *
St Crispin's Day *
The Battle for France *
The Last Knight *
Queen's Knight *
The Knight's Tale

Tales from the Sword I
(Short stories from the Medieval period)

Tudor Warrior series
England and Scotland in the late 15th and early 16th century
Tudor Warrior *
Tudor Spy *
Flodden*

Conquistador
England and America in the 16th Century
Conquistador *
The English Adventurer *

English Mercenary
The 30 Years War and the English Civil War
Horse and Pistol

Modern History

The Napoleonic Horseman Series
Chasseur à Cheval
Napoleon's Guard
British Light Dragoon
Soldier Spy
1808: The Road to Coruña
Talavera
The Lines of Torres Vedras
Bloody Badajoz
The Road to France
Waterloo

The Lucky Jack American Civil War series
Rebel Raiders
Confederate Rangers
The Road to Gettysburg

Soldier of the Queen series
Soldier of the Queen*
Redcoat's Rifle*
Omdurman

The British Ace Series
1914
1915 Fokker Scourge
1916 Angels over the Somme
1917 Eagles Fall

1918 We will remember them
From Arctic Snow to Desert Sand
Wings over Persia

**Combined Operations series
1940-1945**
Commando *
Raider *
Behind Enemy Lines
Dieppe
Toehold in Europe
Sword Beach
Breakout
The Battle for Antwerp
King Tiger
Beyond the Rhine
Korea
Korean Winter

Tales from the Sword II
(Short stories from the Modern period)

Books marked thus *, are also available in the audio format. For more information on all of the books then please visit the author's website at www.griffhosker.com where there is a link to contact him or visit his Facebook page: GriffHosker at Sword Books or follow him on Twitter: @HoskerGriff or Sword (@swordbooksltd)
If you wish to be on the mailing list then contact the author through his website.

Made in United States
Cleveland, OH
06 November 2025